FINDERS TAKERS

Brian Lehman

To Julie Lehman

for her endless love,

ongoing support

and infinite patience.

I shall be telling this with a sigh

Somewhere in ages and ages hence:

Two roads diverged in a wood, and I--

I took the one less traveled by,

And that has made all the difference.

ROBERT FROST

CONTENTS

BRIAN LEHMAN

ONE

June, 1996 – Seattle, Washington

David Steiner found himself standing outside late at night. Even though it was raining he was disturbingly warm and torrents of sweat were rolling down his face. He struggled to pull his sweatshirt hood down off his head but it wouldn't move. It was growing hotter and the rain was pounding now as steam rose up from the concrete. Looking around he saw that just like all the other times, paper money was now fluttering down along with the rain and the bills were beginning to burn.

He awoke with a start and sat up, drenched in sweat along with the pillow case and sheet. He looked at Mary Kay lying beside him.

Her eyes were open. "The dream?" she asked.

He nodded and sighed. "I'm gonna get some water."

He went to the kitchen, grabbed a bottle of water from the fridge and walked into the living room which was softly illuminated by moonlight and the lights from nearby buildings. Standing in his boxers by the large window he sipped the water as he looked out over the lights of Seattle from the 24th floor of his luxury condo.

The dream was always the same but it never completely made sense to him. He knew the heat, the rain and the money were all from that incredible day almost thirty years ago. But it was nighttime in the dream and what in the hell was burning money all about?

He sipped some more water and heard Mary Kay softly padding across the marble floor behind him. She too was wearing only boxers. She pressed up against him and wrapped her arms across his stomach. She knew the dream and what he was thinking about. On that day long ago she had been there too.

Mary Kay Dias confidently guided her black Z06 Corvette at just over a hundred fifteen miles per hour along the final mile of the wide gently meandering country road outside Seattle. Rounding the last curve she down shifted and braked hard to make the turn into her destination.

Every other week before going to the salon for her hair and nails, Mary Kay spent about an hour at a private shooting range. David occasionally joined her for these sessions, but not today. Her time at the shooting range both energized and relaxed her.

She paid a few thousand dollars a month to have the range to herself during her sessions with only her trainer and the owner present. There was an outdoor and indoor handgun range as well as an outdoor rifle target shooting area and another outdoor area for trap shooting or shotgun target practice. She always brought along her favorite shotgun and a few handguns from her collection. The owner and her trainer knew she enjoyed trying out new weapons and they always had one or two for her to check out.

She stepped out of her Vette into a slight mist that had been wetting the area all morning. She was just opening the trunk when Al, her weapons trainer, came out to greet her.

"Hey, Mary Kay. You want to start inside today and see if this half-assed rain lets up later?"

She was dressed in jeans, a purple lightweight sweatshirt and pink Nikes. "You afraid you're going to mess up your hairdo?" she kidded, closing the trunk.

Al rubbed his buzz cut hair and laughed. "Exactly!"

"I'm fine," she said. "It's not really raining and I want to play with the shotgun first. Can you set this inside for me?" She handed him her case which contained a Colt .40 caliber semi-auto and a Ruger .357 magnum revolver.

It was a short walk on a level gravel trail to the shotgun area.

Al caught up after taking her case inside. "I'm just about done setting up the range."

They reached the shotgun range and set the guns on the table. There was a narrow roof built over the row of tables providing some protection from the mist. There were already several boxes of shells set out for her.

"Give me a minute and I'll finish your setup," Al said and walked out onto the lawn area.

He had set up a collection of targets for her. Spaced five to fifteen yards out were some two-liter bottles filled with water as well as variety of targets at various heights including mannequins, water balloons, buckets, bullseye targets and two watermelons.

Al returned and they both put on ear protection. Sitting in front of her was her favorite shotgun—a custom built 12 gauge, pistol grip, short-barrel shotgun with a five shell capacity and barrel length of just sixteen inches. The soft pistol grip and the pump stock were bright pink.

As usual she was using #4 buckshot shells. She knew plenty of so-called experts who touted the penetration and man-stopping ability of the larger 00 buckshot. Over the years she had read a lot on the subject, tested various shot loads on her own and consulted with knowledgeable people she trusted. She finally came to the conclusion for herself that she liked the idea of firing 27 pellets at the target versus 9 from the 00 buckshot. She also liked the comment Al had once made that at close range he thought either type of shell produced about the same amount of deadness.

"Ready?" she said.

"Go for it," he answered."

In less than five seconds she took out a two liter bottle, two water balloons, and punched two holes in two mannequins. She had become very proficient with this weapon and at close range could hit exactly where she intended nearly 100% of the time holding the gun out in front of her or at her hip.

Al always enjoyed watching Mary Kay shoot. Like most men,

he just plain liked looking at her, but he also had a real appreciation for her fierce marksmanship. The combination of that shooting ability and her striking beauty never ceased to fascinate him.

"Okay," she said, "it is getting a little wetter out here. I want to shoot a few more using this other shotgun you have here, then we can go inside."

An hour later Mary Kay arrived at the salon. A middle-aged woman was getting her nails done as she usually did every other week or so.

"There she is," whispered her manicurist, gesturing with her eyes to the other end of the busy shop where Mary Kay had just strolled in.

The two of them had been talking about her right when she entered. The woman getting her nails done had seen this visitor before and the woman doing her nails had seen her several times.

"You said she's like forty?" the customer said quietly. She turned and looked her over again. "She's beautiful. She looks like she's twenty-five, maybe thirty. In fact, I looked older than her when I was eighteen!"

Both women laughed.

The manicurist shrugged. "That's what I heard. Actually I think she's about to turn forty. Christy says she's heard her say it more than once. She's kinda quiet when she's here. Gets her hair and nails done about every other week or so."

"You ever do her nails?" asked the customer.

"I did once a few months ago when Christy was out sick, but usually Christy does her nails. She was nice. The usual small talk about celebrities and crap like that. Nice smile. Ashleigh does her hair. Just some trimming and some highlights, nothing fancy. From what they say she always gives pretty huge tips."

"Wow!" breathed the customer. "She must be loaded, huh? Did you get a big tip?"

The manicurist nodded and smiled. "A hundred dollar bill.

She gives a hundred to whoever does anything for her every time she's here." She did some more filing in silence. "She drives a pretty cool black Corvette."

"This is a nice salon," the customer said, "but you'd think somebody like that would be going somewhere real exclusive where the rich people go."

"I guess she thinks this is fancy enough for her," the manicurist sad. "Monica, the owner, told all of us that Mary Kay doesn't want us talking about her to a lot of people. Monica said that Mary Kay said if a lot of curious people start coming around to see who the rich bitch is then she would have to find another salon."

The customer giggled then whispered, "Well, you're talking about her to me!"

"Oh, you're different."

"So who is she?"

The nail technician shrugged. "Just Mary Kay, that's all I know."

The glossy, straight brunette hair with lighter highlights stopping just at the top of her shoulders couldn't possibly be natural, but Mary Kay wore it with a confidence that said it was. The slender but curvy figure, the clear, large deep-brown eyes, the smooth olive complexion, coupled with her graceful poise always got Mary Kay Dias noticed. When she was a child and young adult everyone always thought she was older. Now that she was older everyone always thought she was younger.

For a number of years now people always asked how she did it whenever they found out how old she was. She was always very gracious about such inquiries and attributed it to the genes of her Portuguese and Greek heritage. That was true enough, but employing the talents of personal trainers, dieticians, cooks and maids certainly had a way of taking care of many of the cares and worries that tended to age the average person. Some guessed she must have had plastic surgeries of some kind, but they were wrong. She was educated, smart, knew she looked good and usually enjoyed the attention it brought her. She was sometimes thought of by those who had briefly crossed paths with her as a single-minded narcissist. In fact. she sometimes presented herself that way just for her own twisted amusement, but she was much more complex than that and a lot more dangerous. Like David, she too had the same secrets to keep and she had her own way of accomplishing that.

Tommy stood ten feet to the side and just a bit behind middle-aged, beginning golfer Jennifer Scott as she prepared to tee off at the third hole of the West Seattle Country Club. Even this uncoordinated bitch can't kill me from this angle, he thought.

Suddenly she relaxed her stance and turned her head toward him. For a moment he worried that he had just said out loud what he'd been thinking. "Can you show me that grip again?"

"Sure, Mrs. Scott." He walked over and adjusted her hands, then stood back again to watch.

As the senior resident pro at Washington Pines Country Club, Tommy Dias had what many people would consider a dream job. He got to play golf whenever he wanted and in return he gave a few golf lessons every week whenever he felt like it and did a handful of speaking engagements during the year for local service organizations. Once a year he helped organize a celebrity golf tournament that attracted enough Hollywood and professional sports figures to keep things interesting. Of course, others did most of the actual organizing, due partly to the fact that Tommy began most days with a bowl of cereal and two tall, double-shot screwdrivers. By the end of a typical evening he would go through ten more plus a few straight shots "just to keep the joints loose." Everyone who knew him could not believe that he hadn't become obese or died from his never-ending alcohol consumption. In fact, Tommy looked much as he had for the past twenty-five years or more—the same slim build, smooth Mediterranean complexion and short hair that just naturally laid flat.

After Jennifer Scott's lesson and one other, he made his way to his regular spot for his usual early lunch at the bar located just off the restaurant. He headed for the far corner of the three-sided bar where Abe, Bart and Charlie, the A,B,C's, could usually be found this time of day—three members who rarely made it out onto the course.

"Hey, Tommy, how's your putter swingin'?" Abe greeted, as usual, and all three men laughed too loudly.

Tommy perched himself onto one of the leather stools. "I told you before, Abe, it's not a putter, it's a driver. A seven wood at least!" The three erupted again as Tommy tossed a couple of hundreds in front of the bartender. "Set us all up, Jake."

The bartender knew to reach beneath the bar for Tommy's special vodka, keep the drinks flowing on Tommy's tab and send for four club sandwiches from the restaurant.

It was still a little before most people's lunch time and just a few patrons were scattered about the bar and the dining room. In a booth on the opposite wall from the bar was seated Jason Oakley, one of the club's board members. Seated facing him was his guest, the new owner of a local Acura dealership who had just moved from the San Francisco Bay area and was thinking about joining. They were both in their fifties and dressed to play a few holes.

"So who's that?" the car dealer asked.

Oakley shook his head a bit as he watched their over-done laughing and kidding. "That is our pro, Tommy Dias," he said, then sighed.

The guest looked over Oakley for a second. "You sound like you're not too happy with him."

Oakley made a dismissive face. "Nah, he's okay, I guess. Kind of a fuck-off, and he drinks more than anybody I ever knew, but I got nothing against him really. He's a nice enough guy. Those three there and a lot of other people like hanging out with him `cause he spends money like it's going out of style. Like that vodka he drinks, Russian stuff that costs two-hundred bucks a bottle. He'll just buy all kinds of shit for everybody and pick up the tab for whoever he's with, and they all know it."

"Was he a player?" the dealer asked.

Oakley nodded. "I hear he was good enough to play the PGA tour off and on for a dozen years or so. He was one of those middle-of-the-pack guys. They don't always make the cuts and they never get much media attention beyond a quick mention, but they're way better than you or me. I don't think he ever won a PGA event, but he's still a fucking good golfer, drunk or sober, but mostly drunk. He's around forty and I only know of a handful of guys around here who ever beat him and those were just once or twice fluke things. He could probably make a million a year just betting on rounds out there on the course and doing trick shot exhibitions."

"Does he fulfill his duties as a pro?"

"He has a couple of younger guys who work for him that do most of the pro work," Oakley explained. "He doesn't need the dough anyway. He doesn't even take any pay for being the resident pro and he donates his own money to pay those two assistants of his. I guess it's just something to do for him."

The car dealer raised his eyebrows. "Really? That's a pretty sweet deal for the club. He could probably keep that job forever. So, if he didn't make it playing golf, where'd it come from?"

Oakley shrugged. "I've heard he's connected with some big real estate and investment firm. Somebody told me that he and his sister and some other people are the owners. Whatever it is they've all got money out the wazoo."

Tommy left the real work of guarding their shared past to David and Mary Kay. He just had to play along and follow the rules laid down by his twin sister and especially by David. The secrecy had even been a factor in his professional golf career. At David's insistence he held back so he would never achieve the notoriety of a PGA winner. He resented it, but he reluctantly understood the need to stay out of the limelight. Most people just don't pay as much attention to the golfers who play great but don't win tournaments.

Tommy was standing at the podium just finishing up his remarks. "So that's who I have lined up for our next Greater

Puget Sound Celebrity Golf Tournament Fundraiser."

The nearly 500 seated at the round tables in the enormous dining room applauded.

"And of course," Tommy continued, "we need all of you starstruck fans to show up for the overpriced events and dinners to show your support for our charities. If you're lucky maybe your favorite superstar will pose for a photo or sign something for you or even have a brief conversation with you. I've told all of them to try to act interested."

Everyone laughed and some shouted remarks.

"So, that's all I've got for now. Everybody enjoy the rest of the evening." Tommy returned to his seat and exchanged a quick smile and nod with Mary Kay who was seated at a neighboring table beside David.

David sipped his whiskey, glancing around and taking in the scene, even smiling a bit. At times like this when he was with the right people and he'd had a couple of drinks and some good food in a relaxed atmosphere, it was easier to think that maybe he had succeeded in keeping their secret for so long that it really did not need so much of his attention anymore. He couldn't really believe it though, especially since a few additional secrets had developed over the years. Still it was nice to relax and pretend once in a while. Nobody watching him would have any clue that he never entirely enjoyed this, or any experience, the way other people were able to. Through his every waking hour, sometimes even in his dreams, David Steiner's thoughts were consumed with the keeping of a commitment he had taken on at the age of twelve, and because of it a region of his brain never slept. His task in life was to protect Mary Kay, Tommy, himself and their financial empire. To accomplish this he was always on alert, continually thinking ahead and planning for possible scenarios in the event anyone learned the truth concerning the secrets he had devoted his life to shielding from the world.

As the applause died down, Mary Kay turned to a couple seated by her. "He has so much fun putting these celebrity bashes together. I didn't want to embarrass him by shouting out anything but tomorrow is his fortieth birthday."

"And yours too," Katie said with a grin.

The couple was a little younger than David and Mary Kay, just into their 30s. Katie served on one of the environmental advisory boards that Mary Kay headed. Her date, Kevin, was not someone Mary Kay knew.

David was toying with Mary Kay's left thigh beneath the table and working his way higher. "You know that guy was a pretty damn good PGA player at one time," he said to Kevin and Katie. "He's still crazy good. Pops up sometimes at Pro-Am tournaments. Almost nobody here at the club ever beats him."

Kevin returned a doubting look. "Really? My dad is a club member and from what I hear that guy is a real ass. Spends most of his time sloshed and doing nothing."

Kevin suddenly jumped as Katie stomped his foot under the table. She started to say something to him but instead covered her mouth with one hand and slowly shook her head. After a few seconds, she lowered her hand and mouthed "I'm sorry," to Mary Kay.

Kevin looked back and forth between the women and blurted, "What?"

David uttered a soft, "Whoa," studied Mary Kay's face and waited.

Mary Kay took a sip of her drink. "Are you referring to my twin brother?"

Kevin stared at Mary Kay for several moments. "Oh, I didn't know. That's just what I heard. Sorry, I…" He sighed and looked around nervously.

"Don't worry about it," Mary Kay said and excused herself.

David watched her walk away and he caught Kevin's attention. "Listen, man, if I was you, I would make a point of apologizing some more."

Much later that night, around 1:00 in the morning, Kevin dropped off Katie at her apartment and drove home. He stepped out of his Audi into the third floor parking garage and headed to the elevator to go up to his 6th floor condo. As he rounded the corner of the wall he was somewhat startled to find a woman standing in front of the elevator facing him.

"Hello Kevin," Mary Kay said.

He stopped a few feet from her. "Wow, it's you. What brings you here?"

"You," she said, unsmilingly.

Kevin sized her up for several seconds, thought back to the awkward exchange at the dinner, and felt himself become a bit concerned. "You came here just to talk to me? Do you live near here?"

Mary Kay gestured toward the wall a few feet away. "Can we talk over here?"

"Sure, I guess," he said. They walked the few feet to the chest-high wall and leaned on it looking out over the landscaping and quiet side street below.

"I don't like anybody talking shit about my brother, my twin brother."

"I'd like to apologize again about that," Kevin said. "I had no idea he was someone to you."

"You know, I'm a lot stronger than most people think I am," she said. "I weight-train and practice kickboxing and jiu-jitsu every week. I could put you in a hold right now and throw you over this wall before you could fight me off. Third floor might not kill you but it would for sure fuck you up."

Kevin was now feeling genuine fear. "You're threatening me because I repeated some stuff about your brother being a drunk? What's the matter with you?" He took a step back from her and pulled out his cell phone. "You better leave or I'm calling the cops."

Mary Kay took a step toward him and in a lightning-fast move reached out, grabbed his phone from his hand and threw it over the wall. She stepped closer and brought her face just inches from his. "I ever hear about you talking shit about my brother again, we won't just have another conversation like this one. You'll never see me coming. You understand, Kevin?"

Kevin nodded. "Yeah."

Mary Kay walked away, calling back over her shoulder, "I think your phone landed in some ground cover down there. It's probably fine.'

TWO

July, 1968 – Bakersfield, California

"This is my best pair of doorbell shoes," David said, referring to his nearly worn-out black Keds.

Tommy smiled then giggled in reply, looking down at his own summer-toughened bare feet propelling him along. His smiles always came easily and he was never happier than when he was with David, especially if they were out to do some mischief.

"Your sister get in much trouble over that fight today?" David asked.

Tommy laughed. "Nah, that kid was pushing me around, then he started crying after she punched him so it was a short fight. My dad almost laughed but he grounded her for a couple of days. The principal said if it happened again she would be expelled."

"That's what he told her last time," David said, snorting a laugh.

It was late July, just after dinnertime. David Steiner and Tommy Dias were on a mission, making their way down the alley. They lived on Second Street just three houses apart from each other on the south end of the block. The alley, the forbidden great divide they were always told to stay out of, ran through the middle of their world between the backs of the houses along Second Street and the covered parking structures of the "four-plexes" along First Street. The boys would be out playing in the blessed, extended early evening of daylight saving time until they finally got hollered at for being out after dark. Tommy's twin sister, Mary Kay, spent much of her time with the two boys, but tonight she was stuck serving her grounding.

The alley was rarely swept and over the years sandy soil had drifted in from the adjacent yards and been tracked in by cars, burying half the cheap pavement. Weeds routinely grew along the edge where the cedar fences bordered the backyards. The sun was low and the apartment parking structures shaded the alley, but it was still hot out since the high temperature had reached just over one hundred degrees only a few hours earlier. The two boys trudged north toward the far end of the block away from their houses, kicking up some dust as they went, and, as always, keeping a sharp eye out for naked women because a story had been passed around for years that someone had once seen one get out of a car and head into the apartments.

David was a few weeks older, but both boys had celebrated their twelfth birthday around the beginning of the summer and would be going into 7th grade when the school year started. He was the taller of the two by three inches and was often taken for a couple of years older. His blond hair was Butch-waxed into a flattop above his freckled face. An only child, he had decided long ago that he liked that situation just fine. Tommy had the same smooth olive complexion and dark brown hair as his sister.

They were nearing the end of the block. "This one?" David suggested.

Tommy nodded.

They quickly checked the alley in both directions to make sure there were no adults around, then turned and walked between the garages into the bowels of the forbidden four-plexes.

David gave the go signal and they both started down their side of the grass courtyard to each ring all four doorbells. Tommy missed the second button, laughed out loud and reached back after a barefooted skid and got it. David flew through the gate on his side just half a second ahead of Tommy, then they ran crouched over behind the wall and met in the middle, writhing on the ground, panting and holding back most of their laughter amid snorts and wheezes.

Tommy managed to whisper, "Did I tell you this is my

best pair of doorbell feet?" before dissolving back into stifled giggling.

Then something happened that had not occurred before. David was about to rise up and peek over the wall when a man leaned over it just above them. He was wearing a tight, strap-style tee shirt that showed three tattoos on both his well-developed arms. He looked to be in his thirties.

"You guys think you're pretty damn clever, don't you?" His voice was stern, but there was a nasal, almost whiny quality to it. "I've seen you two doing this a couple of other times."

Tommy was terrified. David was intrigued, and he figured they could always run if they had to.

"You're Tommy Dias and you're David Steiner. You live around the corner on Second. Tommy, your dad works at Wilshire Paints downtown. David, your dad works at the liquor store up First Street there." He smiled and pointed toward the store which was only a half mile down the busy street.

Both boys stood and faced him from their side of the wall. Tommy thought he might wet himself, but managed to hold it back.

David was extremely curious about how this stranger knew who they were. He stood, looking back at the man's short, thinning, dark hair, the round face with full, reddish lips and long prominent eyelashes, thinking he had seen him before. "How do you know who we are, sir?"

The man laughed a little now, nodding and looking them over in the light of the setting sun. "I'll bet you'd like to know. Why don't you ask your fathers? Tell them you were out ringing doorbells and ran into Mr. Saladino." He laughed harder now. "Get on out of here before I sic all the neighbors on you. Scat!"

Saladino walked back into his apartment still laughing a little. "Shit, it's still hot out there," he said to himself. He reached over to the cooler vent and held his hand up to the not-quite-cool-enough air.

He put the volume back up on his expensive hi-fi set, and

the blaring Italian opera filled the apartment again. He relit his cigar, refilled his glass with a couple of new ice cubes and port wine, and sat down once again to enjoy the rest of the record album. He had no worries about the neighbors complaining about the loud music. His apartment, and only his, was constructed with the latest technology for sound-proofing, with double thickness walls with full insulation and a dead air space between the two thicknesses to cut down on sound transmission.

Vincent Saladino's round pudgy face and receding hairline gave most people the impression he was several years older than his actual age of thirty-four. He had been a very young man when he moved into the apartment and watched as the continuing 1950s and into the 1960s building boom filled up Second Street with single family homes and spread many blocks to the east from there.

It was a nice stable neighborhood and even in the four-plexes not many people moved out or in, but when they did, he knew it. Using the information provided by a contact in the post office and an investigator he used from time to time, he knew the identity of every person who lived in the nearby apartments, every person on the west side of Second Street just across the alley, and a few of those who lived on the other side of Second. He realized it was probably unnecessary to keep track of all that, but he didn't like surprises. He had been known to frequently say, "You just never know who's going to turn out to be someone you should've been paying more attention to."

When he moved in he paid a very talented contractor several thousand dollars in cash to construct the sound-deadening walls, to do a couple of other projects, and to keep his mouth shut about it all. A short time later that contractor disappeared and nobody, except Vincent of course, ever knew what happened to him. An abandoned oil well on some property east of town that an acquaintance owned and a few sacks of cement had done the trick. After all, people could rarely be trusted to actually keep secrets.

Shortly after moving in, he bought the building he lived in and the one across the courtyard. The rent and any problems went to a property manager and the other seven tenants knew nothing about Vincent being the owner. Vincent Saladino's usual business, though, was neither murder nor being a landlord. He was a courier. He drove to Las Vegas two or three times a month and to the Los Angeles area to meet with his bosses, to pass along messages from the casino operators and to deliver a consolidated skim. Collectively, the mob-controlled casinos in Las Vegas were the biggest cash cow ever conceived. The mob leadership had been coming under increasing scrutiny by the FBI and other Justice Department entities and they were all fearful of wiretaps and other surveillance invading their domains. Couriers could deliver the money and information and the bosses could keep their distance.

Vincent wasn't the only courier but he was more than just a run-of-the-mill errand boy. He moved the larger skim after several others were collected and combined. He was one of the few underlings to be working with the higher-ranking bosses. In fact, many people he came in contact with assumed they were being watched by him. After all, he was Dino's nephew.

David and Tommy trotted off down the sidewalk together then slowed to a walk as they rounded the corner at the end of the block.

"Shit!" Tommy exclaimed suddenly. "You think he's going to tell our parents?"

David shook his head, laughing as they continued walking. "I think he was just letting us know that he's nobody to mess with. That guy looks familiar."

Both boys found it unsettling that they didn't know him and, whoever he was, he was living right in the middle of their world and he knew all about them.

"You see those tattoos?" David asked.

Tommy giggled. "We finally saw a naked lady!"

As the boys continued their hike around the next corner

back onto Second Street and their own familiar side of the world, they had no idea that this chance meeting during a few minutes of minor troublemaking would soon dramatically and permanently alter the remainder of their lives.

It had been two days since the doorbell-ringing incident.

"David, Howie is here!" his mom announced.

David smiled and jumped up from the living room floor where he was watching the usual run of Saturday morning cartoons. He was school friends with Howie Williams, but they didn't see each other very much otherwise. Howie lived a couple of blocks past the liquor store where David's father worked, just far enough away that they didn't really share many neighborhood friends.

"What's going on?" Howie asked as they walked down the driveway.

David knew that Tommy and his sister were busy with a visit from their grandparents until later in the morning. "Just hanging around the house watching TV. What you want to do?"

Asking this question of Howie could bring unimagined responses. Howie did whatever he wanted whenever he wanted. His alcoholic single mom fed him and gave him a place to sleep but otherwise left him and his older brother to their own whims. David was very good at keeping himself out of any real trouble and he had learned to be careful when choosing which shenanigans to participate in with Howie.

"I just came from the ditch," Howie said. "The water is way down. It's mostly just a few big pools left. Remember all those baby frogs last year? They're back, but even more. There's millions of them! We need some buckets."

"I think they're toads," David said, "but they might be frogs. Anyway, why buckets?"

Howie began an evil chortle, delighting in his own twisted genius. "I have a great idea! What do you think of filling the buckets with those things and bringing them back to your neighborhood and letting them loose everywhere? All up and down the street we'll put them in people's yards. The whole place will be overrun with toads, or frogs, or whatever they are. Women screaming, men cussing, dogs barking. It might even get in the newspaper or on TV!"

A grin spread over David's face as the bizarre idea took shape in his mind. It was a couple of steps above Howie's usual more basic misbehaving and it seemed the perfect summertime nonsense. "Okay, I'll get my bike and a couple of buckets."

They were joined by Tommy when they returned from their wobbly ride, each with a heavy bucket hanging from their handlebars. Using David's beat-up red wagon to haul the buckets they grinningly went about their mission, up one side of the street and back on the other, with no particular concern about being seen and didn't even try to conceal what they were up to. Running around people's yards depositing handfuls of juvenile amphibians was such a peculiar activity, even for them, they weren't at all sure it was something for which they could actually get into trouble, though they suspected that somehow it had to be.

David and Tommy, usually with Mary Kay, were always out and about the street. You looked outside, you saw trees, you saw houses, you saw cars, you saw the three of them clanking a wagon up and down curbs, pulling each other on skates or homemade contraptions behind their bicycles, sneaking around on military missions chasing Nazis and Viet Cong, pretending they were astronauts, or a multitude of other concocted amusements. They were just another part of the standard, neighborhood environment and had become nearly immune to being particularly noticed by the residents on that block of Second Street. On summer afternoons most people had their windows closed and coolers running, so whatever noise the three were making outside didn't catch much attention.

Every yard on the block on both sides of the street received a generous deposit of the transplanted hoppers. Not one person paid any attention to the three boys or ever knew what they had done.

After gloating for a while over the success of their inspired relocation mission, they decided to head down First Street to Paul's Liquor where David's father worked. Howie rode his bike and Tommy hitched a ride on the back of David's.

"So Mary Kay's still grounded?" David asked.

"Not officially, but she got stuck doing stuff with my grandma and had to go along with it," Tommy said with a laugh. "I was lucky to get out of there!"

"Think your dad will give us any stuff?" Howie asked.

"Maybe, if it's not too busy and his boss isn't there," David said. "He likes to surprise you with it though, so don't act like you're expecting something or you'll probably pay the regular price."

When they walked into the small store, there was just one customer who was leaving. "Hi, Mr. Steiner," Tommy and Howie both greeted.

"Hello, boys," he said from behind the counter.

"Hi, Mr. Steiner," David greeted his father.

"Hey, watch it boy!" his father growled playfully.

All three boys laughed. They opened the lid to the chest style box where many of the bottles of soft drinks were kept. Howie got a Royal Crown Cola, while David and Tommy both fished out a Nesbitt's orange soda.

They set them on the counter and Mr. Steiner popped the caps for them. The boys each laid down a dime and a nickel. All the sodas were either thirteen or fourteen cents, including the one cent bottle deposit.

He looked at all three of them. "You drinking those here?"

They all nodded.

He took just a dime from each of them. "No dripping on the floor. Drink them outside and make sure you bring the bottles back in when you're done."

"Thanks Mr. Steiner!" Tommy and Howie chorused. They both grabbed nickel candy bars from the rack and held them up to show him where the remaining money was going.

David picked up his soda and the nickel. "Thanks, Dad."

His father winked in reply and turned to straighten the beer in the cold box.

The store stood on the corner of First, a busy four-lane, and Terrace, a residential street. Howie lived just a block and a half down Terrace. The three boys sat on the sidewalk in the shade beside the store drinking their sodas and eating the candy bars.

"I saw Debbie Turner the other day," Howie said. "She got a haircut. It's real short and I think she's growing some boobies." He set down his soda and pulled out the front of his shirt to demonstrate. Tommy laughed, choked, and orange soda bubbled from his nostrils.

A black Cadillac slowly made the right turn off of First and parked across Terrace. A man dressed in a cream-colored suit stepped out and strolled across the asphalt toward the boys. Now David remembered where he had seen Mr. Saladino before. The man had come into the store a couple of times when he'd been there hanging around. David had never really paid much attention to him, but he remembered that he had been dressed in a suit, like he was right now.

He smiled as he stepped up on the curb and headed toward the door. "Hi David. Nothing like a cold drink on a hot day like this, eh Tommy?" He walked on into the store.

Howie looked at his companions wide-eyed. "You know that guy?"

David shrugged. "Not really. He lives in the apartments down the alley. We talked to him the other day."

"He lives down there?" Howie said, shading his eyes and looking down the street. "Man, that's Cadillac Vinnie! My brother Gary is always hanging around down here in the parking lot behind the store with his punk friends. Sometimes they let me hang around with them for a while before they tell me to get lost. I've been here a couple of times when that guy pulled up and went into the store. He hangs around talking to your dad or whoever is working. My brother says he's some Mafia big shot. He runs a gambling thing called Numbers."

BRIAN LEHMAN

"How does your brother know him?" David asked.

"He doesn't know him, he just knows about him."

David eyed the Cadillac. He'd seen it around too. "The other day he knew our names, where we lived, our fathers, everything."

"These gangsters have to keep an eye out for everything," Howie explained. "Other mobs might send their guys to get him 'cause he killed one of their guys, you know? He probably has to know who everybody is so he knows when strangers are around looking for him."

David grinned. "You don't know shit."

Howie finished the last of his soda, burped and set the bottle down for David to return. "I gotta go. My mom told me to be back by 2:00."

David and Tommy both looked up at the clock over the front door of the store. "It's almost 3:30 you stupid butt," David said while Tommy giggled.

Howie was just beginning to pedal away on his bike. "That's okay, I'll just blame it on you guys!"

"So, how come we never knew about this Cadillac Vinnie guy before?" Tommy asked.

David stood. "Good question. Let's go in and see what he's doing."

The boys looked over the candy rack as Vincent Saladino talked softly with David's father a few feet away at the counter. David saw his father hand him some money and Saladino put it in his coat pocket along with a small notebook.

He turned and saw the boys. "Ed, one of these guys is yours, isn't he?"

David's father pointed. "Yes, this is David. His friend is Tommy Dias. Boys, this is Mr. Saladino."

"Glad to meet you boys." He gave a quick wink as he shook hands with them. He headed toward the door carrying his bag with a quart of Falstaff beer and two fifths of Gallo port. "Okay, paisan, see you later."

When the door closed David said, "Dad, Howie said that guy's some Mafia gangster and his name is Cadillac Vinnie."

"Some people call him that," Mr. Steiner said. "Some people call him a big shot. I just call him Mr. Saladino. Yeah, I guess he's in with the mob or Mafia or whatever it's called these days. He never causes any trouble around here so I don't care what he does. Buys a new Cadillac every year, so whatever he does I guess he makes a lot of money. But he says he lives down the block from us in the four-plexes, so maybe he spends all his money on cars."

"You play Numbers, Mr. Steiner? Tommy asked. "I think my dad does. I've heard him mention it before."

Mr. Steiner looked a little uncomfortable. "A lot of us do. It only costs a few dollars a week. You can win five-hundred some weeks. Technically it's illegal, but it's a harmless little game so the police just ignore it. I wouldn't go around talking about it though, know what I mean?" He put serious emphasis on the last sentence and leaned down on the counter close to both of them. "That includes talking to mothers about it. Understand?"

The two boys looked at each other and back at Mr. Steiner. "We got it, Dad. No problem. In fact, we never even had this conversation, did we?"

His father stood back up, looked the two boys over for several seconds and pointed to the bucket on the counter. "Have some bubble gum."

"Spy on him?" Mary Kay looked at her twin brother and back at David. "Why? We must have something better to do!"

David threw up his arms. "We don't! This is an opportunity. What better way to spend the rest of our summer than spying on a gangster and finding out more about him? We'd be like the neighborhood cops keeping an eye on the bad guys."

Mary Kay gave them a doubting look, but they had her attention. At least it would be something new, she thought.

David, Tommy and Mary Kay had been friends since their families had moved into the new housing tract ten years earlier. There were other kids in the neighborhood that the three of them were casual friends with, but most of them were a couple years older or younger and mostly lived on the next couple of blocks on Third or Fourth. The three of them spent so much time with each other that other kids, and even some adults, referred to them as the Three Musketeers. David and Tommy spent nearly every waking second together and much of that time included Mary Kay as well.

Mary Kay and David had just as strong a friendship as he and Tommy, but in a different way. She knew how to be one of the guys when they wanted to play football, play army or stage idiotic bicycle wrecks in the middle of the street and wait for cars to drive by. She also had no problem walking away when the boy stuff got too gross, although she was usually entertained enough by it that it was rarely an issue.

They had always been friends but even when they were younger there was a part of their relationship that was a childlike boyfriend and girlfriend. Lately, he'd been taking notice of a new gracefulness in her movements and that lanky frame of hers had changed shape a bit. The Greek and Portuguese background had given her the same smooth Mediterranean skin as her twin brother, but in her, even as a young child, it had manifested itself as striking exotic beauty with grown-up eyes. Over the past year or so, David had become aware of himself taking in a definitely not childlike new appreciation of her head-turning attributes.

Mary Kay liked the idea of having a boy as a best friend. He protected her when she needed protecting, which wasn't very often, and it was nice to sometimes have someone to practice being a girl around besides other girls. She was taking new notice of David lately as well and saw that he was looking older and more attractive in a way she couldn't, and didn't, articulate to anyone. Months ago she felt embarrassed when she caught her thoughts running in that direction, but lately she just enjoyed letting them take their course. The feeling of trust she had always had in him had only increased lately and, as always, she continued to share nearly everything with him, even things she never talked about with anyone else, including her twin brother.

The three of them were sitting on David's front lawn in the late afternoon shade provided by the peaked roof of the garage. "Just because that turd Howie Williams says he's a gangster doesn't mean anything," Mary Kay said.

David and Tommy exchanged a quick look. "It's not just Howie," Tommy began.

Over the next few minutes they told her about their first encounter with Vincent Saladino while ringing doorbells and about the conversation with David's father at the store. She listened intently, fascinated by how the man had known their names and by the information about the numbers game from David's father.

"Wow, guys, that's pretty interesting all right." She asked a few more questions about what he looked like and a change came over her face. "I think I know who you're talking about! You know Janice that lives down toward the end of the block?"

I guess," David said. "I know there's some girl down there named Janice. The pink house?"

"Yes," she continued. "It's the fourth house from the corner. I hardly see her at all anymore, but we used to play once in a while. I got to know her when we were in kindergarten together. That's the year they moved in here. They don't own the house, they rent."

Tommy gave his sister a look. "How do you know that?" It wasn't something they ever considered about other kids.

"Listen, you guys. The last time I was down at her house was probably more than a year ago, but before that I used to be down there once in a while. Sometimes when I was over there a man was doing stuff in the backyard. One time he was painting part of the trim on the house in the back. I asked Janice who he was and she said it was their landlord. I didn't know what she meant and that's when she explained that they rented the house. She called him Mr. S. and mentioned that he lived in the apartments across the alley. He seemed nice but I never really talked to him much. He kept telling me how cute I was. Anyway, it must be the same guy."

David was shaking his head. "A couple of weeks ago I never knew this guy existed. Then Tommy and I run into him at the apartments, again at the liquor store, we find out he's some gangster and now he owns a house right down the street!"

Mary Kay was displaying a smug grin, obviously proud of herself for adding to the intelligence-gathering.

THREE

Vincent Saladino backed his Cadillac out into the alley and pushed the button to close the automatic garage door. He drove slowly north down the alley the short distance to Simpson Street. As he neared the end of the alley he saw David and Tommy standing on the sidewalk. They waved, expecting him to drive away.

Instead he stopped and rolled down the window. "Hey, come here, boys."

They looked at each other and trotted to the open window. "Hi, Mr. Saladino," they chorused.

"You two aren't out looking for doorbells to ring, are you?" He chuckled at their worried looks. "I was going to drive over to your street to see if you were out and about and here you are. Hey, I'm going out of town for a few days. I want you to do me a favor. I don't like the newspapers piling up on my step when I'm gone. The old man next door used to do it for me, but he died. Can you do that?"

They both nodded. "Sure, Mr. Saladino," David answered. "No problem."

Saladino nodded. "Good, good. Also, there's this cat around, black and white. He's not really mine, but I put out a little milk for him every night. Think you could put out a little milk in the bowl that sits on the step in the evenings?"

David nodded. "I think my dad gets milk pretty cheap from the liquor store. We can do that too."

"Thank you. Here's a little something for your trouble, and the milk." He dangled two twenty dollar bills out the window. They both hesitated and looked at each other. He chuckled again. "Just take it. I appreciate your help."

Tommy finally reached out and took the money. "Thank you, sir."

"Yeah, thanks a lot," David added. "How long you going to be gone?"

"Two, three days. Going to Las Vegas and L.A. Okay, see you boys in a few days."

The window rolled back up to keep in the air-conditioned air as he pulled away and then disappeared around the corner onto First Street.

"Wow!" Tommy finally blurted out. "Forty bucks!"

David grinned, thinking about how rich Saladino must be and about how this was making it even easier to do their spying. Nobody he knew gave kids forty dollars for anything, ever. Girls did babysitting for just fifty cents an hour, a double feature movie was a dollar, a half-gallon of milk cost around fifty cents and he knew his dad brought home about a hundred dollars a week. It was a huge deal whenever his dad gave him a couple of dollars just to surprise him. Forty dollars was maybe what your rich grandma might spend on you for Christmas—maybe.

David backhanded Tommy in the chest. "Come here," he said, then trotted down the alley.

They stopped in front of Saladino's garage door. "We gotta start paying more attention," David said. "We've been messing around in this alley for years. I remember now that I've seen his car a few times, but how come neither one of us ever talked about this garage door? All up and down this whole block it's the only door. All the rest are just big wide covered spaces with no doors. What's the matter with us?"

Tommy stared at David, then the door, then both ways up and down the alley. "No, I didn't wonder. It's just been here I guess and it was just how it was." He turned to the door again and gave it an accusing look as though it had deceived them on purpose. "Maybe we've been minding our parents too well and we should've been spending more time in the alley."

"Exactly," David said. "So this is why we've never seen his car parked back here. And did you see how the garage door closed itself?"

"Yeah," Tommy said. "I've never seen anyone do that before."

"My rich grandmother who lives across town drives new Cadillacs every year or two and she has one of those," David said. "I don't know anyone else who has one. Nobody around here. It's pretty cool. She has a button inside the car that opens and closes the door and she lets me press it. My dad says it's lazy."

"New Cadillacs and an automatic garage door," Tommy said. "Is your grandma a gangster?"

David laughed. "Maybe, huh?" He put his hands on his hips and sighed as he walked around in a nervous circle then stopped. "We ran into Mr. Saladino. Then a couple of days later we found out he's some kind of gangster. Now we just figured out that this is his garage and we haven't paid any attention to it at all even though it's the only one like it on the whole damn block! What else have we been missing? We gotta stop thinking like little kids. Stuff is passing us by while we're thinking we're so clever, out ringing doorbells and bullshit."

Tommy nodded in agreement, a grin slowly developing across his face. "Let's go ring his doorbell. I'll bet you twenty bucks he doesn't answer."

David stared, began laughing, then quickly reached down and scooped up a handful of sand and threw it as Tommy ran away screeching with laughter.

Back in 1959 when Vincent had first started working in the organization at the age of twenty-five as the nephew of Nicholas Saladino, he had been nothing more than an errand boy. His uncle was just nine years his senior and a rising star in the Los Angeles mob due to his involvement in a string of lucky money-making transactions in several Las Vegas schemes. This, coupled with his charisma and natural ability to handle the people around him, first through his leadership, then using restrained but quick and quiet violence when needed, had earned Nicholas

Saladino the respect of many of his older associates. His extreme temper surfaced on occasion, but he was smart enough to keep it at bay most of the time. He was given the position of underboss at the young age of thirty-five.

As his uncle's good fortune increased over the years, so had the value of Vincent's role and along with it his monetary compensation. Vincent also benefited from the patchwork of crime organizations that had carved out pieces of the pie in Las Vegas. The Chicago Outfit as well as mob families from New York, Buffalo, Philadelphia, Cleveland, Kansas City and Los Angeles owned or controlled casinos up and down the strip and downtown. They didn't trust each other or even the members within their own organizations. So much money was being skimmed at various levels that some truly lucrative properties appeared to be just barely getting by. In some cases the skim was being skimmed, adding to the confusion concerning just how much cash was supposed to be arriving at the final destination. In addition personnel from some properties worked together while others kept their unauthorized money operations more secretive.

Living away from Vegas and Los Angeles made Vincent less accessible to the very people the bosses didn't trust. People in the organization thought of him as a little odd, but his work was mainly behind the scenes so not many came in much contact with him. His uncle and the few who knew him thought he was maybe just a little stupid for living in a crummy little apartment in the summer-hot and winter-foggy San Joaquin Valley of California. When questioned he always answered that he had family nearby, which was true, but in reality it was just a couple of cousins that he only saw once or twice a year. He had also carved out a little action of his own in some rental property and a small-time Numbers game he ran around his end of town. But the money he made in those activities was a pittance compared to his share of the skim and the other compensation that came his way from the organization.

He only intended to live here for a few more years, then it

would be off to South America or Mexico or maybe Thailand. When the time came he would figure out where the mob would be least likely to find him.

Bakersfield's population of 70,000 was just large enough to warrant an airport, of sorts, but not enough of one to actually have good connections to many places. Getting to Las Vegas involved flying or, God forbid, taking a bus to Los Angeles, then finally a flight to Vegas and only on certain days. Vincent actually enjoyed the desert landscape and the long drives, at least partly due to the fact that every year since 1963 he had treated himself to a new Cadillac. Unless he chose to because maybe he'd had a little too much wine, he didn't need to rely on taxis to get around in Sin City. And showing up in valet parking in a flashy new Cadillac did bring a certain amount of service. Driving also gave him the freedom to travel without the airlines or the FBI getting too curious about his frequent trips. Most of all, driving allowed him to bring certain things back with him with nobody else paying any attention.

Vincent could easily afford to live in the most exclusive neighborhoods of the city where the expensive homes and expansive country clubs sometimes shared property lines. But he felt no desire to rub elbows with doctors and oil company executives and no need for lavish surroundings, at least not at home. He chose to be wined and dined in the hotels and casinos he frequented.

As for why he lived in Bakersfield in the "crummy little apartment" complex, he had good reasons. It kept him out of Las Vegas or Los Angeles except when he traveled there. The less he was noticed the better he liked it. He was just far enough away and just close enough. Four hours to Vegas and less than two hours to L.A. Everyone was busy with their own piece of running things and most people didn't know him or care where he lived. Most of the other couriers were everyday gofers moving small amounts within one property or to a boss in another property. But there were only a handful of couriers like Vincent who moved large amounts that had been skimmed and amassed over a week or two. His large deliveries went to the big bosses in Las Vegas and Los Angeles, often along with special messages that could only be passed along by hand because Vincent Saladino could be trusted.

Later that afternoon David and Tommy met with Mary Kay on the side of the Steiner house. This was open to the front yard, but it was a bare dirt strip seven feet wide that ran down the side of the house to the fence that separated the front and back yards. Here they often dug foxholes, built highways with Tonka trucks or constructed forts and battle scenes with hundreds of plastic army men.

Between the dirt strip and the house next door were several orange and lemon trees that belonged to the neighbor couple who they rarely saw. The trees hid most of the view of the side of the house from the street except for straight out the end. Across the street was the side of a house that faced Michigan Avenue. It wasn't a completely hidden spot. Anyone could walk up from the sidewalk or front yard, but it was hidden enough that whatever went on didn't attract much casual attention from the neighbors.

About a year before, the three of them worked all day just to see how big a hole they could dig. When David's parents first saw it his father burst out laughing, but then he saw the look on his wife's face and hollered at them. "You're mother's right! Somebody's going to fall in and break their neck. Fill it in!" It was five feet across and over five feet deep.

In the summer it was a good place to meet and not be overheard if the cooler was on and the house was closed up. His parent's bedroom window was just above them, but a tall dresser blocked half of it making it awkward to look out the window and David knew that it couldn't be cranked open without a loud squeak warning them.

He pulled the bills out of his pants pocket and handed them to Mary Kay.

"Forty dollars!" she said it in a loud whisper. She put down the latest book she was reading then held the bills for a few seconds and handed them back to David. "He must be rolling in it!"

"Tommy and I talked it over and we think you should get part of it too."

Tommy nodded. "Even if you are my sister."

She laughed and slapped his shoulder.

"Tommy and I get fifteen each cuz we're going to do the papers and the cat. You get ten bucks just because we're a team and it's all a part of our spy mission."

Mary Kay nodded and held back most of a smile. "You know, our parents have been telling us forever not to take anything from strangers."

David and Tommy looked at each other then back to her. "He's not a stranger," David explained. He was trying to sound serious, but a mischievous grin came to his face. "He's a gangster. We know exactly who he is."

Mary Kay returned the grin. "Okay, but how are we going to explain this to our parents?"

"We're not," David said. "I've got a few dollars saved up, so adding some to it won't even be noticed. There's always some new model cars down at the drugstore I can buy."

Tommy added, "Mom will never notice a few extra cokes or comic books. It's not like a hundred bucks or something."

"And we can't tell them we're helping out Saladino with the papers or any of that either," David said.

Tommy nodded agreement.

"Right," Mary Kay said.

David picked up the book she had set down and saw the title was *Mary Poppins Opens the Door*. "You really like these, huh?"

"It's the fourth book in the series," she said. "They're all good. I just started this one. The movie was good too, but these are different. Stories that have nothing to do with the movie."

Tommy said, "And not all that singing like the movie. I've read a little bit of the others she was reading. I don't know. I think they're crap written for girls."

She gave her brother an eye-rolling look. "You might like

them, David. They're weird and funny."

David opened the book and started skimming the first couple pages. "This guy is a sweep?"

"A chimney sweep," she explained. "The story is in England. Sweeps used to clean the inside of chimneys with brooms. They used kids to do the work so they could fit inside the chimneys. People say chimney sweeps are supposed to be good luck. Like shaking hands with one brings you luck."

Just then they heard a loud, "Tommy!" from Mrs. Dias.

Mary Kay laughed and backhanded his shoulder. "Your new deal to take out the trash and make more money."

"Crap, now I don't need it!" he said. "Be right back."

A few seconds later David asked, "So, how are things?"

She knew what he meant—anything and a lot of things. "Okay, I guess. My dad hasn't been hitting me or Tommy much lately, so that's good. My uncle still comes in my room sometimes, but he's not around too much. He doesn't really hurt me. . ." She shrugged, not knowing what else to say.

David nodded thoughtfully. "Tommy still doesn't know?"

She shook her head. "I don't know, he might. Don't tell him, okay?"

David reached over and held her hand. She smiled and brought her other hand over on top of his.

Over the next three days David smuggled milk out of the house every evening after dinner using the World War II canteen his father had brought home from the navy. They brought the newspapers back with them and put them in David's toy chest in the garage. Amid the jumble of various toy weapons, trucks, dirt-caked tools and dozens of other play items, a few newspapers would hardly be noticed or cared about.

On the third night, Sunday, David was pouring the milk into the bowl on Saladino's porch when he heard Tommy utter a soft, "Uh-oh."

He looked up. "What?"

Tommy pointed at the doorknob. "It turns."

David finished pouring the milk and straightened up. "Maybe it's one of those handles that turns even when it's locked."

Tommy shrugged.

David reached for the knob, turned it and pushed. The door popped open a bit. The two boys looked at each other. David pushed open the door about a foot. No chains, nothing against the door. He shut it again. "That's interesting."

"Maybe he came back home already," Tommy said.

David opened the door again. "Mr. Saladino! Mr. Saladino! It's us David, and Tommy. Anybody home?" He waited then shut the door and spoke softly. "If he left his place unlocked he must leave it that way all the time. This might make it easier to spy on him."

Tommy gasped. "We can't go into somebody's house!"

For several seconds David just nodded and thought. "That's true." He lowered his voice further and leaned down close to his companion. "But this is a special somebody. He's a gangster and we're the good guys."

Tommy nodded and looked at the door. "You think the back door is open too?"

"Let's check," David said.

They grabbed the newspaper and walked around to the back of the complex. Saladino lived in the end apartment so they could check the door without walking by other apartments. They discovered this door, too, was unlocked.

It was almost dark and they hurried down the alley and into Tommy's backyard. "Maybe he always leaves his doors unlocked."

"Maybe," David answered. "I know other people who never lock their doors. My grandmother who lives in Iowa leaves her house unlocked all the time. We're going to ask him."

Tommy's eyes widened. "Why?"

"Because it sounds honest. If anybody in another apartment was watching us they might say something to him. We'll just sound like we were concerned and see what he says. Maybe we'll find out if he does it all the time. We won't do anything right now, but someday when we need to, we have a way to maybe find out more about him."

That night, Vincent Saladino arrived back in town from his travels to Nevada and Los Angeles. He turned off of Highway 99 and drove through the agricultural outskirts of the city. It would be another few minutes before he would arrive home.

Vincent was not as simple as he let others think. He kept most of his observations and comments to himself and he was described by most as, loyal, dependable, even bland. His unexpressive face and sometimes awkward social manners caused others to nearly always underestimate him. Some thought him a little dim, many suspected he was gay and several knew damn well he was. He wanted them all to think of him as the dutiful courier who endured the methodical boredom of his mundane job and never rocked the boat.

Shrewd was not one of the descriptions that others offered, but he was every bit as shrewd and calculating as those he worked for and far more so than some. He had figured out long ago that he was in a unique situation, surrounded by such widespread criminal ineptitude, idiocy and dishonesty that it practically begged to be taken advantage of.

Between Vincent, several other couriers who brought money out of Las Vegas each month, other unofficial amounts being moved around or skimmed by casino bosses and their bosses, and sloppy or nonexistent accounting, it was often the case that nobody had a very good idea of exactly how much money was supposed to be in any particular place at any particular moment. The top bosses in Los Angeles and Las Vegas were rolling in it so deep they were giddy. They were using their "legitimate" Vegas businesses to launder money coming in from prostitution, drug sales, sports betting, union kickbacks, extortion schemes and a variety of other illegal endeavors. The officials from the state gaming commission, charged with seeing to it that everything was done properly and everyone was following the law, were paid so much extra by the mob that many gladly ignored the obvious skimming and other financial shenanigans.

Vincent was considered a special courier and it was common for him to be delivering half a million dollars in one trip, sometimes from several casinos to bosses who didn't necessarily honestly share the details of their business with each other. He had learned whom to tell what to, whom to avoid, whom to report about and whom to keep quiet about. Nobody was checking on Vincent Saladino or even cared to. He had figured out early that contrary to their reputation, the various mob bosses were not nearly as bright as some thought, and that if he did it right, he could skim the skim and everybody would still be happy as hell.

So, like most months, along with his normal payment in the trunk was another travel bag with money that only he knew about. Naturally, as time went on, Vincent had given himself regular raises as the business in the Nevada desert exploded beyond anyone's wildest dreams.

He knew it probably couldn't go on forever, but, then again, he sometimes told himself, maybe it could. He knew that whatever future he was capable of dreaming up could easily be paid for. His only real indulgences were nice suits, that new Cadillac every year, some gambling, and escort services in Las Vegas that let him indulge his "special" appetites for the right price. For now he would continue to lead his simple central California, small apartment life. He could figure out later how best to spend his growing retirement fund.

The next day, Vincent answered the knock at his door. "Hello, boys. Hey, thanks for taking care of things while I was gone."

"You're welcome, sir," David answered.

Tommy also mumbled a quick, "You're welcome."

"There's something we need to talk to you about," David said.

"Oh? Come on in and we'll talk." He looked past them. "Just you two? Where's your sister?"

"No, it's just us," David said.

They had seen into his place through the screen door a few times, but this was the first time they had actually been inside the lair of the mobster. He motioned them to a leather sofa and they seated themselves together in the middle of it, feeling smaller and younger with every passing second.

"You boys want something to drink? I've got Pepsi."

They looked at each other and nodded. "Sure," David answered.

As Vincent was busy in the kitchen just a few steps away, the boys looked around, pointing silently with their eyes. A dozen crucifixes and figurines of Mary were either hanging or resting on a shelf around the apartment, most of them visible from where they were sitting. There were too many paintings crowding the walls, a mix of mountain and desert landscapes and Italian village street scenes.

Cluttering nearly every remaining surface were souvenirs from Las Vegas—coasters, ashtrays, coin cups, coffee mugs, champagne glasses, gaming chips, decks of cards, dice, cocktail napkins, matchbooks and more. Most of these items were branded with names like The Mint, Flamingo, Desert Inn, Dunes, Landmark, Caesars Palace, Binions and Tropicana. David and Tommy had little idea of what all the names meant, but the souvenirs, along with all the rest of the conglomeration of art and religious icons struck them as exotic and mysterious. Las Vegas was just a four-hour drive away and the two boys knew next to nothing about it other than people went there to gamble.

Vincent returned with two tall glasses full of ice and Pepsi and handed one to each of the boys. Walking back into the kitchen he retrieved his own tall glass of ice and port wine and seated himself in his large chair facing them.

"So, what are we going to talk about?" After several moments of silence he chuckled. "You guys look nervous. What's up? The cat die or something?"

They both laughed a little. David took a deep breath. "We wanted you to know that when we were getting the paper and leaving the milk the other night we were standing on your step and we discovered your door was unlocked."

Saladino took a swallow of wine and nodded. "How did you

find that out?"

"That's why we wanted to talk to you," David said eagerly. "We didn't try to find out anything. We were just there holding the door handle while we did the milk and stuff and it turned. We looked at each other, then we tested it to see if it was really unlocked. We stuck our head in and yelled for you in case you were home already. We didn't go in or anything. Then we checked the back and it was unlocked too. So we wanted to let you know it was unlocked in case you didn't know. But we thought somebody might have seen us and we didn't want you to think we were messing around or anything."

Saladino switched his gaze to Tommy, who just nodded emphatically, but said nothing. Saladino smiled and nodded again. "You two are good boys. I know you weren't messing around my place. I just don't pay much attention to locking up. I guess maybe I should lock the doors, but I just never got in the habit and I figure people will mind their own business and leave my stuff alone."

"But what about bad guys?" David asked.

Saladino laughed out loud and threw his arms into the air. "Hey, the bad guys don't mess with me! But I guess the business I'm in maybe I should be worrying about the bad guys."

David felt the opportunity to be a little bold. "What business are you in, Mr. Saladino?"

Saladino nodded slowly and let a more serious expression return to his face. "Good question, kid. I'm in the money business."

He stood and motioned for the boys to follow him. He led them down the short hall to his bedroom. He used the wall switch to turn on the ceiling light and pointed to the corner where a four-foot tall safe stood.

"That's where I keep my business money. If anyone ever came in here to steal it they would have a pretty hard time. It's bolted to the floor and it weighs hundreds of pounds. Way too heavy to carry away. They would have to make all kind of noise and work on it a long time to get it open. I think it's pretty secure, don't you?"

Both boys nodded and wondered just how much money was in that safe. "It's open," David observed.

"I'm home," Saladino said. "When I'm not here I lock it closed."

He saw their eyes move to the top of the safe. "Yeah, that too," he said, pointing to the .38 caliber revolver lying on top of the safe. "It sits right there whenever I'm home and it's loaded. Like you said, just in case of bad guys."

He reached for the light switch, stopped and looked down at the boys. "Let's keep this just between us. I don't want other kids getting the wrong idea or coming around. I don't pay nobody else to help me with stuff, just you guys. Capisce?"

The boys nodded and Saladino turned off the light switch and the three of them returned to the living room. Hanging in the air was an understanding. They knew what he was and he knew they knew. They had been given a small glimpse of his life and there was a certain implied trust in that. They would keep being overpaid for small chores and in return they wouldn't talk about it with others.

FOUR

During the next week David, Tommy and Mary Kay spent a good deal of their time on their spy mission. They stationed themselves in the Dias's backyard and kept watch down the alley with binoculars. They also spent some time at Adams Elementary School where they had just finished up their sixth grade year. The northeast part of the playground was across First Street from Saladino's apartment. They went to elaborate lengths to go completely around the school, entering from the opposite side and sneaking across the open playground. Near the fence were several box-hockey sets which stood about a foot high. They laid down behind these and raised up or leaned around just enough to view the front of his apartment through the binoculars. Occasionally they had to jump away from black widow spiders.

Through all this watching and waiting they learned absolutely nothing and by the following Saturday were beginning to tire of the whole notion. David now understood why he had not known about the man before. They rarely saw him even when they were doing practically nothing else but trying to see what he was doing. Vincent Saladino was proving to be a very boring gangster.

Saturday morning they were stationed at their usual spot across First Street at the school, laying in the grass by the box-hockey sets. Mary Kay was reading her Mary Poppins book while the boys took turns with the binoculars.

Suddenly Tommy said, "Hey, there he is!"

He saw him come outside in old work clothes and walk back

toward the alley. Still watching through binoculars, Tommy caught a glimpse of him rolling a wheelbarrow across the alley toward the house that he owned.

"He's going over to Janice's house to do yardwork or something!" he announced.

David was as tired as the others of the lack of action. "How about if we just wander down the alley and say hi when we see him? We could even offer to help."

Tommy and his sister eagerly agreed. They hurried back to the kindergarten area, out the side gate and made for the Simpson end of the alley, nearest Janice's end of the block.

Saladino always kept around twelve thousand dollars in his bedroom safe, just to give anybody who was looking something to find, but he kept his real money somewhere a little more difficult to find. In the bottom of the wheelbarrow, covered by a tarp and assorted yard tools, rode another contribution to his retirement fund.

The backyard landscaping had been planned well. A mixture of trees and shrubs on either side of the yard were maintained by Saladino to block all but the most determined onlookers. Along the back fence which paralleled the alley were more shrubs, but he kept these trimmed lower. He wanted to be able to see over himself, from both sides of the fence.

Between the back fence and the back of the house was a wide lawn and a patio that ran more than half the length of the back of the house. Where the lawn and patio met stood another row of shrubs which blocked the view of half the patio and the chimney from the alley and from one of the bedroom windows.

The brick chimney was outside against this back wall of the house. It jutted out two feet and ran from the ground, where it was five feet wide, up through a space in the eave, narrowing along the way to just a couple of feet square as it rose up above the roof level. It looked like all the other chimneys in the neighborhood. At the bottom, just a few inches above ground level, was a metal door for cleaning the ashes from the firebox under the fireplace inside the house.

Saladino unlocked the alley gate and wheeled into the backyard, latching the gate behind him. He continued forward around the line of shrubs and parked his wheelbarrow near the chimney. He often scheduled his work days when he knew the Boyds were out of town or away at some activity. He enjoyed the peace and quiet, plus if he had a deposit to make he could do that with nobody else around.

He opened the ash cleanout door, knelt down and reached inside. A second later a soft click sounded. After going through the proper steps and allowing himself a few moments of admiring satisfaction, he dropped the tools out of the wheelbarrow and moved the tarp to one side. He quickly transferred the bills into the chimney vault, noting that he would probably have it filled before another year went by. He stood and closed and locked everything back into place

"Mr. Saladino, you back there?" David called over the fence.

It startled him, but he recognized the voice. "Right here, boys." He walked out from behind the shrubs so they could see him. "Come on in." He quickly turned and put the tools back into the wheelbarrow.

David reached over and unlatched the gate and they walked across the yard to the patio just as Saladino walked away from the wheelbarrow. "This is my sister, Mary Kay," Tommy explained.

"I know," Saladino said and extended his hand. She shyly extended her own and they shook hands.

"How did you know who she was?" Tommy said.

He gave Tommy a serious look with just a hint of a smile. "She looks just like you only prettier. I met her before a while back when she was over here playing with Janice. Plus, I know who everybody is around here, remember?"

"Even kids?" David asked, but his eyes were on Mary Kay, verifying Saladino's compliment.

"Especially kids," he answered. "Everybody starts out as a kid, but they all grow up someday. I knew who you guys were." He laughed out loud.

"So what are you doing?" David asked. "You want any help?"

"Nothing much," he said. "Just hitting the weeds and a little trimming and raking. I could always use a hand with the weeds. Most of the yard is in pretty good shape, but that corner there by the side fence is kind of getting out of hand. You want to help?"

The three looked at each other and nodded. David answered for all of them. "Sure. It's better than pulling weeds at home. We're all sick of our own weeds, but I have to run home for a second and take a leak. I'll be right back."

"What about the other side of the house?" Tommy suggested.

"No, don't do that," Saladino said. He tossed him a key ring. "They're out of town. Go in the front door. Wipe your feet. Don't forget to flush and lock the door."

Tommy giggled again and Mary Kay shook her head and smiled as she walked to the patio and set her book on a chair.

"Here, I'll get you guys started on this corner," Saladino said.

David walked through the breezeway between the garage and the house and unlocked the front door. Even though he had permission it felt uncomfortable walking into someone else's house. When he came back out of the bathroom, he stopped on his way through the living room just to gaze around. There were only five different models in the neighborhood and this was one of the most common ones, just like the Dias's house in fact. But something looked different. He stood a little longer just looking around.

Every house in the neighborhood had a fireplace, all with the same outside chimney at the back of the house. He stood staring at the end of the room where the fireplace should've been. Instead there was just a chair and table and a funny painting hanging on the wall above them. All the houses had flat stone or brick on the inside wall around and above the fireplace up to the ceiling. On the way into the yard he had seen the wheelbarrow and tools back behind where Saladino had greeted them and they had been sitting by the outside chimney.

He finally just muttered, "Hm," to himself and walked back

outside, locking the front door behind him. He walked back through the breezeway to the patio and stopped. A few yards to his right was the wheelbarrow sitting by the chimney like he remembered. Saladino was across the yard instructing Tommy and Mary Kay about how to clear the weeds out of the unkempt corner.

David returned his attention to the chimney and began to walk over toward it. "David!" Saladino was hurrying toward him. "They're going to need help. The three of you can probably knock it out in twenty minutes."

"Okay," he answered, and he walked across the yard and joined his companions.

David said nothing then about the lack of a fireplace in a house with a chimney, but he kept watching Saladino as they worked. More than once he saw him eyeing the chimney from different angles, even running his fingers in the mortar lines. The wheelbarrow contained pruning shears, a broom and a folded, dirty canvas tarp.

Over the next half hour David watched Saladino pull a few weeds here and there and use a small pair of hand shears to shape a shrub that grew at the corner of the chimney. He also watered a few of the plant containers around the patio and used the hose to wash off the concrete slab.

"Okay, kids, that's it for today. That corner looks a lot better."

He seemed in a hurry as he ushered them out through the gate and followed them out into the alley. "Thanks, you were a big help. See you later." He turned and wheeled across the alley and through the side door of his garage.

"Bye Mr. Saladino," they called together after him.

"Let's walk out this end and around on the street," David said. "I think my dad's in the backyard."

They walked the short distance to the north end of the alley, out onto Simpson and around the corner onto Second. Mary Kay and Tommy were talking about whose turn it was to wash and dry dishes that night.

Mary Kay turned to David. "Why are you so quiet?"

"Just thinking," he said.

"We're sure not finding out much information," Mary Kay said. She was tiring of the whole affair even faster than the boys.

"I found out something," David said.

Tommy giggled. "How to flush the Boyd's toilet?"

David answered with a loud laugh. "No, fart head. Do either of you know of any houses around here without fireplaces?"

They both looked around as they walked, noting the chimneys that weren't hidden by trees. "They all have them, don't they?" Mary Kay said.

"Janice's house doesn't have one," David announced.

"Are you sure?" Mary Kay said.

"Positive. When I came out of the bathroom I stopped in the living room trying to figure out what looked different. There's just a wall. No stone or brick."

Tommy thought for a bit. "But there's a chimney in the back, isn't there?"

David just nodded.

They reached the Dias's yard and plopped themselves down on the front lawn by the driveway in the shade of an ash tree, hot and sweaty from the yard work and the usual hundred-degree heat of August.

Mary Kay stood again. "Want a popsicle?" Both boys nodded and she ran into the house to put her book away and fetch the popsicles.

"Hey," Tommy said softly. "You notice anything about Mr. Saladino looking at Mary Kay?"

David looked at him blankly. "No, what do you mean?"

Tommy looked back to make sure his sister was not returning yet. "I don't know. I thought he was looking at her, you know, like looking her over."

"You mean like a dirty old man look?"

Tommy nodded. "Yeah, maybe, I don't know." A mischievous grin spread across his face. "Kind of like you look at her sometimes, except you're young."

David reached out and slapped the back of Tommy's head,

which just boosted Tommy's grin to full laughter.

'That's okay," Tommy said, "I can tell she likes you more lately too. So I guess her nose is changing because you smell just as bad as ever, probably worse." Tommy was still grinning, hoping for some kind of huge reaction.

David just stared back at him for several moments. "You know, her nose is probably dead from living with you and your stinky feet." Then he reached out and wrenched Tommy's worn out left sneaker from his foot and threw it out into the middle of the street.

Tommy laughed even harder, pleased with himself for getting just the kind of reaction he was hoping for.

Mary Kay returned a few seconds later. "What are you guys laughing about?"

"David threw my shoe in the street," Tommy said, pointing and laughing.

She looked at the shoe and back at David and Tommy. "Let's see how long it takes until a car runs over it."

The boys looked at each other then broke into renewed laughter.

The laughter soon died down and nobody spoke as they unwrapped their popsicles, all root beer flavored because that was their father's favorite.

"Maybe it used to have a fireplace," Mary Kay said. "Maybe the people living there didn't like it and had it covered over so it looked just like the wall."

David shook his head. "You know what all these houses look like. Your house, my house, everyone's house, they all have stone around the fireplace and running up the wall to the ceiling. That seems like a lot of work to get rid of all of that too."

She just shrugged. "I guess."

"Didn't Mr. Saladino say he bought that house when it was being built?" Tommy remembered.

David nodded. "He said he watched this neighborhood being built and decided to invest in one of the houses."

"A mistake, maybe?" Tommy said.

"Mr. Saladino?" David said. "He would've made sure it got fixed, or else."

They all laughed a little.

"So, what do you think?" Mary Kay asked.

"I think he had it built that way on purpose and the outside chimney is where he hides his money," David said.

Tommy scowled. "He showed us the safe in his bedroom."

"Right," David said. "We're a couple of kids and he showed us where he keeps his money. I believed him, and he probably does keep money there." He lowered his voice and they all leaned their heads closer together. "Why would a gangster like him even want to mess around taking care of somebody's rental house? He had his stuff parked over by the chimney and he never used any of the tools he had in that wheelbarrow. Plus he kept looking at the chimney and touching it."

Mary Kay chewed a piece of Popsicle. "Sounds kind of weird. You really think he's hiding money there?"

David shrugged. "I don't know, but it's kind of strange about no fireplace and the way he was messing around the chimney but not using the tools he brought. And that little door down by the ground, it has a lock on it. We don't have a lock on ours, do you guys?"

They shook their heads. "It's for cleaning out ashes," Mary Kay said. "Why would anyone have a lock on it?"

"Right," David said. "He had a canvas in the wheelbarrow too, like he used it to cover something. So if the other bad guys ever come after his money they find his safe and they figure that's it. Who would ever think of checking across the alley inside the chimney of some house?"

"Those guys are always killing each other over something," Tommy said. "Mom was reading to Dad about some guy in the paper just the other day."

Several moments of silence passed. Mary Kay said, "So, we should be spying on Janice's house, not his apartment."

"I was looking around at the yard when we were back there," David said. "Lots of bushes down both sides. There might be places where you could lay down just on the other side of the fence and see through the cracks."

"Who lives in those two houses?" Tommy asked.

"The one is some guy named Chick," David said. "I guess my dad knows him a little. I don't think they even have any kids."

"I know who you mean," Mary Kay said. "The people with the boat next to the driveway? They're kind of older. Their kids are probably grown up."

Tommy said. "If we knew they were gone or out in front we could sneak over the fence and hide in their yard."

David nodded. "We'll have to check and see if they have good places to hide along the fence. So who lives on the other side?"

Mary Kay got up and walked out into the street, shielding her eyes from the sun as she studied the far end of the block for a few seconds then returned to the lawn. "It's that lady who lives by herself. She drives that old station wagon with the wood sides. I think her name is Mrs. Palmer."

"Oh, her," David remembered. "Anyway, we can't very well ask her if we can come over and play so we can spy on Mr. Saladino."

"So, now what?" Tommy asked.

Mary Kay sighed. "We're probably off on the whole wrong track on this. Janice and her family live in the house and they know there's no fireplace. They must've noticed they have a chimney."

"Saladino could've told them anything about that. He might have told them he had it taken out or even that it was a mistake when the house was built. They probably don't even think about it anymore."

"Okay, so, like Tommy said, now what?"

"I don't know yet." David said. "But we'll think of something."

A few seconds later a delivery truck turned the corner at David's end of the block and rumbled down Second Street. As it got closer they all remembered the shoe in the road. As they stared with anticipatory smiles, the front left tire ran over Tommy's sneaker and then the back tire kicked it up in the air behind the truck. It was some time before the writhing-on-the-ground laughter ran its course.

Over the next couple of weeks the boys, sometimes with Mary Kay, visited Vincent Saladino a few times when he was standing outside his apartment or at the Boyd's house and they were left in charge of the newspaper and the cat again for three days, making another forty dollars. They checked and discovered both doors unlocked again, but did not go inside.

It was just two and a half weeks until school started and neither of the boys were overjoyed at the change that would come over their lives then. Both of them did passingly okay in school, but it was not their highest priority in life. They both loved to read, but not necessarily what they were assigned by a teacher.

Mary Kay, on the other hand, was beginning to become more excited about the upcoming school year and seemed to be placing a lot of importance on the whole notion of being done with elementary school and starting at Fort Kern Junior High. But David thought she was being quieter and seemed different somehow, but he didn't know what was going on with her. There had even been a few times when she wasn't around and when he asked Tommy where she was he didn't know.

On the Monday of their next-to-last week of freedom, the three of them were sitting in the shade on the front lawn of David's house drinking lemonade. Mary Kay announced that Janice Boyd had invited her to her birthday party on the upcoming Saturday.

David gave her a skeptical look. "I thought you two weren't really friends anymore."

She shrugged. "That's true, but I think she's just trying to build up some friendships for seventh grade. I think it's a girl thing."

David nodded, taking notice again of her budding breasts pushing against her thin shirt. "You're probably right."

"It's a slumber party too, so I'm pretty sure that sometime during the evening I can bring up that I noticed they don't have a fireplace. It might be interesting just to see what she says."

Tommy giggled. "Ask her if she knows her landlord is a gangster."

"I found out a little something that may be helpful," David announced in a hushed voice. "Yesterday while you guys were at your never-ending church service I did a little spying on my own."

Mrs. Dias was a devout Catholic and the family attended mass every Sunday without fail. Even Tommy and Mary Kay thought their Sunday routines got a little long. To David, whose family was Lutheran and attended services sporadically, the three hours the Dias's were gone at church every Sunday seemed like it must be some sort of an incomprehensible hell on Earth masquerading as religion. They had invited David to come to church with them before, but he could not conceive of enduring such a time span.

"I was sitting on the wall at the end of the alley yesterday drinking some chocolate milk and watching a bunch of ants when I saw Saladino head across the alley pushing a wheelbarrow."

"He just came back from another one of his trips!" Tommy said.

"He didn't see you?" Mary Kay asked.

David shook his head. "I was back just barely able to see down the alley. I don't think he'd see me from all the way down the block unless he was really looking for someone. As soon as I saw him I jumped back and just peeked around the fence."

"So then what?" Tommy asked.

David smiled. "I ran down our side of the block. I was going to head up the alley from the other side and try to watch him through the fence, but guess who I saw driving away all dressed up for church?"

A smile spread across Mary Kay's face. "Mrs. Palmer!"

"Exactly. I knew nobody was home so I opened her gate and walked right into her backyard like I belonged there. I figured if anyone asked I could say a ball went over from the alley and

I was looking for it. So, anyway, I snuck over to the side fence. She's got some trees growing along the fence, but there's room to crawl underneath and right up to the fence. I found a place where I could lay down and watch between two of the boards."

Both of his companions were leaning forward and waiting wide-eyed. "Well?" they said at the same time.

"He was just closing that little door at the bottom of the chimney and putting the lock back on it. He picked up the rake and stuff he had laying on the ground, put them back in the wheelbarrow, folded up the canvas and left."

Tommy swatted him on the shoulder. "Man, you must be right!"

Mary Kay was smiling and shaking her head. "Steiner, you did good on this one." She lowered her voice. "We're really onto something. We all have to be careful. We can't say anything about this to anybody." She turned to her brother. "You got that?"

Tommy quickly crossed his heart and held up his right hand.

FIVE

Earlier that same day, a meeting was taking place in Los Angeles that would very soon put an abrupt end to Vincent Saladino's retirement savings plan.

Nicholas "Dino" Saladino, though he was Vincent's uncle, was only nine years older than his nephew at forty-three. Having moved up in the hierarchy of the organization beginning at a young age, he was aware that his relative youth was an issue with some of the people he worked with. He sometimes felt he had to try just a little bit harder because of it. The current situation threatened to undermine his authority and his standing in the organization.

He was a good-sized man, six feet tall, a little heavy in the belly, dark hair combed straight back. Women thought him good-looking and he was a smooth talker when he wanted to be. He was standing behind his ornate, Italian walnut desk, having just pounded his fist down on top of a wooden cigarette case, smashing the lid. "How much?"

Standing in front of him was Michael Luna, his most trusted lieutenant, flanked by two of his Las Vegas casino operators. "We're not sure yet," Luna said. "but we know for a fact of three pooled skims in the last two months that came up light between Vegas and you. All three were delivered by Vincent."

"Jesus! You mean somebody finally got around to keeping track?" Saladino's face grew even angrier. "Him and his fucking new Cadillacs! Shit, I guess I've been buying the bastards! How much were we short on those three skims?"

The two men, one a casino cage manager and the other a

counting room manager, each handed Luna a slip of paper. They had been ordered to remain silent and were not going to put themselves in any worse light than they already had. Both were entertaining doubts about their lives continuing beyond this meeting.

Luna had talked over the figures with the two men, but he checked over the figures again before answering. "Round figures, maybe around sixty grand."

Saladino took a deep breath and said nothing for half a minute. Finally he pointed at the two casino men. "I want to thank you for coming to me on this. Don't worry about the fact that it's my nephew. When you guys get back to Vegas we're making some changes so we don't have more of this happening. Let's find out who else knew this was going on. I want those people taken care of."

Both men nodded. "Thank you, sir."

"Wait out front," Luna told them.

Nicolas Saladino was figuring how he could keep this from getting out to too many of his associates and bosses. If it did but it also got around that he ordered a hit on Vincent for it, he might be able to put himself in a better light in this whole mess. "Okay, Michael, family or not we need to send a message on this one. Put Fats and Doggie on this one. They can hit him at his apartment in Bakersfield. While they're at it, have them toss the place and find some goddamn money. We might get some of it back."

Luna walked around the desk and put his arm around Saladino's shoulder. "Sorry it had to go this way, Dino. I assume you want this to be quick and painless?"

Saladino gave a sarcastic laugh. "This is a hell of a business we're in, eh? I guess I owe the thieving bastard that much just because he's family. Damn, sixty thousand! How long has he been doing this? He might've gotten to us for a million by this time."

Luna shook his head. "No way it's that much. We would've picked up on it. He probably just got greedy a couple times and decided a couple more wouldn't hurt."

Saladino nodded. "I pay him plenty. He should've just asked for a raise. I would've cut him in on more action."

The next day David and Tommy walked down the alley and into Saladino's complex. He had told them to come over around 9:00 in the morning and they could help him paint the back fence at the Boyd's house.

It was just after 9:00 when David knocked on the door to his apartment. They waited a bit and then knocked again.

"Maybe he's still asleep," Tommy said.

"Nah, he's always up early. Maybe he ran to the store."

They sat down on the step to wait.

"Where's your sister?" David asked.

Tommy shrugged. "I think she had to help fold laundry or something. She'll be here."

Another minute went by while they fiddled in the dirt in the flower bed by the step.

"Try the door again," Tommy said.

David opened the door just enough to stick his head in. Loud Italian opera music blared out. "Mr. Saladino, it's me, David! Anybody home?"

To Tommy's surprise, David stepped inside and turned around to face him. "Wait here. If he comes, knock on the door and I'll go out the back and come around."

"You can't..." Tommy began, but David closed the door.

Tommy paced back and forth between the doorstep and the sidewalk so he could see Saladino if he came from any direction.

Being inside the apartment by himself struck him as creepier than when they had been in there before and somehow the loud music from the hi-fi made it even weirder. He had no idea what he might find that would be of any use, but he was feeling emboldened by recent events and decided it was time to take advantage of Saladino's unlocked doors. Their summer was coming to a close and they would have much less time to watch their quarry after the looming start of the school year.

Tommy walked out to the sidewalk and kept watch as noisy traffic sped by including several trucks with empty flatbed trailers clanking over a section of rippled asphalt that seemed to never get repaired. He walked back and forth three more times.

The three minutes he had waited already felt like an hour and he was sure every window he could see had someone peeking out at him. Unable to stand it any longer, he opened the door and stepped into the dimly lit apartment closing the front door behind him. The music had stopped. He saw David staring back at him from the other side of the living room where it became the end of the kitchen and the hall.

"What?" David said. "Someone coming?"

Tommy shook his head. "No, I feel like everyone's watching me hang around out there. What're you doing? What if he comes home?"

David said nothing for several moments. He wiped his eyes and then shakily said, "He won't, he's dead."

Tommy's eyes widened and his chest was pounding. He wanted to cry and run away, but he was afraid to do either one. "Where?"

David pointed down the hall. "Come here."

Tommy could not remember ever being this scared. He walked across the room and down the short hall with David.

David stopped at the doorway to the bedroom and faced Tommy. "Don't worry, he's dead. He can't hurt us. Don't touch anything." He held up his hands and wiggled his fingers. "Fingerprints."

Tommy nodded and said nothing.

David reached around and flipped on the light switch with the back of his hand.

Saladino was sitting up in bed staring at them, his head leaning to one side. He was bare chested with the sheet pulled up to his waist. There was a dark hole over his left eye. Behind his head was a splatter of bloody tissue and pillow feathers on the headboard and wall.

Tommy began squealing as he struggled to hold back

screaming, crying and his breakfast. "Shit! Shit! Let's get out of here!"

David grabbed the front of his shirt. "We will, but hang on a second, and don't barf!"

"Look," Tommy said. He was pointing to the open safe next to the bed. The door was ajar about six inches.

David shook his head. "We better just leave it alone. Grab his keys from the hook in the kitchen. Take any other keys you see and let's go."

Careful to touch things as little as possible, they began looking around the kitchen. Tommy took the key chain from the hook and shoved it into the pocket of his cutoff jeans. There were half a dozen keys on it. They looked around quickly, opening a few cabinet doors using a dish towel. They found another key chain with just three keys on it. David pocketed those and they left the apartment.

Out on the step, David called, "Okay, Mr. Saladino. See you later." Then he closed the door behind them and grabbed Tommy's arm. "Walk."

They walked out onto the sidewalk along First Street. It got them out of the complex quicker than walking by all the other apartments back into the alley. They forced themselves to walk until they reached the corner at Simpson where they broke into a panicked run.

They ran right by Tommy's house to the strip of dirt on the side of David's house. David knew his father was at work and his mom was inside ironing and watching television. It was already hot out and the house was closed up with the swamp cooler running.

For nearly a minute they just panted and said nothing. "Go get your sister," David finally said. "Don't tell her anything, just get her."

Tommy got up to leave but David slapped his leg to stop him. "You did good, man. I was scared too."

Tommy managed half a smile then turned and ran to his house.

David moved slightly farther down the wall toward the front yard away from the bedroom window. He pulled the key ring out of his pocket and began studying the keys. He also pulled out the .38 revolver he had shoved into his waistband before Tommy came into the apartment. Holding it in one hand he turned it this way and that, feeling the weight of it. Figuring it was a good idea to take it, he wasn't sure what he was going to do with it, but he knew where to hide it.

Three years ago while the three of them were playing and digging on the side of the house, David had discovered a space at the edge of the foundation right behind the gas meter about eight inches wide and deep. They kept it covered with a small piece of wood and some dirt. So far it had been used from time to time to hide part of a pack of cigarettes taken from Tommy and Mary Kay's uncle, a paperback book full of dirty stories they found in the alley, and a rusty switchblade knife Tommy found sitting in the gutter. All three items had since been disposed of.

David stashed the gun and waited. After a couple of minutes, Tommy returned with Mary Kay. They sat facing David on the short curb that marked the property line between the two houses. She had a way of chewing her bottom lip when she was nervous, which she was doing now while her eyes darted back and forth between David and her brother, finally locking with David's.

"Saladino is dead," David said, so softly it was nearly a whisper.

"We went over to help him paint the Boyd's fence," Tommy explained. "We knocked on his door a couple times. Then. . ." He gestured to David.

"I opened his door and yelled for him and nobody answered so I walked in to see what I could see. Tommy stayed outside keeping watch, but he got nervous waiting and came inside too after a little bit. Saladino was sitting up in bed. Somebody shot him."

Tommy pointed a finger at his own forehead.

Mary Kay silently stared at David for a long time while

Tommy stared down at the dirt and rubbed both hands back and forth through his hair in nervous frustration. She grabbed her brother's hand and held it tight as she broke her gaze from David. "Were you scared to death?"

Both boys nodded again, "That safe in his bedroom was standing open," David continued. "We didn't look in it."

She was shaking her head as he talked, her eyes filling with tears.

Tommy pointed at his forehead again. "Small hole here, big mess on the wall behind him. We didn't look, but I think he had a big hole back there."

She made a face. "Did anybody see you?"

"Don't know," David said, "but we didn't see anyone. I yelled goodbye to him as we left just in case anyone was watching."

Tommy snickered nervously. "Don't worry, he didn't answer."

Mary Kay put her hand over her mouth again. Her whole body began to tremble and tears spilled from her eyes. "Sorry," she managed to get out shakily.

"You don't need to be sorry," David said. He reached over and rubbed her shoulder with his free hand.

He showed the keys in his hand. "We took whatever keys we could find. There might be a key to that little door in the chimney. I've been looking at these. I think it's the same key chain he had me use the other day. Look, this looks like a house key, but there are two other keys on here. They look like they could be to a padlock or a cabinet or something like that. What do you have Tommy?"

He held out the key ring. Two of the keys had Cadillac symbols on them. "That's his car keys and probably his apartment key," David said.

Mary Kay took a deep shaky breath. "Are you actually going to check to see if the money is in there?"

"I've been thinking about that. I want to know if we were right about the money. But besides that, it's bad guy money, right? It's not like we can turn it in and someone's going to give us a reward. It's mob money. I think whatever we find should just be ours."

Mary Kay scowled.

"Think about it," David said. "We'd be taking it from bad guys. In a way we would be helping because the less money the bad guys have the better, right? I'll bet you a dollar there's at least five thousand in there."

She sniffed and wiped her eyes. "So if it's less, you owe me a dollar?" she said.

David nodded. "If it's more, you owe me a dollar."

Mary Kay sighed. "So, say there are thousands of dollars in there. What do we do with it?"

"Hide it," David said. "Hide it and keep it. Use a little of it when we need it. Save most of it and use it when we're older for stuff we need then. Cars, clothes, whatever. You know how they say 'when opportunity knocks'? Well, this is a huge opportunity!"

"How would we keep it secret?" Tommy asked.

"Hide it in a good spot and don't tell anyone, ever," David said. "We just have to be smart about it."

Mary Kay tilted her head and studied his face. "You've been thinking about this."

David nodded.

"Wait a minute," Tommy said. "What if there's no money in there at all?"

David smiled, and didn't believe for a second that it would turn out that way. "Okay, if there's no money in there at all, we both owe you two dollars."

Tommy's face widened into a grin. "Okay! I bet I win. There's probably nothing but spiders in there."

David became serious again. "Listen, I was doing a lot of thinking while I was waiting for you. Except for who shot him, nobody knows he's dead but us. Pretty soon though, people are going to find out."

"How is anyone else going to find out?" Tommy asked. "He doesn't seem to have any friends or anything. In movies sometimes the bad guys want everyone to know when they kill someone. They might call the police so it gets in the news and everything."

David nodded. "Yeah, maybe. You know my Uncle Bill, the fireman? He has all kinds of gross stories about finding dead people. Sometimes people just sort of rot, especially in hot weather like this. The neighbors start smelling something and they call the cops."

Mary Kay made a face and let out a quick nervous laugh as she shook her head, still wiping tears from her eyes. "That is sickening." Her hands were still trembling.

David grinned. "I know. If we just let his newspapers pile up, one of his neighbors will get curious after a while. We probably have at least a couple of days to figure out if there's money in the Boyd's chimney."

Just then they heard Mary Kay and Tommy's mother yelling for them from two houses away.

"Get going," Mary Kay told her brother. "I'll be right there."

Tommy took off running. Mary Kay scooted closer to David, wiped the leftover tears from her face and stared into his eyes for a long time.

"You okay?" he asked.

She nodded, shrugged then shook her head and began trembling again.

He reached and took both her hands in his. "We're going to find his money. I'll make this work. I'll take care of this, of you, of all of us."

Mary Kay leaned forward and for the first time kissed him on the mouth. The first one was just a quick peck. Then she leaned in again and kissed him much longer. "David Steiner, I love you," she whispered.

She reached, touched his cheek and stared at him with the same look he had tried to understand a few minutes before. "Don't tell Tommy," she said, then stood and ran off.

He watched her disappear and he sat and thought for a long time—about her, about Tommy, about Vincent Saladino, about a lot of things.

That night the Dias household was awakened twice by Tommy screaming. When his mother came into his room and shook him awake he said he must have been having nightmares, but he said he couldn't remember them.

In the morning his mother remarked how strange it was having Tommy screaming like that. He never had before. Mary Kay didn't find it strange at all and she knew that he probably remembered his nightmares perfectly well. She always remembered hers.

Late that afternoon the three of them were sitting in the shade on David's front lawn talking a little about when and if to go looking for Saladino's money, but mostly they were sitting in silence, thinking, wondering.

Suddenly Mary Kay sat up straighter. "Janice's birthday party got moved to Saturday night instead of the afternoon. They're going to visit her grandmother on Friday and they're not coming back until Saturday afternoon sometime."

"Let's sneak over on Friday night," Tommy said.

David was staring at nothing and thinking. "No, if we go over at night we'll have to use flashlights and someone might see us. People pay too much attention to noises at night. Plus I don't think I could sneak out of the house without getting caught. We could go over early Saturday morning. Where does her grandmother live?"

She thought for a moment. "Fresno or someplace near there. They were talking about it being a couple of hours to drive. They're having a birthday breakfast and a little family party with her grandparents before they come back. The party here isn't until 5:30."

"Perfect," David said. "They won't be getting back too early. We probably have at least until noon, but just to be safe let's meet in the alley at 9:00. We can watch cartoons early and the usual junk just to keep our parents happy then disappear out playing for a while."

Thursday morning, David, Tommy and Mary Kay spent their time alternating between observing from the school playground, walking down the alley and walking down First Street by the front of the apartment. At Tommy's insistence, they were on the lookout for any strange cars or people who might be coming back to look for the rest of Saladino's money.

They went back to David's house and sat around in the yard and rode their bikes through the neighborhood the other direction, away from the apartments, but Vincent Saladino was really the only thing on their minds. No matter what they were doing or pretending to be interested in, the conversation always came back around to Cadillac Vinnie and his money.

Early that evening the three of them went to his apartment, picked up the newspaper from the porch and left some milk for the cat. Friday they did pretty much the same thing, but late in the morning Mrs. Dias took Mary Kay and Tommy to Sears for some school shopping.

David decided to walk down to the liquor store. He could say hi to his dad and get a free soda or something. He thought maybe he'd go down to the drugstore on the corner and check out the car model kits and comic books. He still had most of the money from the two times Saladino had paid them.

He crossed at the school and began walking the few blocks up to the liquor store. As he was walking by the Assembly of God church he noticed two men sitting in a car in the parking lot. One of them was watching him and looked away when their eyes met. He walked on past the building out of their sight then stopped and turned. He walked through the flower bed and up to the wall of the church, then quietly made his way along the wall to the corner where it met the parking lot. From where he stood he had virtually the same view the two men did from their car just around the corner of the building. They were watching straight down First Street and the succession of duplexes that filled the block.

Crouching down, he slowly brought just his right eye far

enough around the corner of the building to see the two men. Their car was just twenty feet from him. The driver lit a cigarette and said something that made the other man laugh. The other man was chewing on a cigar and as David watched he brought a pair of binoculars to his eyes and pointed them down the street in the direction of the apartments.

David continued on down the block to the liquor store, wondering if there were others watching them. His father was busy helping several customers, which was fine with him. He had a lot of thinking to do and he wondered if it somehow showed on his face. When David set his bottle of orange soda on the counter his father opened it for him and handed it back with a quick wink and his usual "it's free" wave of his hand.

When he left the store he walked on down to the corner drugstore and spent some time looking at the model kits, but his mind was on the two men in the car. After just a few minutes he walked back by the liquor store and continued on down that side of the street. He walked by the church parking lot again and the two men were still there. As he passed by he gave them a quick glance and they were watching him.

After returning home he spent his time hanging around in his front yard or riding his bike up and down the street. He didn't want to miss catching Tommy and Mary Kay when they returned. Finally, about 3:00 he saw their car turn the corner. As they passed his yard he waved and twisted his index finger into his ear, their signal that he had something important to tell them.

Ten minutes later the three of them were sitting on the Steiner's front lawn as David told them his story.

"Maybe they're police." Tommy looked nearly as scared as when they had discovered Saladino's body.

David shook his head. "I don't think so. The car was a Cadillac and the one guy was really fat and, I don't know, they just didn't look like cops. It could be gangsters that don't even know he's dead. Or it could be the ones who killed him and they're just watching to see who comes around, like some other bad guys that they know."

Mary Kay took a deep breath and sighed. The three of them silently looked from one to the other. "So should we still go over on Saturday?" Tommy finally asked.

"Good question." David shifted over onto his stomach and leaned on his elbows. "They've probably seen us, but I can't believe they're interested in us. If they don't know he's dead, or even if they do know, we're just some neighborhood kids. They can't think we know anything about it. We'd be screaming and hollering to everyone about it and we for sure wouldn't still be feeding the cat and picking up the paper."

Tommy thought that over and felt a little relieved. "So, they probably aren't even thinking about us. You think we should go ahead for tomorrow morning?"

David nodded. "I do." He looked at Mary Kay.

She was trying hard to not sound like she felt—sick to her stomach—but she was feeling her growing trust in David. "Let's do it."

The weatherman on the evening news spent a lot of time explaining that an unusually large hurricane in the Pacific off the Baja coast of Mexico was splitting off a disturbance that would likely bring rain to southern California, maybe as far north as Bakersfield. Rain in the San Joaquin Valley in August was not unheard of but it was a pretty rare occurrence.

That evening after dinner they collected the newspaper and left milk for the cat for the last time. The normally clear summer sky was already filling with a grey overcast that brought stifling humidity along for the ride. David was concerned that any real rain the next day could interfere with their plans to find Cadillac Vinnie's money.

Before going home they took a quick trip down the alley in the next block to a spot where they could see between the apartments across First Street to the church parking lot. The car and the two men were gone.

Their first step Saturday morning, after getting out of their houses was to send Mary Kay to the Boyd's front door to ring the doorbell numerous times to make sure nobody was home. In case they were there she was ready with a story about losing her phone number and a question about the time for the party. Nobody answered the door.

Mary Kay and Tommy entered the alley from the Boyd's end of the block while David entered from the other end. They were all on the lookout for strange cars or people and repeatedly glancing skyward at the darkening grey, low overcast, hoping no real rain started so their parents wouldn't bother them to come inside. David was carrying a rake, Tommy a shovel. If anyone asked they were going to tell them they were doing a little yard work for Mr. Saladino.

They entered the yard and jammed the gate closed with the rake and shovel so nobody would surprise them walking in from the alley. They went straight to the chimney. David pulled a small flashlight from his back pocket and the key chain from his front pocket. He flopped down on his stomach in front of the ash cleanout, tried one of the smaller keys and it opened the lock. He opened the small door scooted his face right up to the small opening and shined the flashlight beam inside.

Tommy couldn't stand it. "So what do you see?" he whispered.

David scooted back, rolled over and sat up with his back against the bricks. Mary Kay and Tommy knelt down in front of him. "Nothing. A few ashes, some bricks. It's empty."

Mary Kay looked disappointed. "Well, shit," she whined.

Both boys laughed out loud at her uncharacteristic swearing.

Tommy grabbed the flashlight. "I want a look." He flopped down and looked for a long time. "What are those two little metal things?"

David dropped down next to him and pressed the side of his face against his. "I don't know."

Tommy reached in and wiggled one and then the other and then back to the first one.

They both felt Mary Kay's foot on their butts. "Hey, hey you guys, look! Get up and look!" They stood and looked at her. "There was a loud click here and look. This whole part of the bricks moved." She reached out and touched the chimney and suddenly there was a section swinging out like a door.

David saw the matching door and opened the brick door on that side. They now found themselves staring at a three foot by four foot steel door with a padlock on it. David held up the keychain, looked at his two companions then tried the key on the padlock. It slid in and turned and the lock popped open. He slipped it off and opened up the steel door.

All three of them stared silently.

"God!" Mary Kay finally whispered. She reached in and took out one of the bundles of bills.

"Holy shit!" David whispered.

"I guess this means I'm not getting my four dollars from the bet," Tommy said.

David reached into the front of his pants and pulled out a folded grocery bag he had brought along to carry any money they found. He took a deep breath and let it out noisily. "Well, this ain't going to work."

After staring a while longer he said, "I'm going to check in Saladino's garage. If it's locked we probably have the key here. I think we need his wheelbarrow."

David moved the tools and opened the gate. The side door into the garage was locked, but just as he had thought, one of the keys on the ring opened it. He flicked on the light and looked around. The shiny black Cadillac filled most of the small space. The large wheelbarrow they had seen him using was leaned up against the side wall along with some tools and two canvas tarps. He didn't want to attract attention by opening the main door, so he wrestled the wheelbarrow to the side doorway, threw in the tarps and did his best to just walk rather than run as he wheeled it across the alley and into the yard.

Mary Kay met him at the edge of the patio with wide unblinking eyes. She was holding a bundle of hundreds in her hand as she brought her face just inches from his, pushing her voice as loud as it would go and still qualify as a whisper. "David! This is five thousand dollars! Just this! I can hold it in one hand and that thing is full of these!"

David stared at her and the bundle in her hand and a wide grin slowly spread across his face. "We're never going to forget this day, are we?"

Mary Kay grabbed his wrist. "David, are you sure about this? I think I'm gonna pee."

He pushed some strands of hair away from her eyes. "I'm sure. You trust me?"

She nodded and quickly kissed him on the lips. "I trust you."

"Don't pee," he said, grinning.

In just a couple of minutes they had filled the wheelbarrow over a foot deep. "Where are we going to put this?" Tommy asked.

"My house," David said. "I figured it out last night, but it's going to take a lot more digging than I thought. Okay, step back."

He closed up the bricks and the ash clean out. He grunted as he lifted the wheelbarrow and steered it to the corner of the yard. After laying the tarp over the money he began frantically throwing weeds and a little dirt in on top of it. Tommy and Mary Kay quickly joined in.

"Okay, that's enough," David said. "It's only a little after 9:00. We have plenty of time to come back and get the rest. Let's go."

They went out into the alley and flanked by Tommy and Mary Kay, David pushed the heavily loaded wheelbarrow to the end of alley. They stopped there and he slapped Tommy on the shoulder. "Okay, hop on. If anyone sees us they'll just think we're doing some stupid wheelbarrow rides or something."

Tommy giggled as he climbed on and sat on top of the weeds, dirt and money. It was only filled to about eight inches from the top so he had a little room to settle down in and hold onto the sides. It was easier pushing on the smooth sidewalk and David settled into a jog behind the wheelbarrow. A few large drops of rain started falling but stopped right away. They went right by the Dias's house and as they neared his house David cut across the corner of the front lawn and down the dirt strip along the side of the house. Tommy jumped off as they slowed and David continued all the way to the fence that separated the backyard from the side.

"Right here," he instructed. The three of them grabbed the exposed edge of the tarp and lifted the dirt and weeds down to the ground. David dumped the pile of money at the corner where the fence and the side of the house met. His father kept a small pile of scrap fence boards there for repairs.

He grabbed the tarp and dumped the weeds and dirt on top of the money and tossed the tarp back into the wheelbarrow. The money still showed a little but from a ways back it didn't really look like anything more than just part of the clumps of weeds with the scrap wood behind it. It didn't look so large here out in the open by the fence.

On the way back they put Tommy in the wheelbarrow again just to keep whatever the neighbors were seeing consistent. The second load was about the same size but turned out heavier because they took the time to pack the money in tighter. To their dismay they discovered they could not take it all on this trip and would have to return for a third load. This time they covered it with the tarp and just a shallow layer of dirt to hold the tarp down. They returned for a third trip and discovered that they still could not take it all. It was just past ten-o'clock when they returned for their fourth and final trip. This last load was slightly lighter. They finished it off with the tarp and dirt just like the other loads.

David double-checked the chimney to make sure it was closed up properly and Mary Kay placed the rake and the shovel across the top of the dirt in the wheelbarrow. Tommy opened the gate and they walked out into the alley. They all turned their heads at the sound at the same time.

Heading toward them, now just one house away, was Howie Williams, bouncing a basketball as he walked. "Hey, what are you guys doing?"

For just a second they all looked at each other, then David spoke up for them. "Believe it or not, Mr. Saladino owns this house and we're doing a little yardwork for him."

"No shit?" He held onto the ball as he reached them. "Cadillac Vinnie lives here?"

Tommy shook his head and pointed. "No, he lives in there in one of the apartments. He rents out this house."

Howie looked through the space between the buildings that showed part of the lawn and the wall along First Street. "He does, huh? So does he pay you or anything?"

David shrugged. "A little sometimes. We've been taking care of his newspapers when he's out of town and feeding his cat, stuff like that."

"Hm." He looked down at the wheelbarrow. "Man, must be heavy. You moving dirt out of here?"

Tommy hopped up and sat cross-legged on top of the dirt. "He needs a flower bed deeper so we're taking some dirt to our yards," David said. "Where you headed?"

"There's some guys over at the school playing basketball," Howie said. "I'm heading over to Keith's to see if he wants to play. How about you guys?" Large drops began falling again making loud plopping all around them. He looked up at the clouds. "Weird weather huh?"

They were used to hot summers but the overbearing humid heat of the hurricane weather system had them all sweating profusely.

"No thanks," David replied, wiping his dripping forehead. "As soon as we're done here my mom's taking me school clothes shopping. See ya, Howie. Gotta go."

He pushed the wheelbarrow on down the alley at a near run ahead of Howie and almost dumped the load when they slowed and turned onto the sidewalk at Simpson, but caught it just in time with the help of Mary Kay. They continued on around the corner and down Second just as they had the other times. The drops stopped again.

Howie stood and watched in the alley as they hurried away

and then disappeared around the corner. "That was weird," he said to himself. He started bouncing the basketball again, peeked over the fence into the Boyd's yard, then slowly continued on down the alley toward Keith's house. He wondered for a bit what they were really up to. As a kid who spent most of his time being deceitful about one thing or another, he knew nervous lying when he saw it. But he didn't think about them for long and the whole meeting was soon nearly forgotten.

Tommy fetched a better shovel from his house and David got both of the ones they owned from his garage. This was the same spot they had once shoveled for several hours just to see how big a hole they could dig, so the digging was fairly easy in the sandy soil and in about forty minutes of furious, sweaty shoveling they had a hole roughly seven feet long, five feet wide and over three feet deep. They had wanted to count the money exactly, but there wasn't time, and they quickly realized they didn't need to. Every bundle of hundreds they counted came out to be fifty bills just like the one Mary Kay had first discovered. After counting a few of them they decided all the bundles of hundreds must be the same. Most of the money was hundreds, but there were also quite a few bundles of twenties and even a few bundled fifties. After counting several of these they found they too contained consistent amounts and assumed all the rest contained the same.

So rather than spend the time to count all the bills, the whole time in fear of being discovered on the side of the house, Mary Kay ran home and grabbed a notebook and a couple of pencils and they just hurriedly tallied up how many bundles of hundreds, fifties and twenties they had. They were surprised when they realized they had moved several hundred bundles of bills. This made up nearly all of the money. There were a few odd bundles of mixed twenties and tens that they kept out for their own use now.

They placed one of the tarps in the bottom of the hole, stacked the money on top of it then covered up the stash with the other tarp. They packed the dirt back in on top of it and scattered the rest around the length of the bare strip. It was just 11:30 and the money was buried.

The three of them stood dripping and staring at the result of their effort from the edge of the front yard.

"There's too much dirt," David said. "Isn't here?"

Mary Kay and Tommy just shrugged. David still wasn't satisfied. "Let's go get some of the trucks and stuff from the garage and pile up some dirt and leave it like we're playing."

They did so and ten minutes later they were standing at the edge of the front yard staring again. "I think it looks better now," Tommy said.

Mary Kay nodded. "Me too."

"It'll do," David said. He took a deep breath and blew it out with a lot of noise. The wheelbarrow was leaning up against the fence. "I think we should just keep the wheelbarrow. We can say we found it in the alley and decided to just keep it at my house so we could play with it some more."

"They'll holler at you for being in the alley, but your dad will probably like the wheelbarrow," Mary Kay said.

David nodded. He was still looking over their job and thinking. Sitting next to them was David's wagon where they had quickly stashed the odd 20's, 10's and a cloth bag with a few silver dollars inside two old shoeboxes jumbled in with an assortment of toy guns, sand toys and the small notebook of Mary Kay's where they had written down their hasty tally of the bundles of money.

"My mom is supposed to go grocery shopping pretty soon," David announced. "As soon as she does we can go in the garage, count up our money and figure out how much we just buried."

They pushed the wagon onto the edge of the dirt and sat down on the lawn to wait. Just then a car turned the corner from Princeton and proceeded slowly down Second.

"I don't believe it!" David whispered as the car neared. "It's the guys that were sitting by the church."

The black Cadillac slowed and pulled closer to the curb as it reached them. The driver, the man David had described as being so fat, leaned out the window and attempted a smile. "Hey, kids, how ya doing?"

The three of them stared for what seemed like too long. Finally David said, "Fine, who are you?"

The man chuckled. "We're just some friends of Mr. Saladino. Aren't you the kids who take in his paper and watch things for him when he's out of town?"

David nodded. "Sometimes."

"I thought so. We were just looking for him and wondered if you had seen him lately?"

"No," David continued. "He left town a few days ago and asked us to take the paper and leave milk for the cat like we usually do. He said it was going to be three or four days, but it's been a few days more now. I guess his trip ended up being longer than he thought."

"Right." The driver chuckled again, waved and started to pull away. "Thanks, kids. We'll just see him some other time." The car continued down the street and around the far corner past the Boyd's house. None of the three said a word until the car had disappeared.

"Jesus Christ!" Tommy exclaimed.

His sister slapped his shoulder and they all laughed. "You'll have to put that in confession."

"That proves they've been watching the apartment," David said. "How else would they know who we were?"

"Why ask us anything?" Tommy asked.

David was still staring down the street where the car had gone. "I think they just wanted to see if it looked like we knew anything. They probably haven't seen anyone around except us."

Mary Kay looked worried. "You think we should do anything else so they'll leave us alone?"

It started to rain and this time it didn't stop. A smile came to David's face. He turned and stepped closer to them. "I don't think we have anything to worry about. We're just three kids. It's the perfect cover! Nobody would ever suspect that we knew about

Saladino being killed and just went on like nothing happened and took his money. Nobody would think we did anything. I can't even believe we did it!"

"David!" It was his mother calling from the driveway across the small yard.

"Hi, Mom."

"I'm going to the store now. Please stay right around here. Your father is at work if you need anything." She looked around and up at the sky. "Don't stay out in the rain if it really starts up."

"Okay, Mom. We'll go in the garage."

The three of them stood in the yard as the warm rain started falling heavier and waved as Mrs. Steiner backed out of the driveway in her '63 Chevy and drove away headed for Norm's Supermarket.

They wheeled the wagon and its contents into the open garage. For fifteen minutes, as the rain continued, David and Tommy counted the money behind a lawnmower and edger while Mary Kay sat on a box concentrating hard on tallying up the bundles and figuring out just how much money they had. She was quiet for a long time, figuring and refiguring her calculations. She thought she was making a mistake, but she was good with math and checked it over again several times before she was satisfied that she was indeed coming up with a correct answer.

Tommy and David had long since completed their counting and were just watching the freak August rainstorm waiting for her to finish. She finally looked up and asked, "How much money in the boxes?"

"Two thousand, three hundred forty bucks!" David announced. "That's a lot of models."

Tommy giggled. "And comic books."

Mary Kay was not smiling. In fact her hands were trembling and she was trying not to cry, angry with herself for feeling that way.

"What's wrong?" David asked.

She chewed her bottom lip, cleared her throat hard and took

a deep, shaky breath before quietly asking, "How much do think we buried?"

Both boys shrugged.

"Fifty thousand?" Tommy said.

David laughed. "It has to be more than that. It was four wheelbarrows full. There were hundreds of bundles of hundreds. How about, oh, two hundred thousand? No, no, more like three hundred thousand? I don't know."

Suddenly the noise of the rain stopped and some sun broke through the grey sky. Mary Kay tried to smile, but instead tears came to her eyes. She quickly wiped them away and took another deep breath. Both boys stared open-mouthed at her. She picked up the paper and held it in her trembling hands, looking at it for several seconds before she spoke. "Three million, two hundred twenty-five thousand dollars."

SIX

"But, Dino..."

"But, nothing!" Nicholas Saladino was incensed and just a little bit scared. "How is it possible that he stole two million dollars and we can't find any of it?"

Nicolas Saladino understood he could usually do a better job of accomplishing what he needed to by reasoning and intelligent persuasion, and he was normally able to keep his sometimes vicious temper under control. This was not one of those times.

Flecks of saliva were shooting from his mouth as he bellowed and his face was going dark red. "I have bosses too, you know? How in the goddamn hell do I explain that my fucking nephew took all that money but I don't know where it is? He lived in a shitty little apartment in Bakersfield, for Christ's sake! Where'd all that money go?"

He grabbed a putter from behind his desk and began swinging back and forth, launching all the items from his desk around the room. When there was nothing left to clear he began beating the walnut desk top, denting and gouging it until, finally, the club handle snapped. He stared at the remaining two feet of metal he was holding. "Fuck!" He hurled it at the three men standing before him, then slumped, panting and sweating, into his desk chair.

Michael Luna tossed the handle onto a nearby sofa. Standing with him were the same two middle aged casino managers who had first brought this problem to light and Mario Falco. Falco was seventy years old, a monetary genius and the closest thing in Nevada the mob had to a chief financial officer. However it was just in the past several months that some of the mob casino owners had finally gotten together and provided him with real figures so he could help them stop the shorted skims they were belatedly beginning to worry about.

"They did recover twelve thousand from a safe in his apartment," Luna added. "They said it was sitting wide open."

Saladino leaned back and laughed up to the ceiling. "Twelve-thousand! Wow, all my fucking problems are solved!" He brought his eyes back level. "We sure about Fats and Doggie on this? We believe them about Vincent already being dead?"

"Oh, yeah," Luna replied. "Sitting up in bed shot dead. They thought nobody would believe them and were scared to death to come back. They called in and caused a big scene. They're fine. I gave them an extra thousand each out of the twelve."

Saladino sighed. "Okay. Mr. Falco, what've you got for me?"

Falco cleared his throat. "Well, sir, we can't be absolutely sure about this, but going back over some money amounts and interviewing the people involved..."

Saladino held up one hand. "Mr. Falco, you do know that half the people you interviewed were lying and the other half weren't telling the truth?"

Falco smiled and shrugged. "On top of that, most of them have no idea what in the hell they are talking about and didn't keep any records to refer back to. Back when these skims started they normally went through just one person or maybe two. Then it grew and you people started combining the skims into larger amounts from several sources and entrusting that amount to a few people like Vincent."

Saladino was slowly shaking his head and making noises of agreement. "Hearing you say that now makes it sound like we were all stupid to implement such a system."

Falco nodded in agreement. "Anyway, I've come to two conclusions. One, Vincent acted completely alone. There's no sign whatsoever that he had any accomplices in this. Two, I think he started this way back and figured out a way to just increase what he took as the amount of money he handled grew. Everything went along fine and nobody had any reason to question what he was doing. This one and a half million to two million figure is an educated guess. We'll never know. I think he's been doing this for a long time."

Luna was nodding, "That way there was never any noticeable change in the flow of cash. It increased at nearly the expected rate, but it was light right from the beginning."

"And too many hands in the goddamn pot and nobody knows shit!" Saladino was shaking his head and smiling. "We were just happy as clams because there was so much damn money coming in we couldn't even believe it. I always thought, my whole family always thought, that Vincent was smart enough to get by, but just. . .damn, he sucked us all in." He covered his face with his hands and muttered to himself. "All those years, trusting him, thinking I was so goddamn smart to be using my dim, loyal, faggot nephew. Who in the hell thought it was such a damn good idea to have him living so far away from here?"

Luna folded his arms and sighed. "Dino, you did."

Saladino stared hard at him, slowly shook his head and brought his hands to his face. "Yeah, yeah I did."

"There's something else," Luna said.

Saladino brought his face out of his hands and sighed again. "What else?"

"We just learned this morning that they found a hidden safe at a rental house he owned."

"Saladino looked hopeful. "Really? Who's they?"

"The cops," Luna said. "It was built into a false chimney at the back of the house."

"Great, so the cops got it," Saladino said. "How much?"

The two casino managers shifted their feet nervously. Luna, though, showed no hesitancy. He knew his boss well and was not afraid of his temper. "Basically nothing. It was empty. Just one C-note."

Saladino stood and his eyes narrowed. "Where was this house he rented out?"

Luna answered matter-of-factly. "Right across the alley

behind his apartment building."

Saladino's face was reddening again. "Since when did he own this house?"

"Apparently since it was built ten years ago," Luna answered.

The volume of his voice was rising again. "He's stolen two million dollars from us and a goddamn secret safe in a house just across the alley, a house we didn't even know he owned, has one lousy bill in it!? Who in the hell got to that if it wasn't Fats and Doggy?"

Luna shook his head. "I'm telling you, Vincent, on my life it wasn't them. The cops found the one bill, the padlock and a note."

"A note?" Saladino said. "What kind of note?"

"I'll tell you later," Luna said. "But it's obvious whoever took the money left the note to make sure we knew the money was taken."

"Catalano," Saladino said softly, referring to a mob figure who lived in Las Vegas with interests in some of the same properties that he was involved with. The two of them got along well enough on the surface, but for some reason there had always been an underlying dislike from the man that worried Saladino. He felt that Mario Catalano did not respect him.

Saladino's rage had returned full force and he looked at his empty desk top for something to break or throw. Finding nothing he yanked out the top drawer and flung the contents around the room then pounded the empty drawer on the desk top until it fell to pieces on the fifth blow. "He built a safe to hide that money and they found it empty? Somebody knew about it and hit him before we did. Somebody has that money and I want them found!"

Luna nodded. "We're on that."

Saladino reached into a bottom desk drawer and came up holding a loaded .357 magnum in his right hand. While he talked he held it at arm's length across his desk, aiming first at one casino man and then the other. "And you two. I trust you have procedures in place to ensure that nothing like this ever happens again. Am I right?"

They had, again, been advised by Michael Luna to say nothing. They both nodded vigorously. "Absolutely, Mr. Saladino," the younger, taller one added. "But I think this took place above our level after we made a count and passed it on."

Saladino instantly brought the gun back to him. "What is your name?"

The casino manager swallowed hard. "Lenny, sir. Lenny DiCicco."

Saladino came around the desk pointing the gun at him the whole time and brought the barrel right up against his nose. His voice had quieted now to a barely controlled vicious rasp. "Well, Lenny DiCicco, you better be right about that."

Saladino suddenly brought the gun around, aimed at the other casino manager, lowered the gun and shot him in the foot. Lenny screamed and covered his ears. The man who had been shot screamed louder and fell to the floor where he screamed some more.

"Christ, Dino!" Luna said and, backing up a step, startled but not all that surprised.

Saladino was standing over his victim, his voice returned to its previous high volume. "Hey, buddy, what's your name?"

The man was writhing in pain and holding his foot. "Franco Chivas, goddammit!"

"Okay, Franco Chivas Goddammit, I think we've opened up a line of communication here! Mr. Lenny Fuckin' DiCicco here says you guys think this happened after the money had been passed on by you. Is he right?"

"Yes! Yes! Absolutely!" He was sitting up now removing his shoe and blood soaked sock. "Jesus Christ! Son of a bitch! Look at my foot!"

Luna leaned into Saladino and lowered his voice. "You know they couldn't have stopped this or even known about it. They are way out of the loop on this one."

Saladino, also in a near whisper, said. "I know, but this will get around and maybe get somebody's attention, huh? Make sure they take a look at the people who were living in that house. Also, you tell Franco I'm not going to kill him anytime soon. He doesn't look so good. Better have Doc see him."

Luna almost smiled and nodded. "I'll get right on it."

The Bakersfield Police Department was not unfamiliar with organized crime. Being situated between Los Angeles, just a ninety minute drive to the south, and the San Francisco Bay area farther to the north assured that the city was frequented by its share of shady characters traveling Highway 99 between the two metropolitan areas.

In February 1950 a Los Angeles mob figure by the name of Abraham Davidian was one of several defendants who had been indicted in connection with west coast drug trade. Davidian had made a deal with prosecutors and was going to be their star witness. In the meantime he'd figured central California to be a nice out-of-the-way place to keep his heart beating a little longer than it might have miles to the south in L.A. A few days later he was shot dead through the living room window while sitting on the sofa in his mother's home in Fresno, about a hundred miles north of Bakersfield. Even though it had been nearly twenty years ago, it was a big news story and had put the central valley on the map, so to speak, of famous gangland killings. During the years since there had been plenty of other activities involving organized crime in the valley, including some in and around Bakersfield, that didn't make the news.

Police Chief Britton stood and greeted his two homicide detectives as they entered his office. "Thanks for getting over here quickly, guys."

The two other men who had been waiting with him stood as he made introductions. "Detective Bill Lassiter, Detective Gary Heinz, I'd like you to meet Agent Howard Stone and Agent Alfred Bailer."

Everyone shook hands as Chief Britton continued. "Agents Stone and Bailer are part of the FBI office working on organized crime activity."

The two detectives exchanged a quick look. "The Saladino murder?"

"We're kind of used to local police getting pissed off when we show up," Stone said. "We're not here to fuck up anything you're doing. All we're interested in is an exchange of information."

"And we're talking a two-way exchange," Bailer added. "The way we see it, we can learn some things from you and we can probably add some information that will help you out too."

Heinz, at thirty-four, and especially Lassiter, the older of the two at forty-two, held out little hope for an easy working relationship on the case. They'd had the FBI, the Border Patrol and once the Secret Service crash his cases before. Sometimes it went well, but usually the Feds ended up wanting to run the show, shoving the local police farther and farther away from the firsthand information as time went on.

Lassiter gave his partner, Heinz, another doubting look. "Okay, let's get this case cleared."

Bailer and Stone looked pleased. "Okay," Stone said. "Fill us in on what you know about Vincent Saladino."

Heinz laughed. "We don't know as much as we should. He was one of those guys that just seemed to have a talent for being ignored. We all knew he was a mob connection, but he kept a low profile and never caused any trouble, so he didn't get watched much."

"He ran a Numbers game here in town," Lassiter added, "but it seemed to us it was just a private little deal he did on his own, not really a mob thing. Over the last couple of days we've looked into it more and it looks like it was exactly that, no big deal and probably a dead end as far as this case goes."

"So other than being Nick Saladino's nephew," Heinz asked, "what exactly was Vincent up to? We know he traveled out of town a lot. The few times we did look into those trips it seemed more social than any kind of business."

Lassiter chuckled. "He had a couple of boyfriends in Vegas he liked to see, maybe a couple of girlfriends too. I guess he was confused."

"Oh, a double dipper," Stone said and everyone laughed.

"You're right about the Numbers game," Agent Bailer continued. "Strictly small potatoes. More of a hobby than anything. You're also right about his being good at disappearing into the background. For a long time the FBI didn't pay much attention to him either. Starting around 1963 or so those trips of his got awfully regular. Turns out he was some sort of a courier moving the skim from casinos to the bosses in Vegas and L.A."

Lassiter and Heinz looked at each other and back at the agents. "You hear what we found yesterday?" Heinz asked.

Bailer shook his head. "No, but your chief was just about to tell us about some new development. What's up?"

The chief gestured to Heinz.

"You ain't going to believe this," the detective continued. "This morning there's a bunch of us going over his apartment, the garage and all around and this guy comes over from the house right across the alley and says he pays his rent to Saladino. Him, a wife and a couple of kids, just a regular family been living there for years paying rent. So now some of us are looking around the house and yard and one of the techs happens to notice that there's no fireplace in the house, but there's a chimney at the back of the house with a padlock on this little ash cleanout door. We cut the lock, start nosing around and the goddamn bricks open up like a kitchen cabinet. A steel box built right into the chimney."

Lassiter continued the story. "We'll take you out there to take a look. It's pretty slick. Even after you know it opens, when you're up close to the bricks it looks perfect."

"We'll be interested to see that," Bailer said. "Any money or anything?"

"It was big enough to hide a shitload of money, but it was empty."

"Well, almost empty," Heinz added. "Right up against the inside lip was a hundred dollar bill and sitting on it like a paperweight was the unlocked padlock for the box."

The two detectives had decided not to tell anyone about the third item they had found in the safe.

"One lousy bill," Stone said. "He must've cleaned it out knowing he was going to get killed and all."

The two detectives looked at each other. "Yeah, that's what we figured, too," Lassiter said, holding back most of a smile.

Everyone laughed.

"Okay, you geniuses," Chief Britton said. "I want to see this scene too. Let's all head out there. We can grab lunch somewhere on the way. It's on me."

Long-time Chief of Police Hank Britton was extremely disappointed about the chimney safe being empty. In addition to the organized crime figures who traveled through the city, he and a few of his captains made up one of the most corrupt city police administrations around. There were some individuals who thought that the order to kill Davidian back in 1950 came from someone high up in the Bakersfield or Fresno Police Department—someone who didn't want him implicating any of them in the drug trafficking or related activity he was about to testify about. Being just a hundred miles apart, the two departments had officers and administrative personnel who had worked for both and maintained an active network of friendships, intelligence and criminal contacts that included other small town departments in the valley.

Britton knew that if he or any of his friends in the department had found that chimney safe before it had been emptied it would have been a highly profitable discovery involving just their small club. Lassiter and Heinz had actually thought of their chief and a couple of his cronies first when a dead mobster and two empty safes turned up, however after doing a little asking around it didn't seem to involve anyone in the department.

An hour later three cars parked in the alley between First and Second Street. The FBI agents in one unmarked car, Lassiter and Heinz in another and Chief Britton with a regular cop driver in a patrol car. They took the FBI agents through Saladino's apartment first and then across the alley into the backyard of the rental.

Heinz walked them to the chimney. "Watch this." He knelt down, reached into the ash cleanout door and manipulated the levers.

A soft click sounded and one side of the bricks moved outward. Lassiter opened the bricks the rest of the way and opened the inside door revealing the bare inside.

"Shit, you weren't kidding," Stone said as they examined the cabinet. "This is slick as hell. Show me how to open this thing."

As they closed it up and played with it, Agent Bailer strolled around looking over the yard. Mostly he was admiring how well cared-for it all was. Manicured shrubs, the patio and trim nicely painted, everything clean and neat. He ended up standing at the edge of the patio looking out across the lawn toward the back fence.

"You guys notice this?" The others joined him. "Look how the lawn is kind of worn across here to the gate. The ground's pushed down too. Maybe a wheelbarrow?" He walked out onto the lawn and knelt down to look closer.

"Like one of those big ones the cement guys use with that fat tire in front," Stone said.

Bailer nodded. "From what the tenants tell us, Saladino did most of the yard work and maintenance on the place. They mentioned he'd come in and out of the gate from his garage with yard tools and all that."

Bailer stood and walked ahead of the others out the gate and across the alley to the side door of Saladino's garage. The others followed. "Was the doorknob cranked when you found him?"

"No, that was our guys," Lassiter explained. "His car's still in the garage too and we had to crowbar the trunk. No damn keys for anything in the apartment."

"Really? Interesting. So somebody lifted the keys to this thing," Bailer said, gesturing toward the Boyd's chimney. He pushed open the door and stepped into the garage. "Does the big door open so we can get some light in here?"

"Right here," Heinz said and hit the button for the automatic door opener. The bright August sun filled the sweltering garage.

Bailer looked over the mechanism admiringly. "You don't see many of these around. Probably be just a common thing someday. Your guys do much in here?"

"Don't think so," Lassiter said. "Just the car, but it was clean."

Bailer pointed to the back corner. "Tire marks here. Looks like that's where he parked the wheelbarrow. Is it around anywhere?"

Lassiter and Heinz looked at each other and shrugged. They looked around for a stray wheelbarrow in the apartment complex and the Boyd's garage and yard. Bailer wandered away from the rest of the group again and went out to the alley. After carefully studying the sand up and down the alley both ways from the gate he was reasonably sure that he could match some tracks fifty feet down the alley toward Simpson with others that were around the gate and Saladino's garage. By the time the others reassembled, having found no wheelbarrow, Bailer was fifty yards away at the end of the alley looking down at the sidewalk. The others walked and joined him.

"What's shakin', Sherlock?" Stone said.

"Not much, but look at this." He was pointing down at the sidewalk. "You see the way the sand is pushed away here? And on the cement these dark marks? Looks like tire scuffs to me. If someone was pushing a wheelbarrow down here they'd have to make a sharp turn here to clear the corner of the fence and stay on the sidewalk heading over toward Second." He sighed. "But, could just be from kids' bicycles too."

They all stooped over with their hands on their knees. "Could be," Lassiter said. "But why all the fuss about the wheelbarrow? You guys know something you haven't thrown into our exchange of information?"

"Tell 'em," Bailer said. He walked slowly down the sidewalk toward the corner at Second.

"Well, we don't know anything about a wheelbarrow," Stone explained. "That's just something Daniel Boone here jumped on, but I think I know what he's getting at. According to our sources, Nicholas Saladino doesn't know whether to shit or go blind over this whole thing. The word is they just found out that Vincent here was into them for something like a million bucks, maybe two million."

Heinz whistled and Lassiter just started laughing.

"Holy smokes," Chief Britton said. "Any idea who hit him? They must've got to the money too."

Stone nodded. "You would think, but from what we've been able to learn the hit was ordered by Nicholas. Some other boss may have gotten to him first."

"His own nephew?" Lassiter asked.

"They're a great fucking bunch, huh? Anyway, as far as we know, the guys sent to do the job didn't rip off the money because they're back in L.A. with Saladino. Saladino didn't get the money 'cause he's hopping shitless about finding out who did. So...?" He spread his hands and shrugged. "What's your take on the family living in the house?"

"Heinz and I interrogated the husband and wife yesterday. They're completely flabbergasted by this whole thing. I guess way back Saladino mentioned the fireplace being taken out because of some chimney problems or something. He told them the lock on the ash cleanout was just to keep kids out of it 'cause of spiders. Anyway, they say they hadn't even thought about it in a long time. Just got used to the idea and didn't really even notice it anymore. The house has been searched. They don't feel right for it to me."

"Me either," Lassiter added. "Their main concern is being able to stay in the house. What if the guys who did him in were in with someone else? Maybe they've got the money and Saladino's goons are just biding their time until things cool off."

Stone nodded. "We're watching them, but it's not how these wise guys usually work. If those two are in on it, we'll know soon, but I don't think they are. From what I hear, they were afraid at first to come back home without the money."

Heinz laughed. "It doesn't seem too likely that somebody was pushing a wheelbarrow full of money down the street. Who would it be anyway?"

Bailer shrugged and smiled. "Somebody who wasn't going too far?"

They headed back down the alley to the cars, still kicking around theories on just how much money it might have been.

Lassiter hung back, standing on the sidewalk, intrigued by the whole notion of the wheelbarrow tracks. "That would be a hell of a thing," he said to himself. "A couple of million bucks wheelbarrowed away."

He laughed out loud then headed down the alley to join the others.

David Steiner had, in his mind at least, abandoned his present life and fast forwarded several years. He knew he'd have to live in his kid's body until it caught up with his brain, but that was okay. Everything was okay. He'd never felt so alive, so energized, so grown up.

He was now on an information gathering spree and he had put together an interesting list of financial facts. Among these were: His father made about $6,000 a year working at the liquor store. Their average working class home cost around $12,000. His "rich" grandparents lived in a huge house in a nice old part of town and their house cost about $40,000. Some doctors made $100,000 a year or more. A loaded-to-the-gills Cadillac might cost close to $7,000. The President of the United States made $100,000 a year plus a $50,000 expense account.

All this information, balanced against the reality that Tommy, Mary Kay and he were in possession of over three million dollars had put it in perspective for him. His twelve-year-old mind had suddenly grown new frontiers of complications and possibilities.

His main concern was his two co-conspirators. Even though the three of them had pulled off the caper together, he knew, and so did Mary Kay and Tommy, that the whole idea had really been his. He realized that as the "brains of the outfit" he had an important role in this sudden long-term commitment. He needed to guide both of them through the next several years until they grew into the same understanding that he was certain only he had right now.

Tommy was sitting by the side of the Steiner house along with David and his sister. "The cops were at our house this morning."

"Mine too." David said. "How'd it go?"

Tommy shrugged and gave a worried look.

"It went fine," Mary Kay said. "They had already talked to some four-plexers and found out we were over there sometimes. They knew we fed the cat and took the papers and stuff. We just answered a few questions. I didn't really think they seemed too interested in us."

Tommy brightened. "It was starting to make me nervous and then they just started asking my mom a bunch of stuff about what she knew about Saladino."

David nodded. "Same here. I think they've just written us off as kids who knew him and nothing more. Your mom get on you about being over there?"

"She asked us a few things," Mary Kay said, "but mostly about Janice's family and the house." She chewed her bottom lip.

"What'd they say about finding money or a safe or anything?" David asked.

Tommy giggled. "That part was kind of fun, actually. The guy said that they found a hidden safe."

"Wow," David said, looking concerned, "they found the chimney safe already?"

"I guess," Tommy said. "Mom got all shocked and surprised-sounding. I asked him where the hidden safe was and he didn't answer me. Then my dad started going on about 'that no-good wop' and the cops asked him questions for a while. I heard them say something about Numbers."

"Good, good." David was silent for a few moments. "Listen, I've been thinking about this a lot. They might come back. They might interview somebody who saw us pushing a wheelbarrow around, or somebody who saw Tommy and me go in the apartment that morning. If that happens, just keep it simple. Trust me, they won't suspect us. We're kids. We found his wheelbarrow out by the alley and we were playing. Yes, we stepped in because he was supposed to meet us and then we left. We just go around being the same stupid kids we were before."

Mary Kay snickered. "That will be easy for you two."

Tommy got up and stepped over to where the money was buried, standing right on top of it. "You thought of where we can move it to?"

"I haven't come up with anything yet. We should leave it for a while, maybe a long while. I've been reading about money. You ever leave a dollar in your pocket and it goes through the wash? It comes out okay because it's made out of this special paper. It's more like cloth than paper. Even if it rains and it gets wet, it'll be okay. We'll think of somewhere better to move it later."

Mary Kay sighed. "This is just so huge. You guys think we can really do this? I mean, if we're smart about this, we can do anything we want in the future. But we can't get caught."

Tommy smiled sheepishly. "It makes me nervous, but, yeah, I think we can do this. We just have to be smart, like you said."

"I know we can do it," David said. "We just live our lives as normal as possible. The most important thing is to keep our mouths shut and be patient. When we grow up we're going to be rich, no matter what else we do." David leaned toward them and lowered his voice. "Even if we do nothing. That's why patience is important. We shouldn't even worry about buying stuff right now. When we're older is when we'll need it. Between now and then we can plan, think, dream."

He looked at Mary Kay. "I'm going to take care of you."

She pursed her lips and almost smiled. Her eyes looked both grateful and frightened.

A toad hopped out from underneath the neighbor's orange tree, making a sudden loud crunch in the dry leaves. Tommy looked at it and turned to David with a smile. "Nobody found out about the frogs we got from the ditch. Maybe we are good at this stuff."

"I think they're Toads," David corrected."

"What about frogs?" Mary Kay asked.

"Or maybe toads," Tommy said. "We'll tell you later."

"I figured something out last night," David said. "You know how long my dad would have to work at the liquor store to make that much money?" He pointed at the ground under Tommy's feet. "Over five hundred years!"

"Wow!" Mary Kay whispered.

Tommy looked down and then stepped to one side.

As time went on, even though none of them ever said it out loud, all three of them came to regard the money stash as Vincent Saladino's grave site.

Detectives Lassiter and Heinz said good-bye to the two FBI agents, walked back to their facing desks and sat down.

Heinz sighed. "Jesus, three days with those guys."

Lassiter chuckled. "They weren't bad, but I'm glad they're gone. So, now what?"

Heinz made a noisy sigh. "With this case? Hell, I don't know. Hey, I got something here." He reached into his shirt pocket and pulled out a small notepad. "I was doing a phone interview with that lady that lives next door to the rental."

"Mrs. Palmer?" Lassiter said. "Why?"

"Well, remember that day we talked to her and she was backing out in her car and in a big hurry? I just thought I'd touch base with her again. So, anyway, she's rambling on about a bunch of crap and I ask her about those kids who were hanging around Saladino's. She starts in about how they never cause any real trouble but they're always running up and down the street with wagons and bikes, creeping through yards playing army, acting crazy and raising a ruckus. One day, she says, they were even running up and down the street with one of them riding in a wheelbarrow."

Lassiter laughed. "The goddamn wheelbarrow again! So, when was this?"

"She didn't know for sure. A week or so ago, she thought."

Lassiter leaned back and folded his hands behind his head. "Maybe Bailer knew his tracking after all. So, what do you think?"

"I think it's a bunch of kids playing with a wheelbarrow." Heinz leaned forward on his desk. "I'm not thinking they took any money. There's no goddamn way some kids would do something like that and keep their mouths shut."

"Agreed," Lassiter said. "But we've been wrong before. Making assumptions is a sure way to fuck up."

Heinz nodded. "Okay, you want to go talk to them? Maybe they saw somebody or maybe they know something."

Lassiter glanced at his watch. "Sure, let's head out there."

Heinz guided the unmarked car off of First onto Princeton toward Second Street.

Lassiter pointed left. "Head down the alley first. Let's just see what's shakin'."

They cruised slowly down the block-long segment of the alley. "I'd like to catch those kids out somewhere instead of going to their houses. I think their parents might be a little sick of seeing us."

"No shit," Lassiter said. "I'd like to hear what they say when they're away from their parents. Maybe they know something they're afraid to say around them. Or maybe they know something they don't even know they know. Hey, look!"

Mary Kay, Tommy and David rolled by on skates on the sidewalk just sixty feet in front of them across the end of the alley.

David stopped both his companions. "A car's coming down the alley. I think it's those detectives." He pointed down at the grass strip that ran along the sidewalk. "Sit here and pretend you're fixing your skate."

Mary Kay plopped down and pulled the shoelace with the skate key from around her neck.

"If they ask us anything just stick with what we've been saying. Any new questions just act regular. Remember, we know more than they do." He slapped Tommy's shoulder. "Got it?"

Tommy nodded. "No problem. Just like acting in the movies."

The car came out onto the street and Heinz guided it up to the curb alongside the grass strip. "Hi kids," Lassiter greeted from the passenger window. "Mind if we bug you with some more questions?"

"No, that's fine," David said.

Mary Kay looked up from her skates. "Heck, it's the most interesting thing that's ever happened around here."

Both detectives came around and leaned casually against the side of the Ford sedan as they talked. "We don't want you to get the idea that you're in trouble or anything," Heinz said. "Our job is to ask a lot of questions and see if we can find out any information."

"And to be honest," Lassiter added, "we're not real sad that Mr. Saladino got himself killed. He was in the mob and he was killed by other mob bad guys."

"Yeah, we knew he was a gangster or mobster or whatever you call it," David said, "but he was nice to us and never seemed to cause any trouble around here."

"I guess he caused trouble somewhere though, huh?" Tommy added.

The two men looked at each other and shrugged. "Something like that," Heinz answered. "As bad guys go I guess he wasn't such a bad one."

"Did they really call him Cadillac Vinnie?" David asked.

Heinz nodded. "I guess that was a name that a lot of other mob people called him. He bought a new Cadillac every year so that's where the name came from."

"Here's what we're really trying to find out more about," Lassiter said. "We can't tell you all the details, but it looks like he had stolen a lot of money from the mob and that's probably why he was killed. We're trying to find out where all the money is. He ever talk to you about keeping money or hiding money or anything you can think of that might give us some kind of clue?"

David intentionally appeared to be reluctant to bring up his response. "Well, we didn't want to tell you around our parents, but Tommy and I were in his apartment once and he showed us a big safe in his bedroom."

Tommy took up the story from there. "We said something about being worried about him leaving his place unlocked when he was out of town. He showed us the safe and told us how hard it was to break into and too heavy to carry away. I think that's the only time he said anything about any money."

David nodded. "In fact, that's the only time we were inside his apartment."

"What about you, young lady?" Lassiter said.

Mary Kay shook her head and nervously chewed her lip. "They were around him more than I was. The only thing about money was that he paid us for helping do yard work at the Boyd's and feeding his cat and stuff."

"The safe was empty," Shultz said, "but we think he kept a lot more money somewhere else."

"How much?" David asked.

Lassiter hesitated. "A lot."

"A million?" Tommy asked.

"A billion?" David added.

"A hundred?" Tommy asked, then dissolved into giggling.

Both detectives chuckled. "We can't tell you exactly," Heinz explained, "but we know it was a lot. There was a newspaper article yesterday that said a million or more. That's probably about right, especially the 'or more' part."

"Wow!" Mary Kay said breathily. "You told our parents the other day that you had found a secret safe."

Lassiter nodded. "He had a secret safe inside the chimney in the Boyd's backyard."

"Really? Right there in their backyard?" David was still surprised and a little concerned that anyone had found it so soon. "So, how much was in there?"

"A hundred dollars." Heinz said, referring to the lone bill they found.

David laughed. "Hey, you were right, Tommy!"

Everyone laughed again.

Lassiter continued. "So, whoever took the money just left the hundred to be a wise guy. It was sitting right inside the compartment with the open lock sitting on the hundred dollar bill and a note."

"So, whoever took the money left a note?" David asked. He glanced at Mary Kay and she was staring back. "What did it say?"

"Can't tell you, can't tell anybody," Lassiter said. He pointed to his partner. "Nobody knows but me and him. Might be a clue, we don't know. Anyway, when you were over there helping did you ever see him doing anything around that chimney?"

The kids all looked at each other. David answered, "No, just trimming the bushes by it and stuff. Nothing special."

Heinz nodded. "He used a wheelbarrow to carry stuff back and forth?"

They were prepared for this to come up since they had discussed the possibility but still they hesitated, not knowing who should say what first. Finally, David said, "Yes, he used a wheelbarrow."

"We thought so," Heinz continued. "Some neighbors said they saw you three giving each other rides in a wheelbarrow a few days before Saladino was found."

"But, we didn't find any wheelbarrow in his garage or over at the Boyd's place." Lassiter said. "Was that his wheelbarrow you were playing with?"

"It was sitting outside his garage by the alley," David said. "We were playing with it and it just sort of ended up at my place. After we found out he died, we were kind of scared to say anything about it or take it back, so we just kept it."

Tommy and Mary Kay nodded silently.

"No big deal," Lassiter said. "We kind of had the crazy idea that whoever took the money might've used a wheelbarrow. But if you have it, then I guess not."

"But he didn't usually leave it outside his garage where we found it," David explained. "He kept it in his garage. I don't think we ever saw it before just sitting around unless he was using it."

"Maybe they took it from his garage and left it there before we found it." Mary Kay offered.

Heinz nodded. "Maybe, huh? Okay, kids, thanks for talking to us. I think we're done asking questions about this whole thing."

The detectives got back in their car and waved goodbye to the kids as they drove away.

Mary Kay turned to David. "You left that hundred dollar bill there like that on purpose?"

He nodded and grinned. "I thought it was a nice touch. It has style, kind of like leaving a tip for the cops."

"A twenty would've been enough," Tommy suggested, grinning. "We did all the work."

"And you left a note?" Mary Kay said, careful not to speak too loud. "I thought you were being smart. What if they find out who wrote it?"

David smiled. "I wrote it that morning and had it in my pocket. Don't worry. I wouldn't leave them any kind of clue that would lead them to us. Actually, I didn't think anyone would find the note for a long time. I figured it was going to be down inside that little door, not a whole big chimney safe."

"Was it a thank you note?" Tommy asked with a giggle.

Mary Kay was becoming clearly annoyed at this new development. She sighed loudly. "Well, what did you write?"

David smiled as he looked back and forth between the twins. "Can't tell you, can't tell anyone," he said, imitating Detective Lassiter.

Mary Kay closed the distance between her and David in three quick strides and shoved him hard in the chest with both hands. Seeing the look on his sister's face, Tommy jumped up ready to break up a fight as David fell on his butt onto the grass strip.

Tears spilled down her cheeks as she stood over him in her cut-off jeans and flowered blouse, pointing an angry finger down at his face. "We're in this together, David." She was working hard to control her quavering voice. "For the rest of our lives we're in this together. We have a big secret and it has to stay a secret. I have to be able to trust you. Tommy has to be able to trust you.

You can't just decide to do shit like that note and not tell us!"

David looked up at Tommy standing open-mouthed a few feet away. He stood and faced Mary Kay, slowly stepped forward and wrapped his arms around her. "I'm sorry," he whispered. "I'm going to protect you. I'm going to take care of all of us."

It was Saturday afternoon at the end of their first month back at school. David, Mary Kay and Tommy were sitting on David's front lawn in the shade from the peak of the garage roof. The temperature was still in the mid-nineties.

"I think I'm finally beginning to hear less from kids at school," David said. "Our fame is fading."

"Good," Tommy said. "Makes me nervous."

"It is kind of fun when they ask how we got to know him and we tell them we were out ringing doorbells," David said.

Tommy nodded. "Yeah, I guess. Sometimes everyone just starts telling doorbell-ringing stories."

"I don't like talking about it much," Mary Kay said. She pushed her hair off her forehead and chewed her lip. "I usually just tell them it was mostly you two and they should ask you."

"We've been sort of famous in a 7th grade kind of way," David said.

"Yesterday we had some free art time," Mary Kay said. "That butthole Larry Burns passed a picture to me through a bunch of kids. It was a drawing of Saladino sitting up in bed with a hole in his head and blood everywhere."

"Oh man," David said. He reached and put his hand on her knee. "Sorry. What did you do?"

Mary Kay smiled. "Well, that part was kind of good. I got up and took the picture to Mrs. Campbell. A bunch of kids were watching because he had passed it through so many from clear across the room I guess they were all talking about it before it got to me. She got mad at him, scolded him for drawing gross pictures and made him apologize in front of everyone for trying to upset me and made him stay after school."

Tommy giggled. "Good for her. I don't like that guy anyway,

but I think he likes you. He probably thought you'd be all impressed with how well he could draw a gory picture."

She looked down to David's hand on her leg then into his eyes. "But, yeah, you're right, it seems to be dying out. We'll be back to our old unfamous boring selves pretty soon. You guys want popsicles?"

They both said, "Yeah, it's hot," at the same time, which caused all three of them to laugh. Then they both said, "Jinx you owe me a Coke" at the exact same time which caused the two boys to dissolve into more laughter.

She jumped up. "It was a tie, you both lose. I'll be right back."

A minute later she ran back from her house with three popsicles and plopped down close to David. "Here you go. Grape today."

"I thought you only ever had root beer 'cause that's your dad's favorite." He unwrapped his and popped the end into his mouth.

Tommy laughed. "He's doing some things a little different lately."

David saw a quick exchange of looks between the twins. "Yeah? How come?"

"Can I tell him?" Tommy asked.

Mary Kay sucked on her Popsicle for a few seconds, "I guess," she said.

"Okay, we didn't want to say anything about this because we didn't know how it was all going to turn out. But now it's been almost a month, so…" He shrugged.

"So what happened?" David asked.

Tommy looked around nervously and let out a laugh. "She clocked our dad."

"What?" David said, wide-eyed.

Tommy nodded. "Yeah, it was one of the first few days of school. I said something and he backhanded me up the side of my head. Remember that big book that sits on our coffee table?"

"The one about ships?" David asked.

"Yeah, that one," Tommy said. "Big and heavy. I'm standing there rubbing my head and deciding if I should cry or not and she picked up that book and swung it like Willie Mays and hit my dad square in the face. It was loud, man, like a big pop and blood from his nose flew everywhere! He let out this weird loud scream and dropped down on the ottoman holding his face."

"Seriously?" David said, eyes wide.

Mary Kay nodded, pulled the Popsicle from her mouth and said matter-of-factly, "It was September 6ᵗʰ."

"But that's not all," Tommy said. "He's sitting there holding his face, bleeding all over and she walked up to him and told him if he ever hit me or her or mom again she was going to kill him in his sleep. She didn't yell. She just said it calm, like a teacher, like she really meant it."

David gasped. "Shit," he said softly. "What did he do? What did your mom do? What happened?"

"Well, I guess she was pretty damn convincing," Tommy continued. "My mom stood and stared and then led my dad into the bathroom to help him clean up. He hasn't hit any of us since."

"And he buys grape popsicles now," Mary Kay said, and stuck the end of hers back in her mouth.

David laughed nervously. "Aren't you afraid he's just waiting to beat the shit out of you?"

David and Tommy both stared at her waiting for an answer.

She bit off the end of her Popsicle, chewed it and said, "No, I'm not afraid of him anymore. I think he's afraid of me."

As David stared, her eyes shifted to meet his. He could see in that moment that something was now behind those eyes that didn't used to be there. She looked away after a few seconds, but he could still feel it and he decided it was something he would need to be wary of.

SEVEN

David Steiner was letting several seconds of silence pass between himself and Agent Ron Parker of the Internal Revenue Service. He had been ordered to come into the Seattle IRS office for an open-ended audit.

"Well, let's see." He gazed upward and appeared to be thinking, before continuing with his well-rehearsed responses. "My Aunt Elnona died in 1976 and left me just over two hundred thousand dollars. That was the start of my international real estate investing. Before that I was just a regular working guy and I was still going to college."

David waited, pacing himself as he had been for the last twenty minutes, not wanting to appear quite as knowledgeable as he actually was. He had been anticipating and planning for this meeting for years. In fact he was surprised it had taken this long. He could have brought in a team of lawyers and accountants but he figured bringing in a financial and legal team would just make it appear that he actually had something to hide and invite even more scrutiny. So far he thought it was the right decision.

Agent Parker was fifty-three years old and had just started his twenty-fifth year at the agency. He knew his job and he considered himself a pretty good judge of people and very good at spotting if someone was lying. Something smelled about this whole thing. Parker hadn't decided if David Steiner was lying, but he did know he wasn't exactly telling the truth. He knew ten minutes ago that he'd never get to the real bottom of it, but he was intrigued just enough to keep asking more questions. *This guy is only 28 years old, so maybe he'll fuck up somewhere along the line.*

"Yes, that's in your paperwork," the agent said. "I don't see how all the pieces come together to lead us from three-hundred thousand to twelve-million dollars of income over each of the past three years and a net worth that you report to be in the vicinity of ninety million dollars. Frankly, Mr. Steiner, your records from 1977 up to now, although extensive in volume, are actually quite incomplete."

He leafed again through a stack of photocopies. "For instance, it appears you have several money transfers of more than a half million dollars between your overseas investing company and your bank accounts here that were not accurately reported by the banks, as required by law."

David shrugged and put on what he hoped was his best good-old-boy kind of smile. "Agent Parker, you and I both know that the Bank Secrecy Act was not really fully understood or adhered to for several years after it supposedly became law. Banks were just not set up to report all these transactions yet."

Parker returned a long, squinting gaze that slowly turned into a condescending smirk. "Actually I'm well versed in just how that particular law came into practice, Mr. Steiner. It's an unpopular law and probably doesn't even accomplish what it was intended to do which was to stop money laundering by organized crime and drug dealers. Reporting of large cash transaction by banks is still spotty, but most financial institutions are at least trying to appear to be following the regulations. You were using these country bumpkin banks in sleepy little towns that seemingly hadn't quite caught up with the times. Makes no sense for you to do that unless you didn't want those transfers looked at too hard." He thumped his finger on the stack of papers. "And this whole deal about Aunt Elnona's two hundred thousand becoming millions in just a year or two? Some of those companies you were working with didn't make a damn dime during that time period."

David now matched the agent's expression with a smirk of his own. "True, Agent Parker. Shrewd international investing, plus I had a lot of insider information about the markets I was dealing in. Several short-term loans made a huge amount of money in just a few weeks. I got in and got out at the right times. Sometimes I was only invested on paper with no real cash put in and I got lucky. I would've been in a bind but I made a ton of money and didn't have to cover my bets. Inflation was pushing prices so hard there were times I literally made millions overnight on buying and selling land and real estate." He shrugged. "Smart timing, lucky timing, maybe a little of both."

"I will agree that you benefited to a great degree from inflation," Parker said. "The inflation rate from the mid-70s on into the 80s was something to behold. Drove up prices, priced people and businesses out of purchasing or expanding. Drove some businesses into the ground by completely pricing people out of buying their products. But for every loser there's a winner. For the business you were in, crazy inflation couldn't have come at a better time, Mr. Steiner. Still, that doesn't explain everything. And you know it doesn't. All your answers and all your paperwork almost answer the questions, but not really, do they? "

Parker held his gaze for a bit on David, nodded at his own comments and kept nodding as he looked down again and leafed through some papers. "You have been operating under two privately held companies. We've got Multinational Key Dealings, and Transcontinental Development, usually referred to here as MKD and TD. So, not too long ago you started up Domain Motion Transactions International or DMT International. I'm sure it says in here somewhere, but just what does that company do?"

To the world at large they were nothing more than letters, like AT&T or IBM. Just letters representing dull technology and business words, used so routinely that people often had difficulty recalling what the initials originally stood for. Over the years, because he had gone to great lengths to keep their names out of circulation as far as being connected to the financial empire he had built, nobody knew that the initials of the three companies could stand for Mary Kay Dias, Tommy Dias and David, Mary Kay and Tommy.

David forced a small chuckle. "So far, DMT hasn't done very much. We are positioned to invest in coastal commercial properties in Europe, Mediterranean North Africa, some parts of Asia, North and South America. We haven't done a lot yet but we've got big plans." He pointed to another folder on Parker's desk. "DMT is the overall umbrella company now and the other two operate as subsidiaries. Overseas land deals may be a little out of your experience, Agent Parker. Anyway, I've paid quite a lot in taxes over the last few years, wouldn't you say?"

Parker nodded. This was going just exactly where he thought it would—nowhere. Plus, what the hell did he care where this guy's money really came from?

He reached out and closed two open folders on his desk and stood. "You're right, Mr. Steiner. I guess you were just one hell of a lucky investor and yes, you have indeed paid a pile of income taxes. I don't see any point in the IRS pursuing this any further. Thanks for taking your time to meet with us for this audit. I think we're done here." He extended his hand across the desk.

David stood and smiled his friendly smile and shook hands with his inquisitor. "Thank you, Agent Parker. I'm glad I could clear this up. I'll be happy to answer any questions that come up in the future."

Parker sat back down and leaned back in his chair. As David walked out of his office, the agent's thoughts immediately went to an item on the wall behind him. He had received it a number of years ago from a friend who had retired from the agency. Among a clutter of photos and certificates of various sizes, hung a framed document. It was a humorous twist on a well-known quote from the French writer Balzac. On an important-looking certificate in ornate lettering it read, "Behind every great fortune there is a crime, or at least a lie, or maybe just somebody smarter than you, or luck, but probably a crime."

David left the meeting eager to move forward with his plans. There might be more meetings in the future with the IRS but this one had confirmed for him that he had succeeded in muddling, confusing, concealing and stirring his finances to the point that nobody would or could take the time or trouble to trace it all back to the original three million. It was clear to him that the IRS had little concrete information and now probably little interest in how it all began. As he stepped into the waiting limo he was confident that he was now ready to shift gears into the next phase of his plan.

Already seated in the limo, facing each other, were Mary Kay and Tommy.

"Go like you wanted?" Tommy asked.

David let out a quick sigh and smiled as he sat next to Mary Kay. "Pretty much. In fact, I was over-prepared. He didn't even ask me about some details that I was sure he would."

Mary Kay nodded and pulled a pen from the pocket folder on her lap. "We moving forward on these right away?"

"Not all of them," David answered. "Mark the Group 3 Zurich accounts and the Group 4 Milan accounts. That's about, let's see, twenty-four million. And liquidate the Milan and Amsterdam properties. Contact the last best offers made and take their deal. Those two total right around nineteen million. That comes to about…"

"Forty-three million," Mary Kay offered.

"Okay," David said, half to himself. "I like that number. Transfer all that to the seven Alfa accounts and start buying up the properties we already discussed. South America will use up more than half so start there. Next go for the African Med resorts."

"Got it," she said, nodding and writing notes on the papers in front of her. "Dammit, I'll be glad when they finally make laptop computers good enough to actually use."

"I'm glad you two know what the fuck all that means," Tommy said, scowling at the papers in his sister's lap.

"It's just details," David said. "All it really means is as far as the IRS is concerned, we're legit."

David allowed himself a satisfied smile as he watched the city scenery slide by.

Tommy pressed the button to lower his window and leaned toward it, breathing deeply, eyes closed. This was a technique suggested by his therapist that he had been using with some success when his bouts of claustrophobia came upon him. It wasn't so much being closed inside the limo that was bringing on another of his recurring attacks, but the completely irrational sensation that the interior was stuffed with stacks of money, leaving him no room to breathe.

Seattle, Washington – September, 1990

Maxwell Nguyen was just thirty-one years old and had been working for DMT International as a computer science engineer and all-around technology geek for several years. Recently he had begun to describe himself as an IT specialist, a term that was coming into more common usage and seemed to describe well his job and his skill set. He knew there was someone at the top named David Steiner whom he had never met and would not have recognized if he was standing at the next urinal. This morning he was contacted by a secretary and asked to report to his office on the 29th floor.

Nguyen checked in with the secretary who had contacted him and sat down in a small waiting area. Looking around as he waited he noticed several framed photographs and art pieces. One was a picture of two men and a strikingly beautiful dark-haired woman, standing on a beach with a yacht a couple hundred yards offshore in the background. Another was the same three people standing aboard the yacht with a beach in the background. There were others of just the one man posing with a band on stage with their instruments.

Nguyen stood and walked a few steps to get a closer look at the framed pictures arranged across the opposite wall. The same blond-haired man was in several of the photos. Seated astride a black and tan motorcycle, another one with the same group of musicians, one standing in front of a private passenger jet. There were several photos with just moose, elk and what looked to be grizzly bears.

"Excuse me," he said to the secretary. "The man in most of these pictures, is that Mr. Steiner?"

"Yes it is," she answered in a friendly tone. "The two with the yacht were taken somewhere in the Caribbean. The moose and elk and bear were taken on photography trips in Canada and Alaska."

"I see," Nguyen said, looking over the pictures again. "I don't remember ever meeting him before or even seeing a photograph."

The secretary smiled. "He likes to stay behind the scenes. I don't even see him that much. He's not here in his office all the time."

Nguyen nodded. "Who are these two with him in the yacht photos?"

"He has told me more than once they are his two best friends in the world. They grew up together. Mary Kay and her twin brother Tommy. I have met them both up here a couple of times and, yes, she is just as beautiful as she looks in that photograph. Actually more so in person."

The door to David's office opened. "Please come in Mr. Nguyen."

David motioned him in and closed the door.

"You go by Max, right?"

The man nodded as they shook hands.

"Would you like anything?" David asked. "Water, coffee, soft drink?"

"Water would be fine," he answered as he seated himself in the chair David motioned him to. He hadn't expected the boss to be wearing jeans, boat shoes and an unbuttoned tropical print shirt hanging out over a yellow tee shirt.

"Nice office," he added.

David chuckled as he returned with a bottle of water from a small fridge in the corner. "It's not just nice, it's ridiculous. It's way bigger than anyone really needs, and look at this view. I guess it's technically an office but I don't do much work so maybe it's just a place for me to hang out and enjoy the view. I actually have had a few small parties and some catered dinners with a few people up here."

David seated himself behind the large desk and opened a folder and leafed through a few sheets of paper as he talked. "You've been doing a great job for the company, Max, but that also is not why I want to talk. I've gone to a lot of trouble to choose who I think is the right man for a job I'm going to offer you. I chose you for a number of reasons. You seem intelligent, you have no family living other than some aunts, uncles and cousins who you don't seem to be in any real contact with, and you are thirty-one years old. Is all that correct so far?"

Max was nodding. "I like to think that I'm intelligent and, yes, I have no close family living and I am thirty-one years old."

"Okay," David said, returning the slight smile. "I think it would be fair to say that the job position is one of being a caretaker and it would require you to relocate to Bakersfield, California. You would have to maintain the strictest secrecy to others about this job. It's a huge responsibility but requires very little in the way of time or energy. Starting pay is one million dollars a year.

Max sat up straighter and took a swig from his water bottle.

Over the past several months, David had put together an incredible amount of information about Maxwell Nguyen. Other than Tommy and Mary Kay, this man had become the single individual on earth that David knew the most about.

"I used the term caretaker," David continued. "Mainly your job will be to check every day at one of my properties and just check around and make sure everything looks okay. This should only take a few minutes daily. You'll also have some computer monitoring of information you'll need to do from home for alarm settings and things like that, but that won't be very time-consuming either. You'll have to be close by and available in case any problems arise but you'll be living in a house that's provided, not on the property but in the neighborhood. As time goes along you may have some additional duties but they will still not amount to anything strenuous or taking up much of your time. You will not be allowed to share with anyone just what it is you actually do for a living or any details about the complex. You will need to use your own good judgment but any friends or romantic entanglements that arise will also need to be kept in the dark about just what it is your job involves. We will come up with a proper title on paper for you with the company. Maybe something like executive property manager, financial property review, property security—some boring-sounding technical gobbledygook."

Max chuckled softly. "It sounds like my first assignment should be helping to invent a title for my position that sounds both high tech and obtuse at the same time."

David pointed and nodded. "High tech and obtuse. I knew I picked the right guy."

He stood and began pacing back and forth behind his desk as he continued with his presentation. "Your contact person will be me and only me for every aspect of this job. Most importantly, the one trait you need to possess to succeed in this position is a complete absence of any curiosity about why you are being paid such an enormous salary for such a seemingly simple job. I anticipate this position lasting for quite a number of years. As time goes along, I will probably be required to bring you more into my confidence and you will have increasing knowledge of the role your position fulfills. But that will be my decision. If you ever breach any of my rules about keeping this secret or if you ever attempt to do any investigation of your own concerning any aspect of this position, I will find out and the consequences for you would be very grave. That would include not disclosing to anyone what is talked about in this interview today. If you excel in this position, as I fully expect you will, you will become one of my closest confidantes. So, Max Nguyen, that's all I have to say at this point. Any questions?"

Max took another sip of water. "I have no questions other than when do I start?"

"Great," David said. He stood and came around the desk and shook hands as he patted Max on the shoulder. "This is very important. We will meet again in the next few days to arrange your move, sign some papers, visit the site and work on that name for your job."

Max nodded and took another sip of water. His curiosity had certainly been aroused, but he sensed that to show how intrigued he was would be a serious mistake, so he pushed it down and kept it to himself, for now.

August, 2002—Seattle, Washington

Tommy sat in a comfortable chair facing Dr. Lindsey Robbins, the therapist he had been seeing off and on for almost two years. Tommy was forty-six and she was several years younger. He thought she was pretty, easy to talk to and he liked her well enough.

"It's good to see you again, Tommy. It's been almost a month."

He nodded and took a sip from his screwdriver. "Yeah, I just didn't feel like coming for a while there, but I do miss our little talks."

Nearly a year earlier she had begun keeping a small liquor and mixer stash just for him. She had never known anyone who could and would drink as much as Tommy Dias. So she made a deal with him that he could have one drink during their hour-long sessions if he agreed to not show up already tanked, even though that was a little difficult to gauge with him. She rightly figured that allowing him a bit more when he met with her couldn't possibly add enough to matter to the daily damage he did on his own. Some extensive alcohol rehab was in his future, but she knew him well enough to know that he would get nowhere drying out until they could get to the bottom of some of his other demons.

"How has your claustrophobia been?" she asked. "Had any serious episodes lately?"

"A couple," he said. "They didn't last very long."

"Did you do the visualizing being outdoors, on the golf course, with wide expanses of lawn and trees in the distance, blue skies and puffy white clouds? You've said that a previous therapist had you doing something similar and it helped you."

Tommy nodded. "Yeah, I didn't stick with that before. Anyway, I've been using the visualization and I think it has helped. I think it shortened the episodes."

"Good," she said. "Did you still see the dead man sitting up in bed when the feeling began to overwhelm you?"

Tommy took another sip and stared straight ahead, trying to see the man and at the same time, trying not to see him too clearly. "Yes."

"Still having him pop up in dreams?" she asked.

"Not every night," he said. He took another sip. "But it's still too damn often sometimes."

Dr. Robbins let several seconds of silence pass. "You know, during the two years you've been seeing me, we've never gotten to the real depths of where this vision came from to begin with. You've only said it was from your childhood, but you have always blocked our conversation from getting to the real source of this picture in your head. I think if we can take you back to that time maybe we can help you to take some of the fear out of it. Care to elaborate today?"

Tommy adjusted himself in the chair and took another small sip of his drink, rationing the contents of the tall glass so its contents and his session would run out at approximately the same time.

For many months he had rehearsed this moment, vacillating between almost blurting it out and deciding to just keep it to himself like he always had, like all three of them always had. He decided to go with her suggestion today and see where it led. "It didn't come from my imagination. When I was twelve years old my friend David and I found a man sitting up in bed in his apartment shot dead."

Dr. Robbins was mildly surprised at this leap forward after all this time. "So, it's not something you just imagined from a book or TV or a movie?"

Tommy shook his head.

"Who was this person?" she continued. She still doubted the reality of his haunting vision. "Was this someone in your family or your friend's family?"

"No," Tommy said. "It was a mob guy who lived in an apartment down the alley from our houses. We had spent the summer spying on him and also helping him with yard work and feeding his cat when he was out of town. I guess you could say that we had kind of become friends with him."

She raised her eyebrows. "A mob guy? Well, what happened? Did you tell your parents? Were the police called?"

Tommy sat silently for a time as he thought back to that day. "No, we took his keys and left the apartment. The police found him a few days later."

Dr. Robbins again let silent moments pass as she tried to make some sense of what he was saying, and tried to decide how true it might be. "You took his keys? Why were you spying on him?"

Tommy leaned forward in his chair. "I know you told me this before, but everything we talk about here is confidential, right?"

"Of course," she said.

He stared at her for a long time. "No matter how strange or criminal or anything?"

"Well," she said, hesitating, "if you tell me you have abused a child or that you're planning to kill or hurt someone or yourself then I am bound to report that. Crimes in the past such as, say, robbery, burglary, car theft, fraud are not anything I would report. So, generally speaking, except for the examples I stated no matter how 'out there' what you have to tell me is, yes, it is confidential information."

Tommy thought this over for a bit. "So, if I stole a bunch of money from a dead mobster and nobody ever found out about it, that's something that would stay confidential?"

"That's right." She looked him over for a bit. "Did you steal money from a dead mobster?" Already, she was putting together scenarios in her mind that would somehow lead to him imagining that such a thing actually happened.

He glanced over at a small clock on the table and saw that he still had twenty minutes left, then picked up his glass and downed the remainder of the contents. Setting the glass, containing only abandoned ice cubes, back onto the table, he leaned back in his chair. He thought back over the time he had been seeing her and realized she was one of the very few people in the world he could trust.

"Is it stealing if the person is dead?" he asked. "I've thought about this. Maybe it's just finding since it doesn't really belong to anybody anymore."

Dr. Robbins smiled. "That would be an interesting discussion topic."

"We were spying on him," Tommy continued, "because it was summer, we were bored and we thought it would be fun. After a while we figured out he was hiding money. We found him killed, took his keys and a couple of days later, along with my sister, we found where he had been hiding his money, more than three million dollars."

"Three million dollars is a lot of money," she finally managed to say. "What did you do with it?"

He stared at her for a time, feeling both annoyed and amused by her tone which made it clear that she didn't quite believe what he had just told her. He felt a grin beginning to spread across his face. He leaned forward in his chair. "What did we do with it? We took it and hid it and nobody ever knew how it disappeared. It was the greatest kid crime ever committed! When we were old enough we used it to turn ourselves into some of the richest goddamn people around."

He suddenly felt like he had done something wrong. He had just broken a rule that had been in place for thirty-four years, but this was different, he was telling himself. This wasn't just bragging. This was Dr. Robbins. This was private. Still, he had a rising panicky feeling in his chest that he was trying to push down and away.

Tommy leaned forward again in his chair and his smile faded. Very quietly he said, "We got away with this all these years by keeping our fucking mouths shut about it. You're the first person I've ever told about this. You better keep your mouth shut too, or something bad could happen."

Dr. Robbins was stunned and trying hard not to let it show. She often had patients confess inappropriate behavior and even minor crimes, but this was something quite different and the fact that it was accompanied by a threat she never saw coming had her heart racing.

"I see," she said as calmly as she could manage. "This could be quite a breakthrough in helping you with your claustrophobia and panic attacks."

As for Tommy, he felt like a burden he had been carrying around for decades had been, at least partially, taken away.

She flipped through the calendar on her desk and cleared her throat. "I've been rearranging my schedule for a little over a month from now. My high school is having a twenty year reunion. Originally I wasn't planning to travel after all the mess caused by 9/11 but it seems that flying has gotten a little more back to normal so I'm going to go ahead and go. I'm flying to San Francisco and visiting with some friends while I'm at it so I'll be out of town for about ten days."

"Some people like reunions," Tommy said. "I never go. My twentieth was a few years ago. I didn't go. I think I'd probably get claustrophobia or something. Maybe even bullshitaphobia."

She smiled as she continued checking over her calendar. "I didn't go to my ten year reunion. I'm wondering if I really want to go to this one, but some friends called me and talked me into it. But now I'm a little concerned about developing bullshitaphobia. So, if you come every week like you're supposed to…" She looked up and gave him a good-natured scolding look. "…we will have two more sessions, then we can take a two week break while I'm gone. We can touch base again on the exact dates

114

when the time comes. Does that sound okay?"

He nodded. "Sure. Hey, I didn't mean to sound so harsh a couple of minutes ago. I just got worried after I said something. This is just between us, right?"

"Just you and me," she reassured him.

She was relieved that he had backed off his attitude. But she had made some notes and she intended to check the news stories from back then and see if there was anything that sounded like the story he had just told her.

David and Mary Kay were in bed lazily enjoying the easy quietness that came after a quick energetic lovemaking session. Her head was on his chest as she toyed with his knee and he absently stroked her hair.

"Tommy told me something pretty disturbing this morning," she said.

David rolled his eyes. "Wow, how surprising," he said, adding a sarcastic snort of a laugh.

"Be nice," she said, protective of her brother, as always.

"You know," he said, "there are times when we still get along just like when we were kids. But, sometimes he just pisses me off. I wish he could get a handle on his drinking. Anyway, what did he tell you?"

Mary Kay sighed, moved over and leaned on her elbows so she could look at David's face. "He told Dr. Robbins that when he was a kid, he and his sister and a friend took over three million dollars of hidden money from a dead mobster."

David raised his eyebrows and sat up. "Jesus! Why?"

"Oh, hell, David, you know why. He's never felt right about it. It haunts him. I guess it just came out in their session. He said he could trust her and it felt like a weight had been lifted off him."

"Did you ask him how much he went into detail about this with her?"

Mary Kay nodded. "I did. I was kind of shocked just like you are. Apparently he didn't say anything about exactly who we are or any details about it. He just told her when he was a kid he stole three million dollars from a dead mobster."

David was sitting all the way up on the edge of the bed, feet on the floor. "He actually said three million bucks, huh? Did he say how she reacted?"

"He said she acted like she didn't really believe him, like he was just making something up."

"That'd be nice," he said. "But what if she gets curious and does a little checking? Wouldn't take much to find out where Tommy grew up or who we are. But even then, she probably wouldn't believe the part about us taking the money."

"Maybe," Mary Kay said. "What if she talks about it with her husband or boyfriend or some family person who starts getting curious and digs deeper?"

"Well, what about the whole doctor patient thing and privileged information," David said, not trusting it even as he said it.

"That's just some damn rule," she said, raising her voice. "We can't trust in that."

David knew how Mary Kay could get and at the moment he was mainly concerned about keeping her calm. "You think he could tell her that he was just throwing that out there as a joke kind of thing? Maybe something like telling her the three of us always talked about it as kids like a fantasy thing because nobody ever found out who took the money?"

"Anything's possible, I guess." She leaned forward becoming more exasperated. "I think this could turn into some serious shit, David. We can't just wait to see what happens."

"Okay," he said. "Let's not jump to any conclusions just yet, okay? I'll have someone research her a bit and find out more about her. Maybe we can find out if she can be trusted or if we have to come up with a cover story or something."

Mary Kay backed off and tried to calm her exterior, even managing a small smile. "Okay, let me know."

Inside she was seething and panicking. She had already found out some things about Dr. Robbins and this situation needed some quick attention. More than anything she didn't want

Tommy to be blamed for anything that happened. She would do what she had to do to protect her twin brother, then David would have to take it from there. She knew she could always count on him to protect her.

Dr. Robbins was out on her patio in Seattle putting polish on her toenails and holding the phone receiver between her shoulder and neck listening to the ringing on the other end.

After a few rings there was an answer.

"Hi Mom, how's the weather in Sacramento?"

"Hi Lindsey. Kinda hot and probably dryer than where you are."

Dr. Robbins chuckled. "It's actually pretty dry and nice today. So listen, I've got a question about some relative I barely remember. Dad's sister married a guy named Saladino, right?"

"Yeah, that was Aunt Lillie's first husband. They only lasted about ten years. Wow that was a long time ago. Where's this coming from?"

"Can't say," Dr. Robbins said. "It's boring anyway. Something a patient said that got me thinking. So I seem to remember hearing stories later from you guys and grandma that when I was really little something happened to a friend or someone in that guy's family. Something to do with organized crime?"

"I'm not sure I have it all straight now or ever did," her mom said. "Her husband had something to do with a Los Angeles crime gang and a guy that was killed in Bakersfield. Supposedly the guy that was killed had been stealing from the gang and hiding the money in a secret safe the police discovered after he was killed but all the money had been stolen. So Aunt Lillie's first husband was a cousin to that crime bunch, I think, or some relative. I think that's all I can remember about it."

"So this guy's money from the secret safe disappeared," Dr. Robbins repeated. "They ever find out what happened to it or who took it?"

"I guess not," her mom said. "I don't know really. You were little, like three or four I think. We were living not too far from

Bakersfield at the time and it was on the TV news and in the newspapers for a few weeks and then it just went away. Oh, wait, I remember they had these three neighborhood kids on the news who knew the gang guy who was killed. They had been helping him do yardwork and feeding his cat. Two boys and the twin sister of one of them. Some reporter was asking them dimwitted questions and all of a sudden the girl says, "Hey, mister, why don't you leave my brother alone and ask me one of your stupid questions instead?"

Dr. Robbins and her mother were both laughing.

"I hadn't thought about that for a long time," her mother said. "Everyone seemed all shocked for a few seconds, then the reporter just looked into the camera and said something about returning to the people in the studio."

"Wow, that's something," Dr. Robbins said.

"It is, huh? So, anyway, I don't think I really know anything else about that whole deal. A few years later he and Lillie divorced. I was only around him a handful of times. I never heard him talk about it. I just heard some things from her and your dad."

"That's fine," Dr. Robbins said. "Like I said, something a patient said got me thinking. Okay, I gotta go. Thanks for a good story. Love you."

"Bye, Honey, love you too."

Doctor Robbins returned to polishing her toenails and quietly thinking over what she had learned. It sounds crazy, she thought, but Tommy had sounded so adamant. She was sure he was one of the three kids her mom had just told her about. She wondered if maybe the three of them just got together and concocted a story to entertain themselves.

Mary Kay walked into the café and saw Jerry, an investigator she used from time to time, waving at her from a booth near the back. After a quick hug they sat across from each other.

"Wow, we haven't talked for ages," she said. "You must have something really juicy for me."

Jerry smiled. "I don't think it's too juicy. I guess I could've just told you this over the phone, but I was in town and we hadn't seen each other in forever. So, you told me to tell you if I ever heard of anyone looking into you three, and especially Tommy."

The server brought their drinks as they sat silently for several moments. Mary Kay smiled. "That's one of the reasons I keep you on the overpaid payroll. So what's up?"

"So one of my sources in Bakersfield tells me that a couple days ago some psychiatrist called and asked about some information from back in the summer of 1968."

"Let me guess," Mary Kay said. "Dr. Lindsey Robbins?"

Jerry looked a little surprised and gave a quick chuckle. "Pretty good. Do I even want to know how you know?"

She shook her head and put on a teasing half smile. "No."

"So, anyway," he continued, "she told my source that she was coming to a high school reunion in September in a nearby city and she would make a point of coming into Bakersfield to talk to a couple of people about it. And she asked if my source knew anything about the three kids who were on the news back then and the girl who smarted off to a reporter on live TV telling him to quit asking her brother stupid questions and ask her."

Mary Kay stared for a couple of seconds then launched into loud laughter that made several nearby people look. Jerry watched and smiled.

She finally composed herself, took a few sips of water and took a deep breath. "I haven't thought about that for at least twenty years. That girl was me."

"Must be quite a memory," Jerry said, smiling broadly.

Mary Kay chuckled a little more as she slowly shook her head. "Yes it is. Okay, listen. It's really good you brought this to my attention. I'll have to keep you on the payroll longer now. If you can, find out when she's flying into the area, where she's staying, appointments, anything even if it seems insignificant."

EIGHT

Kewalo Basin Harbor, Honolulu, Hawaii – March, 2003

The meeting in progress was jokingly referred to by David, Tommy and Mary Kay as the "annual meeting" whether they had met a year before or just a few weeks. If it was just the three of them and it was an official meeting, it was an annual meeting. David and Mary Kay lived together and they saw Tommy fairly often, so the three of them saw each other unofficially all the time. These so-called annual meetings, usually called by David or Mary Kay, happened whenever any concern came up that required their united attention. Sometimes it was personal, more often it was business or money-related. It might involve just touching bases on some idea or David informing them of recent financial news. Occasionally they met for no reason whatsoever except to just have a nice dinner at someplace new and spend some time together.

This one was being billed by Mary Kay and Tommy as one of those gatherings of the three that was just social and for no particular reason. David knew better but hadn't said anything yet. They knew he was probably aware of the reason but everyone was sticking with the game so far. The real topic had come up frequently over the last year or two.

This time they were gathered aboard David's 142-foot luxury yacht anchored offshore. He had been there for a couple of days with Mary Kay and Tommy had flown in the night before. Half of the crew of six, including the captain, had the day off and were ashore busily spending money, eating and scouting out women. Of the three who remained onboard, one was in the engine room monitoring generators and various other readings while perusing the latest issue of Playboy. The other two were topside keeping a general security lookout and enjoying the mild sun. One of them was also a reasonably good cook.

It was just past noon and Tommy was behind the main salon bar mixing his third drink of the day. Mary Kay was standing at one end of the bar and David was seated at a tall round table just to the side of the bar.

"By the way," Tommy said, "here's a weird thing. Remember I told you a few months ago that my shrink, Dr. Robbins, must've decided to take a longer trip or something? After a few more weeks went by I called and they told me she was on a hiatus for a while and they were referring patients to a few other shrinks, which I did not want to do. So, a few days ago her office called again. The receptionist was all upset and told me that they were just stalling before and have no idea what happened to her. She left town to go to her high school reunion back in September and nobody's seen her since. They are calling all her clients and letting them know the office is closing permanently."

"I saw something about her on the news a while back," David said. "You get any referrals from her office for a new person?"

Tommy nodded as he cut a lime and squeezed it into his drink. "Yeah, but I don't want to go to anyone else. I think she has helped me do better. I'm just going to talk to myself." He took a long swallow and made a satisfied noise. "So, back to the current topic, what do you think, David? Ready to relax a little? Ready to finally stop looking over your shoulder? Nobody remembers that far back. It's ancient history. The world has moved on." He took another long swallow from the tall double screwdriver. "Look at us. We were twelve years old when this whole thing went down and we're all turning forty-seven in a few months. You've done an anally admirable job of keeping us all safe and practically unknown to the world. Take a break."

Mary Kay was standing quietly at the end of the bar sipping an iced tea. She set down her glass and folded her hands under her chin and gave him her familiar pleading look.

"So, tell me again," David said, "Why a Vegas hotel and casino?"

"Because we need to make some more money!" Tommy said with a sour laugh and took another long swallow.

Mary Kay sighed, gave him a glaring look, and returned her attention to David. "We might not make any money at all," she continued. "If we go with the design plans we discussed a few months ago, construction and opening costs will be right around a billion and a half. We won't have any investors to keep happy, no real financial pressure. We can have the fun of being in on the design and planning of everything and then leave the headaches of building and running it to others. We could be as involved in running it as we want to be. We could recoup our initial cost in five years or so, but whether we do or not isn't the point. Unlike just about anybody who has built one of these, except maybe Steve Wynn and that guy that owns the Venetian, what's his name?"

"Adelson," Tommy answered. "Used his own money, spent a goddamn ridiculous fortune on that thing to get it exactly like he wanted it. That's what I want to do, spend a goddamn fortune, every fucking penny."

Mary Kay ignored him. "Anyway, unlike most people who do this, we can actually enjoy the experience."

David gave her a long, serious look while he thought over the whole concept of enjoying the experience. Maybe this would be different, he thought.

"Tommy can be the resident golf pro," she continued. "He can work as much or as little as he likes. He's already been doing celebrity golf tournaments in Seattle. Think of the line-up he could put together in Vegas."

"It would be perfect for me," Tommy said. "Getting others to do my work, as usual, playing golf and bullshitting people into playing in those tournaments are about the only things I'm good at. And the chicks, well, you know it's the perfect location. A rich guy always looks younger to them."

David nodded and smiled. "Younger and better-looking. I've

noticed that."

Tommy stepped around the bar and moved to the table, his face just a couple of feet from David's. "Think of it, man. For once we would be having fun with something! Building a really cool place and giving thousands of people another place they can come and have fun. It's been a damn long time and now we don't need to be so careful. I think we're all tired of always looking back over our shoulders, especially you. It's been thirty-five years for Christ's sake! Nobody's left who gives a shit about Vincent Saladino's lost money. Plus you've seen to it that there's probably nobody left who remembers us. All ties to family and friends were severed decades ago. It's all ancient history, man. We're all in reasonably good health. We should be enjoying ourselves."

David was silent for a long time, slowly nodding as if agreeing with his own thoughts. "So, let's say the construction costs inflate to two billion. Things look good right now but let's say the economy goes south for a long time and we lose a billion a year for ten years. That would come to twelve billion. If I went and cashed out twelve billion from cash reserves right now and burned it, our lifestyle would be exactly the same." He shrugged. "So, there really is no money issue."

Tommy stood and began slowly and loudly applauding. "Bravo! I like your thinking. Let's start burning a billion every year. Hell, let's go for two!"

Mary Kay slapped the bar with both hands. "Tommy, will you fucking shut up! You wanna move into a box on a sidewalk somewhere?"

David and Tommy looked at each other while Tommy laughed and returned to his drink.

"You know, besides what Tommy calls my anally admirable work of keeping our lives as private as possible, the two of you have kept me busier than normal at times. Tommy, your incalculable alcohol consumption and related escapades have caused some difficulties over the years."

Tommy spread his hands and put on an expression of

grudging agreement. "I think my inherent charm makes up for some of it, though."

David gave Mary Kay a long look and she held her own stare as he did so. "Mary Kay, that famous over-protective streak of yours has sometimes caused some logistical problems that I needed to take care of."

Mary Kay cleared her throat and said nothing.

"What?" Tommy said. "My perfect little sister, seven minutes younger, is not so perfect after all? I can't believe it!" He chuckled, quickly lost interest in whatever the details might be as he walked back behind the bar and began lining up the ingredients for his next drink.

"Well, I don't think that will be a problem," she said. "I'm with Tommy on this. I don't think anybody cares or remembers after so long."

David looked back and forth between the twins, but said nothing.

Mary Kay clapped her hands in excitement. "Come on, David, what do you say?"

David began to smile. It was one of those times that he felt like they were all about twelve years old again. He stood. "Hope you two are right about nobody caring anymore, because something like this will sure as hell attract the media attention. But, hey, let's spend some of our filthy richness without worrying so fucking much about it."

Mary Kay ran the few steps to him and hugged him. Tommy reached and patted him on the back.

David wanted to sound genuine and he wanted to believe in what he had said, but he still couldn't be as happy about it as he was sounding for them. It was a risk, but after so long a time a part of him wanted to just declare that they could afford to finally be a little less careful. He would still need to maintain control over their situation and he just hoped the rest of the world thought thirty-five years was long enough, but he couldn't convince himself to really believe it. So, for him, nothing had changed much. They were about to embark on a very public enterprise that would need him to maneuver more than ever to keep them as private as possible.

September, 2003 – Los Angeles

Howie Williams hadn't been drafted into the Army just after high school as he thought he would have since the draft was ended the year before his 1974 graduation. He'd been given some good advice from some relatives and a few friends and he had enlisted instead. By the time he had finished boot camp in early 1975, the Vietnam War was long over and done. The closest he had come to any combat was duty in the Philippines as part of a security force patrolling the jungle around the perimeters of several American bases where they occasionally exchanged fire with ragtag bands of guerrillas who were supposedly supporting various independence movements. During his three years in the army he worked as a military policeman and became interested in law enforcement. After his discharge he returned to Bakersfield and, in spite of his previous disdain for school work, mustered the motivation to complete an associate degree, attend the police academy and become a proud member of the Bakersfield Police Department.

A few years later, after inquiring into the comparatively high salaries and moving bonuses being offered by the Los Angeles Police Department, he and his wife and two kids pulled up stakes and moved to Encino. The money had only been part of the draw, the kicker maybe, because Howie had grown bored with life and police work in his hometown. There was nothing really wrong with it, it was just that he felt like he had seen and done everything there was and he longed for what he called "bigger" police work. Everyone warned him that the Los Angeles area had the big city problems that weren't as often a part of the job in Bakersfield, but that was exactly what he wanted.

His personal life took a nosedive after the move and two years later he joined the swollen ranks of divorced cops. As divorces go, it went cordially enough. For his career, though, things went just the opposite. He thrived in the southern California environment. He was a good cop, a smart cop, as reasonably honest a cop as he needed to be and he rose through the ranks to become a detective. The year he made detective he was thirty-five years old and they partnered him with a senior grade sergeant by the name of Gary Heinz who had a few years left before retirement. Detective Heinz had left the Bakersfield Police Department for L.A. the year Howie finished the academy. Howie remembered hearing his name around and he also knew that he had been one of the lead investigators on the Vincent Saladino case.

They had gotten along well and being from the same hometown helped create a bond. Just once they talked briefly about the Saladino murder and the mystery surrounding the supposed lost mob money. They were partners for a few years until Heinz retired in 1990.

Over the next few years Howie worked a number of positions on several crime task forces as well as regular duties in homicide and property crimes. These were with a series of training partners or temporary partners between assignments.

As Howie was nearing his fortieth birthday, he was caught up in a messy and controversial police brutality lawsuit and he elected to resign from the force and take an early retirement. He had been wanting a change in what he was doing with his life and this gave him a chance to do that. Since then he was happy doing some part-time work as a bodyguard and some private investigation of his own on jobs that interested him.

Now that he was forty-seven he was enjoying his PI work which allowed him to work as little or as much as he cared to. He kept in decent shape and hadn't put much weight on his six foot one frame. He worked out at a local health club a couple of times a week and jogged a mile every other day or so. A few years ago after the entire top of his head had gone bald he began keeping his head shaved.

At the moment he was drinking his morning coffee, skimming through the newspaper and watching the Today

Show. For the second time that morning he was watching a brief mention in the news segment about the groundbreaking of a new hotel casino resort in Las Vegas to be called Chill. It was going to be built a few blocks off the strip across I-15 near the Rio. It would be taking the place of a rundown strip mall, a few aging apartment complexes and some warehouses. There was a quick shot of several company officials at the announcement ceremony shaking hands with the mayor of Las Vegas. In the background, seated with several other people on the platform he recognized David and Mary Kay.

A few days earlier Howie had noticed a couple of small articles about the Vegas project buried in the financial section in the newspaper that had mentioned DMT International and the CEO David Steiner. It had gotten him thinking about some things and people he hadn't really contemplated in a lot of years. He had been looking over high school yearbooks and doing a lot of reminiscing about people and events from more than thirty-five years ago. He did a little research on DMT International and his brain began making connections about the events of the summer of 1968.

He was recalling memories long dormant. He remembered a couple of times when they were still in high school when David threw some money on the table and paid for a group of seven or eight of them after they ate at a coffee shop. Another time, David chipped in a twenty dollar bill for gas when everyone else was coming up with quarters and ones and gas was twenty-five cents a gallon.

Over the years these seemingly small gestures were not remembered or much noted by anyone and just faded into the sea of irrelevant snippets from their high school days. Now, though, Howie was piecing them together in a new light and fitting them into the puzzle that was becoming clearer every day. When the Saladino murder happened it got around that David, Tommy and Mary Kay had known the mobster and had been talked to by the cops. He remembered that the three of them were minor celebrities for a while. But, as always, the story faded fast and after a time just went away as 1968 and on into the 70s rolled out an endless stream of disconcerting events and a viscerally polarizing war that pushed the sensational murder and its money mystery to the far reaches of everyone's awareness.

Howie had remained casual friends with David, Tommy and Mary Kay all through high school, but mostly David. They didn't spend a lot of time hanging around together, but they talked here and there and, because they had some mutual acquaintances, frequently ended up at the same places or parties. After graduation they had gone their individual ways and on to their separate lives.

It seemed strange to him now that over the years he had done so little thinking about that time because for the last couple of weeks it was practically all he thought about. Somewhere over the last few days he just put it together, and when he did, it surprised him that he had never carried his thinking that far before. It seemed so obvious to him now, especially after his research had brought him to the knowledge of just how wealthy the three had become, and one interesting detail really cemented it for him.

A couple of days later Howie arranged a dinner with Gary Heinz, his former partner, and another man by the name of Angelo "Trap" Trapani. Both were in their early seventies. Trapani was someone who Howie had gotten to know a little over the years. He was a person who enjoyed the notion of other people thinking he was in the mob. The reality was he just had a few cousins, uncles, people he grew up with and people he barely knew who were connected.

Trapani loved to talk, people loved to talk to him and he was a good listener. Long ago, Howie had come to realize that Trapani was always on the edge of things enough that sometimes the man actually knew stuff, usually without really understanding the importance of what he knew. Howie had invited him this night because one of the people Trapani had been friendly with over the years was Dominic "Dino" Saladino.

They met at an Italian restaurant in Glendale. Howie knew the owner and arranged to be seated in the most out-of-the-way booth. He arrived well ahead of time and when Heinz and Trapani arrived, bruschetta, mini meatball appetizers and a couple of bottles of red wine were already on the table. Neither of the two had been told the reason for the meeting or that the other would be there. As the evening progressed they didn't ask, knowing Howie would get to it in due time. Nearly an hour passed while they drank down the wine, ate their ravioli and linguini dinners, talked about the lousy condition of the world and crazy stuff that used to happen back in the day.

"Okay," Howie said. "As you may have guessed, I invited both of you here for a reason."

"No shit?" Heinz offered. "I thought you just missed me and this was like a date."

The three of them laughed and then the lull of curiosity settled back over the table.

"I would like to be able to know that our conversation from this point on will remain just between the three of us," Howie said.

"My lips are sealed, pal," Heinz said.

Trapani chuckled. "Sure, so what's up?"

Howie didn't believe Trapani for a second but figured it wouldn't really make much difference.

'Vincent Saladino," Howie said.

"Jesus Christ!" Heinz answered, then shook his head while he quietly chuckled.

Trapani looked a little surprised, slowly nodding as he seemed to be thinking. "Wow, we're going way back." He looked across at Heinz. "You worked that case."

Heinz nodded, pointing at Howie. "I did, and this guy was a snot-nose kid living in Vincent's neighborhood in Bakersfield." He turned to Howie. "So, you really do miss me and you haven't had anyone to talk to about this?"

"I figured you two were the right ones to discuss this with,"

Howie said. "Trap here used to pal around with one Nic Saladino, Vincent's uncle."

"Yeah, I remember that," Heinz said. "So, what are we discussing?"

Howie ignored the question. "Trap, how old is Dino now? He must be in his eighties, huh?"

"He just turned seventy-nine." Trapani said. "I saw him about two, three months ago. He looks good. Getting around okay. He looks more like seventy or so. So, like your partner here asked, what are we talking about?"

"We're discussing how Vincent's money disappeared," Howie said.

Heinz stared for several seconds. "Why the hell … okay, what about it?"

Howie smiled. "I know, I know. Just hang with me here for a bit." He turned his attention to the other man. "Trap, besides no money being found, what was the big problem surrounding that whole deal?"

Trapani leaned back and thought. "Well, supposedly, Dino sent some guys to hit Vincent up in Bakersfield and when Dino's guys showed up Vincent had already been hit. They grabbed a few grand from a safe in his apartment and reported back to Dino. Dino went fucking crazy and had a mob guy by the name of Catalano killed because he was sure he'd ordered the hit and for a while he thought he took the money too. But that's just what I heard."

Howie looked at Heinz, "I remember you saying something like that too."

"Right," Heinz said. "The word we got was that Dino was not only hopping mad pissed but also worried about the money disappearing and somehow he blamed this guy Catalano. Mario was his first name, Mario Catalano. Something about one of Catalano's guys had been working with Vincent."

"So, did Catalano kill Vincent?" Howie asked. "Did Dino go after the right guy?"

Trapani shrugged. "I know some people who think he was the

wrong guy. I know Dino never got to the money."

"I remember you telling me," Howie said, "that whoever cleaned out the safe left a single hundred dollar bill with the padlock and the key sitting on top of it."

Heinz nodded.

"I remember hearing something like that," Trapani said, "but I seem to remember there was a note with the lock too."

"No shit?" Heinz said. He gave Howie a look and the beginning of a smile. "We purposely never put that info out there. Figured it might come in handy someday. How'd you find that out?"

Trapani shrugged. "Hell, I don't know. I just remember that being said back then. I guess Dino or somebody. I don't know."

"Wow," Howie said, eyebrows raised, staring at Heinz, "you are a tight-lipped bastard. You never said anything to me about a note. Who knew that besides you and Lassiter?"

"Nobody," Heinz said, smiling. "We didn't even tell the FBI guys. Some uniform saw the lock and key sitting on the C-note. The dumb ass picked them up and grabbed out the bill and the slip of paper fell. He picked up the note and looked it over before he gave it to Bill. A couple minutes later we chewed on him a little for touching shit and told him to keep quiet about the note. So, I guess that nitwit might've said something. Also, don't forget whoever wrote the note knew about it."

"What did the note say?" Howie asked.

"That was weird. It said 'We cleaned your chimney for you. The sweeps and Mary Poppins.' Bill and I must have read that note 5,000 times."

Trapani laughed. "Yeah, I remember it was something like that."

Howie was watching this with his mouth hanging open. "Holy shit," he finally said. "Those three kids I knew, the ones who were helping Vincent? They sort of adopted the cat that Vincent was feeding and letting it hang around. They named that fucking cat Mary Poppins!"

"What kids?" Trapani asked.

Heinz slowly shook his head. "These three kids were hanging

around Saladino's place, helping with yardwork at the house and taking care of his cat when he left town. Hell, we checked them out. You know, my partner and I thought about them, but we just couldn't take the idea seriously. We paid attention to the families for a year or so. No money stuff was happening. Same old jobs, same old lives. I parked my ass on Second Street a block south a few times and just watched. The kids were starting into their teenage years and everybody was just having your normal, average, fucked-up existence. It just went away after a while. As far we we're concerned, there was no real victim. This case didn't stay real high on our list after a while. So the mob lost some money—fuck `em." He looked hard at Howie. "They named the cat Mary Poppins, huh? By the way, we told the kids about finding the note, but didn't tell them what was in it."

Howie poured the last of the Pinot into his glass. "Trap, you ever hear anything back then about three kids?"

Trapani looked around thinking back, slowly shaking his head. "No."

"I grew up with David Steiner, Tommy Dias and Mary Kay Dias, Tommy's twin sister. I think they took the money. In fact, I know they did. I've had this in front of me all these years and I finally put it all together. The last time I checked, which was just a couple of days ago, David Steiner is the sixty-fourth richest dude in the U.S. Mary Kay sits on the board of his company, DMT International. They're both worth a ton. Also, I ran into them the day they ripped off that safe in the chimney."

Heinz gave him a wide-eyed, silent few seconds. "Jesus, Howie, you've been sitting on that all this time?"

"Nah, not really," Howie said. "I didn't know what they were doing. I just happened along down the alley. They were acting nervous as hell, and I was a trouble-making little fucker and I knew when someone was hiding something. They acted just like all kids do when they get caught by surprise. I only talked to them for a minute and went on about my business. I didn't know then what had happened to Saladino. By the time you guys talked to them they had covered their tracks and stuck to their know-nothing story. Anyway, they're in the news the last few weeks. They're breaking ground on a big hotel casino in Vegas."

Trapani cleared his throat. "So what's the Mary Poppins shit in the note?"

Howie shrugged, smiling. "That would be just like David to do something like that. So, Gary, you ever get anywhere with that note?"

"Nah, nothing," he said. "The Mary Poppins thing was just some smart-ass stuff."

"So you think these three kids took the money?" Trapani said.

Howie nodded.

"You think they killed Vincent too?" he asked.

Howie sighed. "We were kids, man. That's pretty hard to believe, but I bet they know who did."

"So you're all hot on this because they're opening up a joint in Vegas?" Heinz asked.

"Seeing it on the news got me thinking," Howie said, "but then I discovered something else that really fits in with that note. David Steiner, one of those three kids, the main kid really, has a big-ass yacht. Its name is <u>Chimney Sweep</u>."

"Did you know that chimney sweeps are supposed to be good luck?" Trapani said.

Heinz scowled. "Who says?"

It's like a legend," Trapani said. "It's even supposed to be good luck for brides to shake hands with a chimney sweep at their wedding."

Howie chuckled. "Well, these three sweepers sure as hell got lucky."

"It's like that song from the movie Mary Poppins," Trapani said. Then he softly sang a couple of lines the chimney sweep character sings in the movie.

There was silence around the table for several moments as Trapani beamed a huge smile.

Finally, chuckling, Heinz said softly, "Mary fuckin' Poppins."

The next day Howie came by Gary Heinz's house as they had

agreed.

"Hey Howie. Have a seat at the kitchen table. I'll be right back."

A minute later he came back from the hall closet with a storage box, set it on the kitchen table and pulled off the lid. "I used to keep news items about the cases I worked and some that I was just interested in."

He removed a bulging photo album from the box and set it on the table. "I got a little deeper into it on the Saladino case."

Howie smiled and tapped the front cover. "That's all on the Saladino case?"

Heinz nodded. "Probably a lot of shit in there that don't matter, but I just threw in everything that had anything at all to do with it. I have no idea if there's anything you need or want but you're welcome to it."

Howie began thumbing through the pages and articles in the album. "Well, like I was saying last night, I don't know how they pulled it off, but I realize now that they somehow convinced themselves to just sit on it for a long time." He looked up and thought for a moment. "No, I think David convinced them and somehow kept it all together. He's the smart one and the only thing he was interested in through high school was business and financial shit."

Heinz reached into the box and grabbed a manila envelope, opened it and slid the contents out onto the table.

Howie picked up the plastic bag and held it up. "The padlock and the note left in the chimney?"

Heinz nodded.

"Ever check for prints on the lock?"

"Yeah, we found a couple partials on the door of the safe door and the lock that maybe belonged to Saladino," Heinz said. "There were a couple of smudges on the door that never checked out. That kind of lock doesn't have a nice smooth surface for prints."

"You know they've got better stuff now that might bring them up," Howie said. "Plus, back then those kids' prints weren't in the system. A partial now might match up with one of them."

Heinz shrugged. "Have a go at it, but then what?"

Howie took a deep breath and sighed. "I don't know what I'm looking to do, but I think I need to go see David Steiner."

"Oh, there's a news article in there and some notes attached to it about a cop named Zuber. Don't know if it's anything really, but it's one of those strange little things that gets your attention, you know?"

"Half my life is strange little things," Howie said. "So, who's Zuber?"

"I didn't really know him," Heinz said. "He was with some other department or the county sheriff maybe. It's in the article. I only met him once. This was back in, I don't know, maybe the late 80s. The first time I ever met him he came up to me at some training conference and said he heard I used to be on the Bakersfield P.D. Asked me about the Vincent Saladino mystery. I told him I was on the case back then and how it went nowhere. We talked for maybe two minutes. He said he knew some people there. Said he was retiring soon and he was going to find out what happened to that money. I didn't think much about it. Couple years later I see this small article in the paper about his family petitioning the court to have him declared dead. I do some asking around. Turns out the guy just disappeared about six months after I talked to him."

"So what do you think?" Howie asked.

Heinz opened his hands in front of him. "Hell, I don't know if I think anything. It's just weird that this guy comes up to me out of nowhere and talks about the Saladino money and a few months later he disappears. Probably what it adds up to is a great big nothing, but he's in the box with the rest of the shit. You love these cold cases, so here you go."

NINE

Johnny Saladino ended the call and laid the phone on the kitchen table, staring at it for a long time recalling the conversation and thinking. Finally he said, "Hm," slowly nodding, picked it up again and punched in a number.

"Uncle Dominic, it's Johnny. I got something you're going to find interesting, but I don't want to talk on the phone. You gonna be around today?"

Dominic Saladino chuckled at his nephew's question. "Johnny, that's all the fuck I do is 'be around.' Come on by at 11:30 and we'll go have some lunch at Zee's place."

An hour later, the two of them were sitting in a comfortable booth in a restaurant called The Mediterranean East. It was a family joke that so many of them, though Italian, leaned more toward Middle Eastern food. In the distance the San Diego skyline could be seen along with just a sliver of blue from the bay.

At forty-six, Johnny was Dominic's youngest nephew and regarded as one of the most ambitious men in the family. He was involved in certain areas in the criminal enterprises of the organizational family, but was also a businessman who made "legitimate" money from a chain of fourteen convenience stores in the San Diego area. To enhance his earnings he did, of course, divert around $1000 a month from each of the stores to a company that consisted entirely of one person—himself. This arrangement alone netted him about a $170,000 a year off the books on top of any real earnings from the chain of stores. He called it his fuck-off money.

The two of them talked fairly often about mob business, but at seventy-nine years old Dominic was semi-retired. He was still in good health, but the day-to-day running of the organization had been handed over to two other men over the years while Dominic enjoyed his remaining years playing golf, painting, and puttering in the yard. He no longer ran things directly, but he knew what was going on and he got involved from time to time when he felt he should or when his advice was solicited.

He was as friendly as he needed to be to his nephew but he didn't necessarily trust him. He thought he was not very smart and he held him in somewhat low regard because of the many stories he had heard over the years concerning Johnny's penchant for unnecessary violence. Although no angel himself, Dominic had always prided himself in his ability to influence others through the force of his personality, which some described as having a certain charisma and charm. He did have a famously explosive temper, but he usually did a reasonable job keeping it in check. In the business he was in there were, of course, times when violence and even murder, or just shooting somebody in the foot, became necessary, but he preferred to save it for those times when other options were not possible.

Johnny, on the other hand, seemed to lack his uncle's personality and finesse and often resorted to bloodshed as a first course of action. He considered himself somewhat of a ladies' man and could be charming when he wanted to be, but people around him were always a bit wary and didn't trust him.

Dominic broke off a piece of pita bread, spooned up a large glob of hummus and shoved it into his mouth. "Damn, they make the best in town," he said with a full mouth.

Johnny nodded agreement. "So, I haven't heard you talk about Vincent in a long time."

Dominic glared at his nephew and took a sip of beer. "So?"

"So I thought you might be interested in hearing about something I learned."

"That's what you want to talk about?" Dominic said. "The traitor, the fucking black sheep, faggot, thief of the family?"

Johnny grinned. "Yeah, him. You really think he took that money?"

Dominic sighed. "Hell, I know he took it."

"You ever try to find it?"

"We tried for a while, but it was a big fat dead end. Some people had the idea that the safe was just a fake, or he'd used it for a while and then come up with somewhere else to stash it. Whoever cleaned out the safe left a note, so I know somebody took it, I just don't know who. It just became one of those unsolved shitty things. Maybe it's buried somewhere or it's sitting in a fucking bus station locker or somebody got rich and spent it all. That money went somewhere, but who knows?" He took another bite of bread and hummus and chased it down with some beer. "This is old business, Johnny. Why we talking about this?"

"There were these kids back then that were hanging around Vincent's place. Anyone suspect them of taking the money?"

Dominic made a dismissive face. "We thought about them at first. I even had some guys go back and check them out a couple of times. Hell, they were just kids. They wouldn't have known what to do with that much fucking money even if it was given to them. Another dead end."

"You ever hear of a company called DMT International? Financial investing, commercial real estate, shit like that."

Dominic shrugged. "I don't know, maybe. Why?"

"I never heard of it either. I think they stay out of the public eye and don't attract much attention from most people. Privately held, no stock trading. Anyway there's this PI, a retired L.A. cop, nosing around for some information. He's taking a hard look at three people—Mary Kay Dias, Tommy Dias and David Steiner. DMT International was founded by David Steiner. The other two, Tommy and Mary Kay are brother and sister. Even without the company, they're loaded. We're talking billionaires."

Dominic gave an impatient look. "Okay, so why is this cop nosing around these three and what the hell does it have to do with Vincent and that whole shitstorm?"

Johnny leaned closer across the table and gripped his uncle's wrist, stopping another bite of pita bread in midair. "They are the three kids. They're the ones who were hanging around Vincent's place."

Dominic stared for a long time trying to digest this piece of information, trying to make it fit into his mind somehow where it would make sense.

Johnny loosened his grip and Dominic set the uneaten food down. "And if that ain't enough, the one guy, Steiner, has a big-ass nice fucking yacht. You know how they paint the name of boats across the back? Guess what the name of his yacht is?" He put his hands out in front of him as if he was looking at the stern of the boat. "Chimney Sweep."

Dominic began speaking normally enough, but it wasn't long before his volume rose to an attention-attracting level. "Chimney Sweep," he muttered and mulled that over for a few seconds, remembering a taunting note he hadn't thought of in decades. "So those three kids grew up in that crummy little neighborhood in Bakersfield and now they're billionaires? They own this big shot company and we just lost track of them? The cops didn't stay after them?"

His famous temper wasn't seen as often anymore, but this revelation had let loose a torrent of emotion that had been bottled up for 35 years. "Why can't anyone I work with pay any goddamn attention? Back then nobody knew Vincent owned that house across the alley, then they don't check out those kids enough and now. . ."

The old man sat silently and gazed around the restaurant, then muttered softly, "Billionaires. A fucking yacht named Chimney Sweep." He sighed and said much louder, "Chimney Sweep! Fuck! One swipe of his arm cleared everything from the table onto the floor. He wanted to say more, but it was all he could manage. "Fuck," he repeated, not quite as loud. "Let's go!"

As they stood, Johnny fished a hundred dollar bill from his wallet, held it up for the owner, who was standing by the door to the kitchen, to see and then laid it on the table. "Sorry about the mess, Zee. See you later."

They climbed into Johnny's Audi and he started it up. "Uncle Dominic, take it easy. You're gonna have a goddamn heart attack or something."

Dominic buckled his seat belt and let out a deep sigh. "You're right." He took a few deep breaths as they pulled out of the lot. He ran the fingers of both hands through his still thick, graying hair. "I'm okay. Jesus, you know I was lucky to be alive after that shit that Vincent pulled? Listen, put a couple of guys on this. No, put yourself on this. Find out everything there is, and I mean everything, but don't do anything, and don't confront this Steiner guy or the others yet. Save that for me."

Just two days after the dinner with Heinz and Trapani, Howie was surprised to get a phone call from Trapani. As requested they met at a bar near downtown Long Beach. When Howie walked into the dim light, Trapani waved at him from a booth in the corner.

Howie slid into the seat across the table. "You know, it's not like we hang out together. Until the other night I hadn't seen you in years. How'd you even know how to call me?"

"Well, you're not exactly hiding out, you know," Trapani said. "You're a private investigator for Christ's sake. I just asked around a little." He tapped the bottle of Zinfandel.

"Yeah, I guess so," Howie said.

Trapani poured a glass for Howie and topped off his own.

Howie took a couple of sips and nodded his approval. "Not bad. So, what's up?"

"Maybe nothing. He nervously rubbed the top of his nearly bald head and took a sip of wine and a bite of bread. "But I got to thinking after our dinner. I did some more thinking this morning. Some things came popping into my brain that I wasn't really remembering the other night."

Howie nodded. "Like what?"

Trapani took a long swallow and refilled his glass. "Listen, I don't know how legit any of this is. I hear a lot of things, just like

140

you, and I don't always know what's bullshit and what's the real shit, you know? But, well, there's some stuff from years ago that you jarred loose in my brain and I thought maybe you should know."

Howie waited. "Me too. Been doing a lot of thinking back over some stuff about those three that I'd forgotten about. So what've you got?"

Trapani sighed. "Ever hear of a guy named Moley?"

"Moley?" Howie raised his eyebrows and smiled.

"He had squinty eyes and buck teeth," Trapani said. "I guess somebody thought he looked like a mole. His real name was Tito Janelli. Some half-Mexican half-Italian guy."

Howie chuckled. "Yeah, I hear that combination always makes mole people."

"Will you shut the fuck up and listen," Trapani said, reluctantly cracking a smile. "Anyway, he disappeared in 1992. I hear he went to Nic Saladino and told him he had an idea about Vincent's money and he wanted him to know he was going looking and he would let him know. Wouldn't tell him what he thought or where he was going but I hear that he went to Seattle."

"Wait a second," Howie said. "Janelli. I remember a guy I went to school with named Jesse Janelli. He was like a year or two older. He had that squinty-eyed buck toothed look. I didn't really know him well, but I remember some people called him J.J. Hm…"

"No shit?" Trapani said. "So, this guy is from Bakersfield? Maybe Tito or Jesse is his middle name or something."

"Yeah, I'll have to look into that. So, he disappeared?" Howie said. "Hell, maybe Nic helped him disappear, you know?"

Trapani made a face and used both his hands to wave off that idea. "This is from a guy who talked to Nic back then. He told me that Moley called from Bakersfield and said he had flown into L.A. from Seattle, rented a car and driven to Bakersfield. He told Nic he was onto something and he would get back to him in a day or two. Never heard from him again."

"So, what're you telling me?" Howie asked. "It's bad luck or something to go looking for Vincent's money?"

"Nic sent some guys to Bakersfield to see what they could turn up about him," Trapani continued. "No car, no nothing, gone. The car rental company never got their car back either. Anyway, I thought maybe you're not the first guy to stumble onto the connection with those three kids. Maybe he knew one of them and picked up on something."

Howie was staring into space, thinking. "You ever hear of a cop named Frank Zuber?"

Trapani shook his head slowly. "I don't know. Who is he?"

"Just somebody Heinz was talking about from way back," Howie said. "Probably no connection, but he vanished too."

"Seems to be a lot of that going around," Trapani said.

"Well, there's one thing I've learned over the years," Howie said. "It might be what you think or it might be something else."

Trapani began laughing out loud. "No shit, Sherlock!"

Tommy Dias was driving his Porsche Twin Turbo at just over a hundred ten—not even a stretch for this car. It was three in the morning and traffic was thin. The car could handle it just fine. The problem was Tommy, and the 70 mile per hour speed limit, of course. His license had been suspended two months earlier for a drunk-driving conviction and there had been some others over the years that David had managed to make disappear or reduced to small misdemeanors. In the last three hours he had consumed seven Corona's and four shots of Belvedere vodka. In spite of his alcohol intake he was doing a superb job of keeping the car between the lines, possibly because his current state was more familiar to him than being sober.

A quick-thinking Washington State trooper in an unmarked car knew that a driver reluctant to pull over with a super car like this one would leave him in the dust. He was staying a half mile behind. No flashing lights, no siren. A probably drunk idiot speeding over a hundred was preferable to the same drunk idiot going even faster to outrun the cops. Also, he had a pretty good idea of which drunk idiot it might be. The car was well known in the area.

When Tommy reached his luxury condo complex adjacent to the Lake Washington Country Club, there were three squad cars blocking the gate. As he pulled to a stop, another one pulled in behind him blocking any possible escape. Seconds later he was ordered out of his car, given a breathalyzer test that produced some eyebrow-raising results, handcuffed and put in the back of a squad car.

Most of the cops knew who he was. He was the local rich guy with connections to DMT International who did some good things but was generally regarded by the police as a pain in the ass. They knew he'd be bailing himself out by the end of the coming day, but in the meantime they planned to grind it out for as long as possible.

Tommy started feeling better and complaining around noon. For the fourth time in fifteen minutes he called out from his cell and this time an officer walked slowly up to the bars. "I'm sober, goddammit! I want to make bail and get the hell out of here!"

"Not that simple, Mr. Dias," the officer calmly explained. "You were driving under the influence at an excessive speed and on a previously suspended license. This time won't be simple bail. You gotta go up before a judge first and get bitched at before you can bail."

Tommy sighed and lowered his voice, resigning himself to the seriousness of the jam he was in. "Okay, when's that?"

The deputy smiled. "Night court convenes about five P.M. Might as well relax. That's another five hours and you ain't the first in line. Want some lunch?"

Tommy shook his head and started looking angry again. "You know who I am?"

The officer stepped closer and his smile disappeared. "Yeah, we know who you are. You're a rich shithead who's in need of some booze rehab. You're in here by yourself instead of the drunk tank, so don't complain too much." He stepped back and his smile returned. "There's a pay phone on the wall there. It don't take money, you gotta call collect, even local. Just press zero."

Tommy nodded and the officer walked away.

Howie Williams landed at Seattle-Tacoma Airport a little after 2:00 in the afternoon. A couple of weeks earlier he had contacted an acquaintance of his on the Seattle Police Department, Detective Sergeant Dan Cavazos, just to get some addresses and the local spin on DMT International and his three former schoolmates.

As Howie neared the baggage claim area he saw Cavazos wave. After greetings and small talk, Howie grabbed his one bag, checked in at the rental car desk and the two of them rode a shuttle to the rental car lot.

When they reached the car Howie said, "I assume you need a ride back to your car?"

"That's what I had in mind," Cavazos said, settling into the passenger seat. He reached into his inside coat pocket. "Here's the info you asked for. There's just not much available on these three or their companies. I got you some addresses, brief profiles, a little about the company and some copies of news articles that might interest you. Something else that might interest you. Tommy Dias was picked up early this morning on DUI, excessive speed and driving on a suspended license. Depending on who you talk to he's either a great guy with a drinking problem, a total asshole with a drinking problem or just a stupid bastard who never grew up with a drinking problem. Anyway, he's still sitting in lock-up until late court convenes at five or so. He can't bail until then. They're not cutting him any slack on this one."

Howie checked his watch. "That's still a couple of hours. I think I'll drop by and say hi."

"So, you want to tell me what you're doing here?"

"Not really," Howie said with a smile.

"You PIs." Cavazos pointed at the envelope. "I know you like to think of yourself as a cold case specialist so there's something in there that you might want to get into. A few months ago a local shrink by the name of Lindsey Robbins disappeared."

"Why would I want to get into it?" Howie asked.

"You might not," Cavazos said. "It's a cold-as-ice cold case with nothing but dead ends, so I thought it might pique your interest. Also, one of her patients was good old Tommy Dias. He'd been a patient of hers for a couple of years. She didn't disappear here, though. She was out of town attending her high school reunion in Tulare, California. Lot of people saw her at the reunion. She had a ticket for a couple days later to fly back here out of San Francisco. Didn't use the ticket. Nobody ever saw her again. You grew up in Bakersfield, right?"

Howie nodded. "Yeah, I did."

"I looked on a map and Tulare is about this far from Bakersfield." He held up his thumb and index finger a half inch apart. You just never know who knows who or who knows what, huh?" Cavazos said. "Something else kind of grabs at you about this case. Dr. Robbins had an uncle named Saladino. Distant cousin to the mob bunch. Doesn't seem like her part of the family had anything to do with the other family business, but interesting, huh? Anyway, your ex-partner, Gary Heinz, worked that Vincent Saladino case back then when you were a kid in the neighborhood, didn't he?"

Howie gave him a look. "Did I ever tell you that?"

Cavazos nodded. "I think you did. My car is right here." He got out and walked around to the driver window. He patted Howie on the shoulder. "Take it easy, Magnum, and let me know if you need anything."

Tommy looked up briefly from his cot at the two men walking by his cell. Then the footsteps stopped, a buzzer sounded, his door opened and the deputy motioned the stranger into his cell.

Tommy eyed him for a second then yelled at the retreating officer. "Hey, I thought I had a private cell!"

"You do, Tommy. I just dropped in for a visit."

He sat up on the cot and then stood. "I've already got a lawyer. You from his office?" Being sober and waiting for hours had put him in a foul mood.

Howie smiled. "It's me, Howie, Howie Williams." He extended his right hand.

Tommy stared for a bit then slowly extended his hand. "Howie! No kidding? Damn, what are you doing here?"

"I'm in town, I heard you were here and I just stopped by."

Tommy ran his hand through his hair. "Man! What's it been, thirty years or something? What are you doing with your life?"

"I was a cop, a detective with the L.A. police department. I retired a few years ago. Now I do some security work, a little private investigating when it interests me. I play golf whenever I want. I'm doing okay. Still living in L.A."

"You, a cop?" He gave a laugh, but he also became just a little wary, even backing up a small step. "And a PI? So what brings you to Seattle?"

Howie was silent for several moments while he considered how to answer. "You and Mary Kay and David. You three brought me here. I've gotten a little more curious over the years so I thought I'd come visit you. The three of you have done quite well for yourselves."

Even in his present circumstances, Tommy's wariness came to full alert. "Yeah, we've done damn good all right." He cleared his throat. "Curious about what?" He wished he hadn't asked, because the look on Howie's face made it all too plain to him.

"Curious about Cadillac Vinnie's money and just what might have happened to it. You know, just reminiscing about the summer of '68." He said it completely routinely as though he was saying he'd just come to buy some bread and milk.

Tommy stared into Howie's face for a long time. "You know, of course, I have no idea what you're talking about."

Howie chuckled and sat down on the edge of the cot, motioning for Tommy to sit down by him. "Okay, let's just talk. How the hell did you end up in here?"

Tommy was wondering where every comment or question

was really leading, but this line seemed safe enough. "That, I know. I have this tendency to get shit-faced on a regular basis. I've got a hot car and I was driving it pretty hot, and..." He spread his arms wide and viewed his surroundings. "Here I am! Court convenes a little later and I can't make bail until I appear. Something about them not appreciating me driving with a suspended license from a previous DUI."

Howie nodded slowly, leaned his arms on his knees and folded his hands in front of him. "You don't have any clout around here?"

Tommy smiled and slowly shook his head. "You need a celebrity golf tournament put together? I've got clout out the ass for that. For this..." He made a sweeping gesture at his surroundings. "Not so much."

They made small talk for another few minutes and then Howie stood and called to the deputy. He extended his hand again to Tommy. As they shared their grip, he said, "I'm going to be around for a few days. I'm sure we'll be seeing each other again. I want to visit with the three of you. We have a lot of catching up to do, huh?"

"You can catch us up on what happened to your hair," Tommy said with a chuckle and waved as Howie stepped out of the cell.

TEN

After eating dinner alone at the hotel café, Howie went back to his hotel room and decided to just let things stew until the next day. He was wishing he wasn't seen as a cop in this situation. Retired or not, that's how he was still perceived. It just complicated everything. He had seen the look on Tommy's face as soon as he told him he'd been a cop and how he did some PI work.

About 7:00 p.m. his cell phone rang. "How are you, Detective Williams?"

Howie recognized the voice. "Saladino?"

The caller chuckled. "Please, you can call me Johnny. I'm calling to let you know I'm in town."

"Why?" Howie answered. "You're gonna fuck things up. I told you to let me contact them first."

Saladino chuckled again. "Well, I like to keep close tabs on the projects I'm most interested in. You go ahead and meet with them, but do it tonight. Tell them you heard I was in town. Tell them you checked them out and all that and somehow your inquiries must have tipped us off. Anyway, I'll give you a couple of hours and then I'm coming over to Steiner's place to meet with him."

Howie was taken aback. "Why would you do that?"

"I'm getting kind of anxious and I've decided I have important business to discuss with them that really can't wait," Saladino said. "Don't worry. I'm not saying a thing about us. We don't know each other as far as they know."

"So how am I supposed to know you're in town?"

"You're a genius PI. Tell them you've got sources," Saladino said. "Anyway, sport, you have until 10:00 or so, then I'm showing up over there with an offer he can't refuse. You make friends and all that. You might even want to stick around to hear what I've got to say. I think you'll find it interesting. See ya then."

He sat for several minutes thinking back over the couple of times he and Johnny had talked in the last two weeks. He looked up David's number and called. Voice mail screened his call. He left his name and number. Two minutes later his phone rang.

"Hey, Howie, David Steiner. Tommy told me you were in town."

"Hi, David. I was going to just kick back and call you tomorrow, but a little problem has come up. It seems someone I hadn't counted on just came to town as well. I just found out Johnny Saladino is in town. I guess I may have awakened a sleeping giant, as some Japanese admiral once said. I think we need to meet."

David sighed. "Damn, Howie. Okay, meet me here at the condo. It's on the top floor of the Pac View Building downtown. Just follow the signs to guest parking under the building and take the elevator up to the lobby. The security force will let you up. I gather you've been researching me and you know exactly where I am?"

Howie smiled. "I know where it is. Hey, I came to talk to you, Tommy and Mary Kay. I didn't think anyone would come along to cause you a problem."

"Okay. I'll see you in a few minutes."

David clicked off the speaker and looked across the table to Mary Kay. She was wearing nothing but a knee-length full slip. "What do you think?"

She downed the last sip of a strawberry daiquiri and held the glass while she talked. "You know what I think, but if we're going to keep this civilized then I think enough money will send him home quietly."

"Maybe," David said. "Remember how we always kind of

wondered if he suspected something? We played it out for so long we figured he lost interest just like everyone else. Tommy said Howie told him he'd just been thinking back over some things and getting curious."

"What about Johnny Saladino?" Mary Kay said. "That scares me." She rubbed down the goose bumps on her forearms with both hands.

"Howie, what the hell did you stir up?" David said to the wall of glass before him. "Anyway, call your brother. Tell him what's up and have him come over so we can all talk to Howie. And tell him to take a fucking taxi!"

She called three times and left messages on his answering machine and cell phone. Several minutes went by but he did not call back. "I guess he's not home, and he's always leaving his phone lying around somewhere. I hope he remembers we're all flying to Vegas tomorrow for some final design meetings." She stood. "I better get some more clothes on before Howie gets here."

David was wearing his usual jeans, an untucked tropical print shirt and tan boat shoes with no socks. "I think I'm fine," he kidded, grinning, "but you're right about getting more on. By the way, I noticed you aren't wearing any panties."

All the exercising and dieting seemed worth it when little moments like this came along. She glanced back over her shoulder, smiling as she headed toward the hall. "I know, I saw you notice."

Gary Heinz never knew what hit him. It was just a few days after his seventy-first birthday. As he did most evenings, he was sitting in his recliner watching Jeopardy and sipping some hot chocolate. He mentally congratulated himself for splurging on a big new television a year earlier. Football looked great on it. Hell, everything looked great on it, even Jeopardy.

Between the TV being so loud and his fading hearing, he didn't hear the quick crunch as the intruder broke the cheap door knob and came in the back door and through the kitchen.

Just before Alex Trebec read the Final Jeopardy question, a .40 caliber bullet tore into the back of Gary's skull and bulldozed through his brain, the mushroomed soft-nosed bullet boring a large path of destruction as it went just to the inside of his forehead then stopped. The intruder sent two more through just to be sure.

Around the same time, Angelo Trapani was sitting in the passenger seat of an almost new Ford Taurus parked in front of a bar in Pasadena. His companion had gone inside to collect a quick debt, then they were going by Trapani's house so he could follow in his car and take the man home after returning the rental car.

Trapani had been surprised when the man had called him at another bar where he had spent the afternoon. He hadn't seen him for a year or more. He thought his story sounded fishy, but Trapani wasn't worried. He figured the guy was keeping something from the wife or there was something about the car that wasn't right. Whatever it was he didn't really care.

He was about to relight his cigar when the end of a five foot long crowbar smashed through the closed passenger window and into the side of his head. Confused, bleeding but still mostly conscious, he turned to see what in the hell had hit him. In a split second he saw a well-muscled young man in a t-shirt and a Bud Light baseball cap holding the crow bar as it once again smashed into him, this time catching him just under his left eye and pulverizing several facial bones as it penetrated a good two inches.

The attacker opened the car door, grabbed the front of his victim's shirt and pulled him out of the car where he had more room to finish his job. Trapani, now mostly unconscious, but with just enough awareness to try to stand, was leaned against the side of the car. In the two seconds he managed to stand before his legs wobbled and began to collapse beneath him, the attacker took aim again. Holding the bar like a baseball batter, he connected with a massive swing that caved in Trapani's forehead several inches into his frontal lobe.

Three blows, less than fifteen seconds and the job was done. Angelo Trapani never really knew what hit him either.

Fifteen minutes after Howie's call there was a phone call from downstairs. "Mr. Steiner, a Mr. Williams says you are expecting him."

"I am," David said, "but let me talk to him."

A few seconds later, Howie said, "Hi David, it's me."

"Good," David answered. "I just wanted to check and make sure it wasn't someone saying they were you."

"You mean a rich guy like you with this setup isn't watching me on camera right now?" He was waving toward a camera he could see in the ceiling.

David smiled. "Yeah, I see you, but I haven't seen you in a long time. Just making sure. Put the security guard back on."

A second later. "Mr. Steiner?"

"Yeah, Cecil. If anyone else calls or asks to see me, give me a call. There shouldn't be anybody else coming up except for Tommy, by himself."

"Yes, sir."

A few minutes later, Howie Williams walked through the front door and the two men met each other for the first time since just after high school graduation in 1973. They awkwardly shook hands, then embraced tightly.

"Hey, baldy, what the hell are you up to?" David said as he reached up and touched Howie's shaved head.

As they made their way to a leather seating arrangement, Mary Kay walked into the room barefoot, wearing a low-cut, ankle-length, slinky satin, flowered house dress, and nothing else. A small silk gardenia pushed back the right side of her shoulder-length straight brown hair.

"Hi, Howie," she greeted, seating herself next to David and draping her arm across his shoulder.

"Damn, girl," Howie blurted. "You age better than most of us."

She smiled. "Thank you. You look like you're doing okay

enough. I like the look." She touched the top of her own head.

Howie gestured back and forth between the two of them. "You two an item?"

"Sort of," David explained. "Best friends."

"We're going steady," Mary Kay added, with a playful smile.

Howie looked her over for a few moments trying to figure out if she was making a joke, then gestured toward the bar. "Vodka with a twist?"

David nodded, walked across to a black granite and stainless steel bar by the kitchen and brought back a tall glass of Grey Goose over crushed ice with a twist of lime. "So, what the hell got into you to look us up?"

Before he could answer, Mary Kay interrupted. "Why are you here? Would a million be enough to make you go away? Two million?"

Howie looked at them both and took a long swallow from his glass. He tipped his glass toward David. "Good stuff." Then he looked again at Mary Kay's completely serious face. "I didn't come here for money."

"Why did you come here?" she asked again.

Howie took a deep breath and sighed. "I know this sounds lame, but I'm not sure. I guess I came here just to see if I was right. I really hadn't thought much about the Three Musketeers in years. I didn't know a damn thing about you until a few weeks ago. I saw something in the paper about "Chill" and a few days later I saw David and you in the background on TV at that groundbreaking in Vegas."

"What?" Mary Kay shrieked. "You came here because you saw us on TV talking about Chill? Oh my God." She turned to David, managing to look and sound apologetic and angry at the same time. "I guess Tommy and I were wrong. Thirty-five years isn't long enough."

"I did a little research," Howie continued. "I discovered DMT and I looked you three up and found out how goddamn loaded you are and it just all came together for me. I just knew. I am a retired cop, but I'm not here to bust you. I'm not even sure if there is anything you could be busted for."

David slowly nodded and gazed around the room. "So, just what is it you think we did?"

A smile came to Howie's face as he took another swallow and sighed. "Well, look, I know what you did. What I'm really interested in is how you pulled it off. It must be one damn amazing story."

David stood and walked to the glass door leading out to the terrace. The night lights of Seattle seemed so clear, so peaceful. "You know, I'm not very goddamn happy that you stirred the pot and attracted the attention of Johnny Saladino of all people. We thought enough time had finally passed that nobody would be paying any attention anymore. Chill was going to be a big fun project after so many years of staying out of the limelight."

Mary Kay sighed shakily. "David, I'm so sorry," she said softly.

Howie cleared his throat nervously. He looked across at Mary Kay while she stared him down. "I can't believe Saladino popped up either. You know, his Uncle Dominic is still around too. That's who Vincent was working for when he was killed." He spread his hands. "I sure didn't mean to fuck things up for you."

"How'd you find out he was here?" David asked.

"I'm a retired cop and a pretty decent PI." Howie said. "I've got a lot of people out there who just tell me stuff."

David turned from the window, gave him several seconds of a skeptical look and walked up behind the sofa where Mary Kay was sitting. He softly massaged her shoulder while he talked. "All the shit from back when we were kids, withholding evidence, lying to the police, that's all dead because of how young we were and the amount of time that's passed. The IRS might be a problem. All that statute of limitations crap gets a little murky and you can't depend on it. It gets to be a bunch of legal maneuvering and who knows where the hell a bunch of lawyers can take it. But I've got all kinds of other things since that I don't want to be made public. Anyway, why should we trust you? Why should we share anything with you? And that goddamn Johnny Saladino is sniffing around and that makes me wonder about the two of you and if you're working me together."

Howie looked down into his drink as he slowly swirled the ice around the glass. He took a sip and looked up at David. "You know, if it occurred to me, then somebody else might have a sudden realization about this too. Maybe it would be smarter if you didn't share anything with me, but look, I'm not here as Howie the ex-cop or the PI. So, let's say you deprived the mob of some money. That's no big crime as far as I'm concerned. And I swear I am not here with Johnny. I didn't have any idea he would show up and we're not a team. If that asshole is on your trail, then you might need me on your side."

David leaned down and looked at Mary Kay.

She rubbed his arm and gave him a small nod. Then she looked at Howie and he saw her expression transform even though she seemed to not move a muscle. "Hell, he already knows. We can always kill him if we have to," she said, with no emotion. After several awkward moments she slowly let the barest hint of a smile return to her face, but it was only intended to punctuate the alarming iciness she had already conveyed.

"That day you ran into us in the alley, that was our last load," David said. "We moved the money using that wheelbarrow."

Howie shot up from his chair laughing. "I knew you were up to something that day!" He sat down and chuckled a few more times. "So Dominic found out Vincent was stealing money and sent a couple of guys to Bakersfield to take him out. The story is Vincent was already dead when they got there and apparently whoever killed him also cleaned out the chimney safe that Dominic didn't know existed until afterward. He thought he knew who did it and had this other mob guy killed. But a lot of people think he killed the wrong guy. Apparently nobody knows for sure who took out Vincent."

David walked to the bar and poured himself a Wild Turkey on ice, exchanging a look with Mary Kay as Howie's speculation filled the room with a prolonged silence.

"The three of us had spent half the summer spying on him just to entertain ourselves and we kind of got to be friends with him," David explained. "We already thought he was hiding money and the chimney had something to do with it. A couple of days before we moved the money we were supposed to meet him to help him do some painting. He didn't answer his door, so I went in. I found him sitting in bed shot dead. Tommy came in and we looked around for keys and took them. That morning when you ran into us, the Boyds, the family who lived in the house, were out of town, so we went in the backyard and figured out the fireplace safe."

Howie was still smiling and shaking his head. "How much?"

David hesitated then managed a smile. "We were hoping it was a lot of money, but, hell, we would've been overjoyed if we had found a thousand bucks. We had no idea what we had gotten into." He motioned to Mary Kay.

In a soft, unemotional voice, with just a hint of that young-girl shakiness from thirty-five years before, she recited, "Three million, two hundred twenty-five thousand dollars."

Howie's mouth was hanging open.

"We kept out about twelve hundred that wasn't bundled and buried the rest on the side of my house."

"Jesus!" Howie whispered. "Three million bucks in 1968. Today that would be like..." he spread his arms, at a loss for words.

"Twenty million or so," David said. "What would you do if someone handed you three million dollars back then, Howie?"

"Jesus," Howie said again, softly. He finished his glass of vodka. "You were a kid. We were all kids! You and me, we were like twelve years old. What the hell did you do? How is this possible?"

"It isn't possible, except for this one time we did it," David said. "A hundred things could've gone wrong that day. Parents, neighbors, you tipping over the wheelbarrow, the weird weather opening up on us, but nothing did. It took us four goddamn trips running through the neighborhood with that thing and we got lucky. Nobody paid a bit of attention to us."

"Like the frogs!" Howie said, smiling wider.

"Exactly," David said. "Between then and when we graduated in 1974 I studied everything in existence about banking and investing. I could've passed college courses on the subject when I was sixteen. And I think they were toads."

Howie chuckled. "Okay, man, toads."

"The smartest thing he did was make us wait," Mary Kay said. "I can't believe anyone else, kids or otherwise, would've had the patience to just sit on that money for that long. He just kept telling us all the time how much money we would have someday. He doled out a little money to us but not enough to attract any real attention. Mostly he distracted us from thinking about what we could have then by telling us how much we would have someday. And he promised to keep our secrets, protect me and take care of the three of us."

"There was really no other choice," David continued. "We were kids, and there was no way we could do anything with the money at that age. We had to wait and control the situation."

"You just sat on it for six years? Jesus! I would've gone into your old man's store every day and bought wagonloads of cokes and candy bars for the whole damn neighborhood! I'd have bought so much stupid shit that they would've arrested me by the end of the week. I don't get how the three of you kept your mouths shut all that time."

"I can still remember all those times walking around school or sitting by the side of the house," Mary Kay continued. She was looking past them as though she was trying to picture the scene from all those years ago. "He would tell it just like telling a story. We were the characters in the story and we could see ourselves in the future. He made us believe, really believe. That's the only way we could've done it. He protected us back then and all this time. He's been protecting me since I was a kid and he still is." She sent an admiring glance in David's direction.

Howie thought she looked and sounded like a kid when she talked about David protecting them all this time. "Did it turn out like he said?"

Mary Kay gestured around the room. "Better."

"So, David, when you turned eighteen, you didn't just dig it up and start spending it, did you?"

David smiled. "A little of it. Tommy's GTO, some clothes for all of us. It made some things easier, but that was just a little of it. Luckily the money laundering regulations that came into law in the early 70s took a few more years to really get rolling like they were supposed to. In the meantime I was able to do a lot of stuff that didn't get reported like it does now, plus it helped that I had the money to bribe a few of the right people to help it along."

Howie stood and walked to the bar to pour himself another drink. "I'm all ears, David."

"We can talk about the details some other time," David said.

"So what all does DMT International do?" Howie asked.

"The old DMT is all sold off," he explained. "It was commercial real estate all over the world, and high tech research in North America and Europe. I think it was boring as hell and it was my own shit. It was all sold off to several other companies, but I retained the DMT name. All we do now is invest. It's all very low-key and pretty much off everyone's radar since it's privately owned. On paper the total current net worth of the company including all property and assets is right around, oh, thirty-five billion dollars. There are a few other companies we own—a specialty medical supply business, a chain of funeral homes and some others. All privately held too, no stocks. All nice quiet companies."

"A chain of funeral homes?" Howie smiled. "I guess that would be a nice quiet company."

David nodded and gave Mary Kay a look. "Plus there's a steady stream of business with an endless clientele. Anyway, those companies are worth another billion or so. But even if every business we have goes belly up and we lose every last dollar there's still a bundle we each keep out as cash and private investments. We'd still have enough to get by as multi-millionaires forever."

"Get by, huh?" Howie said. "I don't remember hearing anything about you until just a few weeks ago when this Vegas project of yours was in the news. Even then your name was only mentioned once that I heard and I never have heard Mary Kay or Tommy mentioned by name. I'm pretty good at this and I had a hell of a time turning up much information about you three."

"Good," David said. "My strategy all along was to keep a low profile without looking like that's what I was trying to do. It's hard to do without attracting more attention to yourself for looking so secretive. At one point I thought about having our names changed, but that's a double-edged sword. If anyone starts nosing around and happens across the fact that you changed your name then it just spikes their curiosity and they start looking into why you did that. I created a lot of dead ends and false information about our backgrounds. We cut ties with anybody from back in the day and moved out of the area hoping everyone would just forget about us. Less of a chance of our names coming up and someone getting reminded about anything. Our parents are all gone now, but for years they thought we had these really great jobs traveling the world and doing something completely different. I worked hard to keep our names and faces out of the media as much as possible. Now that we're only doing behind-the-scenes financial stuff it doesn't catch much attention. Chill was supposed to be a chance to finally have some fun and just go for it."

"Chill was sort of our coming-out event," Mary Kay said. "We all figured that so much time had gone by with no problems that nobody was paying any attention to us anymore. The whole idea was to make a big splash, get a whole lot of attention in the media, have some fun and quit worrying about the past. Even if we didn't make any money it was still going to be fun."

"So," David said, "what the hell is going on that brought Saladino to town?"

Howie sighed and took another swallow of his drink. "It's my fault. I talked to a couple of people when I was digging up information on you guys and it got around to him. So, now what?"

"If he wants money, we've got plenty of that." David offered.

"But I'm guessing that's not it, or at least not all of it."

"It's never just money with these wise guy assholes, no matter what they say about it being just business," Howie said.

"You said Dominic Saladino is still around," David said. "From what I hear he took a lot of shit back then for Vincent being his nephew."

Howie nodded. "And even more for the safe being empty and that money never turning up."

Mary Kay was looking back and forth between the two of them. "So, what's he want, the interest?" she said sarcastically.

David gave her a smile and rubbed her thigh. "He might want that too, but we made him look bad and I think what he really wants is us."

She looked at Howie. "Is that why Johnny Saladino is here?"

Howie shrugged. "He may just be on a scouting mission." After several moments of silence, he said, "Where's Tommy?"

"We've been trying to call him," Mary Kay said, annoyed. "I hope he's not out driving on his suspended license."

Howie stood. "Hey, I almost forgot, I've got a souvenir for you." He walked over to his jacket draped over a chair back, reached into the pocket and pulled out a small clear plastic bag. "Here's something you haven't seen in a long time." He tossed the bag to David.

David caught it, saw the lock and the folded piece of paper and smiled. He opened the bag and unfolded the note. "Wow, where did you get this?"

"One of the detectives on the case was Gary Heinz. He and his partner kept the note and lock and never told anyone about them. He was my partner for a few years before he retired and I never knew a thing about it until a few days ago. He gave it to me."

"The note you left in the safe?" Mary Kay asked.

David nodded, stood and handed the note to her. "Man, she was pissed at me when those detectives told us someone left a note in the safe."

She gave him a look as she read it. "I never did think it was very smart. I thought it put me in danger, and all of us."

"So how'd he know to give it to you?" David asked.

"I had a dinner meeting with him and this other guy named Trapani who I knew had contacts who might know about Saladino from back then. He's not a mob guy, just some wannabe dumbass. Then Heinz and I met again and he told me he had this. So, were you just being a smartass with the Mary Poppins and chimney sweep shit? Oh, and your boat, nice name, very ironic. Why tempt fate like that?"

Mary Kay wagged an accusing finger at David. "Told you not to name it that."

David smiled and shrugged. "Only means something if you already know the rest. I guess you're right, just being a smartass. I didn't think anyone would find that chimney safe right away. I sort of felt like I was putting that note in there like a time capsule for the future. So you told Heinz about us?"

"I was meeting with him to check on some details of what happened back then," Howie said. "Yeah, I told him what I thought."

David eyed him for a second, wondering what else would come out. "Shit, Howie. Doesn't sound like you were thinking much about keeping our little secret. What the fuck are we going to do with you?"

Just then the phone rang. David answered. It was the security chief from downstairs. "Mr. Steiner, there is a Mr. Saladino here who would like to come up."

David clicked the television over to the security view. "Saladino is downstairs. He wants to come up."

"Oh, Jesus," Mary Kay whispered.

Howie walked close to the screen. "Is he by himself?"

"Is he alone, Cecil?" David said into the phone.

"Yes, sir."

"Hang on a second, Cecil, I'm putting you on hold."

David took a step toward Howie and looked him over for a second. "Are you and Saladino working me? I don't like the feel of this whole thing."

Howie put both hands up in front of him. "I may have dragged him into this but not on purpose."

"Son of a bitch. He's here so I might as well talk to him." He raised the phone to his mouth again. "Cecil, I know you were a cop so you should be good at frisking, huh?"

"Yes, sir."

"Okay, move Mr. Saladino to the mark facing camera one. Pat him down good and then turn him around so we can see him from the back too."

"Got it," Cecil said.

The three of them watched as the security guard did as he was told. After thoroughly searching him he turned him so his back was to the camera and returned to the phone.

"Get his jacket off," Howie said.

"Cecil, have him take off his jacket."

Cecil did so and searched through the jacket as well. He had him raise his arms straight up and searched his torso again. He returned to the phone. "Everything all right, Mr. Steiner?"

"I think so, Cecil," David said. "Go ahead, let him up. Have one of the officers go with him in the elevator. A friend of mine will meet him at the elevator and bring him into the condo. You did good. Thanks."

A minute later the elevator opened and Johnny Saladino stepped out into the hall outside the penthouse condo. He was dressed in a well-tailored navy blue suit, tan loafers, light blue shirt and tie.

"That's fine, I'll take him from here," Howie said to the security guard. The doors closed. "Lift your arms," he instructed Saladino.

"Hey, man, they searched me downstairs."

"I know, but I'm going to search you again," Howie said.

With a smirk, Saladino lifted his arms and quietly said, "Whatever you say, Detective Williams."

Howie eyed him for a second and proceeded with his pat down. He'd watched the security guard and thought the man had done a good job, but he was looking especially for anything that might be a bug. He looked carefully at buttons and even made him slip off his shoes for a look.

As they walked into the condo and on into the living room, Howie kept Saladino in front of him. David and Mary Kay were standing by the sofa and chairs where the three of them had been talking. David kept his distance, didn't offer his hand and motioned to a side chair.

David and Mary Kay sat in a love seat opposite Saladino and Howie seated himself at the corner of the sofa near him.

"What can I do for you Mr. Saladino?"

He smiled. "Johnny, please. No need to be formal. Could I get something to drink?"

Howie rose.

"Scotch and soda?" Saladino asked.

David nodded and motioned Howie toward the bar.

"Okay," Saladino continued. "Let's get straight to it. It seems you took something that belonged to my uncle a while back."

"A while back?" David said with a smile. "What would that be?"

Howie handed Saladino his drink and sat down again.

Saladino took a sip. "Thank you. I believe it was a couple of million dollars."

"Do you have any proof of this?" David countered.

Saladino motioned around the lavish surroundings. "Nothing that would stand up in court, but I know enough. My uncle wants you dead and if I don't come up with something for him, he'll probably get what he wants."

"We were just kids," Mary Kay said.

"At one time we were all just kids," Saladino said. "You're not kids anymore. And, Miss Dias, I might add that you have done a stunning job of growing out of your childhood."

Mary Kay responded by saying nothing, pushing her hair behind her right ear and looking down at the table in front of her as she reached for her wine glass.

"Let's say we did take his money." David said. "Would it satisfy your uncle if I returned his two million?"

Saladino made a small chuckle and took another long sip. "Mr. Steiner, I think you could probably reach in your pants and come up with two million. I think a nice start might be two million plus thirty-five years of compound interest at, say, a nice conservative eight percent. According to an accountant friend of mine, that would bump it up to right around forty-five million."

David thought that over for a few seconds. "With the kind of money and resources I've got I could have you and your uncle wiped off the face of the earth. Nobody would ever know what happened and they'd never find a body."

"Good idea," Mary Kay said. She stared at Saladino.

"So, why wouldn't I just do that and keep my money?" David continued. "In fact, what if you never left here alive tonight?"

Howie studied David's face trying to judge his seriousness.

Saladino sipped his drink and let just a hint of a smile come to his face. "Very good. I thought you might say something like that. I put myself in your place and tried to figure what I would do. I decided I'd kill me. So, before it comes to that let me ask you a question. Would you like to ever see Tommy again, alive?"

Mary Kay gasped and put a hand over her mouth. David and Howie exchanged a quick look. David reached over and put his hand on Mary Kay's leg. Johnny Saladino went to great trouble to appear as oblivious as possible, taking another sip of his drink as he glanced around the room at the furnishings and wall treatment.

An alarming mixture of panic and loathing came over Mary Kay as she stared at Johnny Saladino. She suddenly felt they had let a monster into their home who had just thrown off his disguise and transformed into an immediate and very real threat to her twin brother. "You are a fucking lowlife cunt!" she hissed.

David put out his arm to stop her, but it wasn't necessary. She merely leaned forward and pointed at Saladino. "If anything happens to my brother you won't be safe anywhere in this world." She sat back, gave a small smile and calmly added, "Oh, I didn't say anything when you complimented me on how well

I had grown out of my childhood. So just let me thank you by suggesting you take this glass coffee table and shove it up your dick."

The intentionally annoying smile faded from Saladino's face. "Listen, you two are in no position to issue threats right now. I've got Tommy and he's fine. As long as a money agreement happens without any problems, he's going to stay fine."

"You said your uncle wants blood," Howie said. "What's to stop you from taking the money and killing Tommy anyway just to satisfy Uncle Nic?"

Saladino looked at each of the three in turn. "Nothing."

Mary Kay continued to burn a silent stare in his direction.

"I'm not going to give you forty-five million dollars," David said.

"Well, listen," said Saladino, "I thought that figure was a little excessive considering the money was never going to be sitting in a bank collecting interest, but I figured I'd throw it out there. How much is Tommy's life worth to you?"

David stood and took a step toward Saladino. He delivered his words with calm, measured menace. "Listen carefully. We're not putting a value on his life. Here's my offer. I'll give you ten million dollars, but not for Tommy. You're going to give Tommy to us, unharmed, no matter what. If you don't, the money won't matter and I'll have you and everyone else involved killed. So, the money is just a goodwill gesture on my part and to make everybody happy enough to leave us alone from now on."

Saladino made a great show of considering the offer, fingering the rim of his glass as he looked upwards and seemed to be figuring as he slowly nodded, but it was clear to David that the man was taken a bit off guard by his show of force. It was a long time before he answered. "Okay, Mr. Steiner, ten million. I want it in cash, bundled hundreds. You and I can work out the delivery details. And, as you said, we're going to release him to you regardless. The money is just, what … a little thank you and apology to smooth over any past transgressions that may have occurred?"

"Where is he?" David asked.

"Come now," Saladino said, letting a renewed condescending smile spread across his face. "He's safe. I'll let him talk to you later. At the moment he's my life insurance."

"He's probably in Vegas," David said. "I know a lot of people, a lot more than you might think and you don't know what connections I've got. Maybe I can find him without you." David leaned forward inviting a response. "Maybe you're the one in no position to be issuing threats. Maybe you don't have as much insurance as you think, Johnny."

Saladino stood and so did Howie, thinking there was about to be a fight. "Don't do anything stupid, Mr. Steiner. Don't underestimate my ability to stand up to whatever you think you can do. Let's keep this civilized."

He turned to Mary Kay. "Tommy will be fine so you need to just calm that sweet ass of yours down a little to make sure he stays that way."

Mary Kay rose from the sofa and locked her gaze onto Saladino. All she had really heard was a threat directed at Tommy. She turned and casually strolled around the end of the couch then suddenly turned and sprinted to the doorway that led to the bedrooms.

David stood, took a couple of steps to follow her but realized he wouldn't get to her in time.

He turned back just as he heard a closet door closing. "Shit! Stay behind me, both of you."

Mary Kay emerged from the doorway in a full speed power walk holding her pistol grip sawed-off 12 gauge shotgun. She slowed and held the gun in front of her pointing at the three men.

"Mary Kay!" David yelled. He was holding his arms outstretched to further shield the two men standing behind him. "Put that goddamn gun down. We need to get Tommy back."

She ignored him and continued walking forward until she was just eight feet from them. "Listen here, Mr. Johnny Saladino, don't think that I won't use this!" She fired into the high ceiling just above the three men, showering them and half the room with bits of sheetrock and plaster.

"Mary Kay!" David yelled. "What are you going to do, shoot me?"

She looked at him and her face softened. She lowered the gun slightly. "No," she said angrily.

David took a couple of steps toward her. "You can't shoot anybody. Give me the gun. We have to work on getting Tommy back."

She lowered the barrel until it was pointing at the floor and David took the gun from her. Her face was passive, blank, and she took her seat again on the sofa.

Howie said nothing and walked toward the bar. Johnny Saladino remained standing in the same spot, also saying nothing but eyeing Mary Kay with a look of mixed shock and anger as he brushed bits of ceiling from his hair.

David walked to his phone still holding the shotgun. "Cecil, please send one of your people up to accompany Mr. Saladino back down. See that he leaves the building and then call me to let me know."

He set the phone down and remained standing. "Nothing happens until we get to talk with Tommy. I may have some requirements of my own when it comes to exchanging the money."

Saladino walked to the door, expecting Howie to accompany him again, which he did. Before David realized what was happening, Mary Kay stood, grabbed a heavy glass dolphin from the table and pitched it with a big league overhand at the back of Saladino's head. It missed him by two inches and shattered on the marble door frame just in front of his face.

Both men jumped. Saladino spun and faced Mary Kay.

"I missed on purpose you sack of shit!" Mary Kay shouted. Then changing to the voice Howie thought of as her little girl voice, she quietly added, "I just wanted to tell you I'm gonna have your balls sitting on this table in a souvenir jar, assuming you have any. Good night, Johnny."

She folded her arms and put on the same ice-cold smile she had shown earlier. Howie and Saladino turned and continued out of the condo in silence.

A minute later, Howie returned. "Wow, I don't think that's quite what the son-of-a-bitch expected from you two."

Mary Kay was wiping tears from her face. "Is he really going to let Tommy go?"

The two men looked at each other. "Here's what I think," Howie said. "He just might go through with the deal, let Tommy go, take the dough and leave you alone forever. That might be easier for him and he might think you won't want to stir the pot and attract any more attention to yourself. The money is enough that he and Uncle Nic can call it a win. But, man, after this little meeting he's got to be rethinking things."

"What do you mean?" she asked.

Howie hesitated, glancing at David. "What I mean is he might be thinking that he's up against something bigger than he thought. He might be worried that you're coming after him whether Tommy is safe or not."

"He agreed to ten million awful damn easy," David observed. "I don't think he's leaving me any choice, but what I really want is Tommy safe and everything back to normal. Think he'll go with that?"

Howie sighed and thought for a few moments. "Who knows? Maybe he and Uncle Nic just want blood anyway."

"Oh, shit." Mary Kay squeaked out, stifling a sob.

David reached over and rubbed Mary Kay's arm. "He knows we've got the money and the clout to take him out even if we get Tommy back. If anything happens to Tommy then he damn sure knows we'll be after him. So, it seems to me that his real plan right from the beginning was to kill all three of us or at least just me and Tommy. He might've figured that leaving Mary Kay wasn't as dangerous, but now he's gotten to know her a little better."

"No shit!" Howie added with a laugh. "I think you scared that idea right out of him. I've never heard a girl, or anyone for that matter, tell a guy to shove a table up his dick. And then the shotgun. Jesus, you are something else!"

Mary Kay sniffled and managed a small laugh. "The fucker," she said quietly.

"Did you really miss with that dolphin on purpose?" Howie asked.

Mary Kay looked over at David then back to Howie. "No," she said disgustedly.

"Were you really going to shoot him if David wasn't in front of him?"

David knew the answer to that question.

Mary Kay sighed and took a deep breath before raising her voice several notches to answer. "Yes, I was going to shoot him. Quit asking me questions and fuck you, Howie, for bringing all this on us! I should shoot you!"

After a long silence, Howie said to David, "You going to keep the deal?"

David looked over to Mary Kay and put his hand on her thigh. He looked back at Howie. "Two things are going to happen. I'm going to do everything possible to get Tommy out of this alive and I'm going to make damn sure that they won't be able to do this again. I've spend my entire adult life preparing for what might come our way. Johnny Saladino doesn't realize who he's dealing with."

Johnny Saladino left the parking garage of the Pac View Building with a mix of emotions as he headed back to his hotel near the airport. One of his concerns was David Steiner. He figured out how to work his windfall into a multibillion dollar financial empire. That meant he was dealing with someone who was intelligent and patient. Those qualities coupled with the access to enormous amounts of money made him a dangerous opponent, too dangerous to leave alive if he managed to pull this off.

Then there was Mary Kay. She had made it pretty clear, he

thought, that she would be coming after him no matter what happened to her brother. He smiled a little. "Man, that broad went fucking ape shit!" he said out loud. He would need to take all three of them out, and that PI too, but he needed to figure out how to pull more money for himself out of the deal first.

ELEVEN

Tommy woke up. It was early morning, just getting light. He got up and checked the locked bedroom door like he had the last ten times. He flopped back down on the bed, staring up at the ceiling and trying to think. He didn't know exactly what was happening. His three guards brought him food and checked on him occasionally, but never said much. Obviously, he thought, the only reason he would be held captive would be money. Howie Williams had come to see him and now this. Was there a connection? Was Howie after a piece of the action? It wasn't the cops or he wouldn't be here, so it had to be Howie working on his own or with the mob. Did the mob find out about them after all these years?

He'd been thinking all this over since last night when they had thrown him into a private jet and he had reached a couple of conclusions. One, if it was Saladino and the mob then no matter what David and Mary Kay did, they were probably going to kill him and maybe all three of them. Two, he wanted a drink! They had given him three cans of beer late last night, but it felt like a tease. He had to figure out a way to escape or to let David know where he was.

The only furniture in the room was the bed and a dresser with a mirror. The small closet was mostly empty. The dual pane window was barred and locked and his view out of it was of a narrow side yard and a brown concrete block wall.

He surveyed the room for what seemed like the thousandth time looking for something he could use, some edge, some way out of the nightmare that had befallen him. It was no mansion, but it seemed like a pretty nice house, pretty big, one story, and he knew he was in Las Vegas. He could see the Stratosphere Tower in the distance. It looked to him to be several miles away and it seemed like his vantage point was somewhat uphill from there. Beyond he could see a section of bare chocolate-brown mountains that he recognized as being beyond Henderson to the southeast. So, he figured that he was roughly somewhere in the northwest part of Las Vegas.

As he sat thinking all this over he realized he was staring at a phone jack in the wall between the bed and the dresser. He knew that up on a shelf in the closet were folded clothes, plastic bags, a couple of reams of printer paper and an old rotary dial desk phone with the wall cord wound up around it.

It was mid-morning when David walked into the kitchen of the condo and, as he had figured, found Mary Kay there.

"Sleep any?" he greeted, pulling himself up onto an upholstered stool at the counter.

She sighed. "Not much." She was standing across the counter eating a piece of toast. "So, my brain won't shut off, and here's one thing I thought of. How do you come up with 10 million bucks without someone knowing? No matter what you liquidate or sell, or even if you just take it out of an account, it will trigger a paper trail. Eventually somebody will want to know what you did with 10 million dollars, won't they?"

David smiled, reached across and stole the other half of her toast and took a bite. "Listen, you are totally in the loop on all the big financial stuff, but there are private accounts that are just mine. There are also a couple of places I keep good old-fashioned cash, you know, like a chimney."

She smiled, nodded, holding back tears for what seemed to her like the thousandth time. They sat in silence for a minute while she poured him some coffee and he drank a couple sips of hers. "Poor Tommy," she managed. "Can we make this happen?"

David took another drink of coffee and finished off the piece of toast. "I slept a couple of hours. The rest of the night I was on the phone, my laptop and thinking a lot. Howie still asleep?"

"I guess so," she said.

David lowered his voice. "Listen, I'm going to make this happen. I don't want to give you or Howie all the details, but I'll tell you when I can. I don't know if we should trust Howie or if we should even try to, but sooner or later, we'll find out. I feel like we can trust him, but as soon as I think that I start feeling like we should treat him like any other threat. So, I don't know what I think about him yet."

She looked hard into his eyes and tears started falling from hers. "I'm so sorry about this Vegas deal bringing all this attention. We should've never worked on you so hard to give in to what we wanted. You were right to be wary." Her voice dropped to a whisper. "You've taken care of us for the last thirty-five years, you're not going to stop now, are you?"

David shook his head, reached out and stroked her hair. "I'm going to take care of all of this. Keep trusting me."

They heard a door open down the hall and Howie's shuffling footsteps. At David's urging, he had driven to the hotel during the night, grabbed all his belongings and moved into the guest room. He was wearing black sweatpants and a grey tee shirt. He grunted a sleepy, "Good morning," and headed for the coffee maker. He poured himself a cup and took a sip. "This stuff real?"

David made a face. "Half real, half decaf. Can't take the full bore stuff all the time anymore. Screws up my sleep and my stomach."

"Me too," Howie said as he took another sip and let out a disgusted chuckle. "Shit, we're all turning into our parents. So, what's the plan with Saladino and the whole mess?"

David's and Mary Kay's eyes met for just a beat.

"I'm working on it," David said.

"Why don't you just go to the police after the exchange?" Howie suggested. "You can go public with the whole thing and be protected."

David nodded slowly and sighed. "There would still be no guarantee they wouldn't just murder us once the story died down. We can't have a security force with us for the rest of our lives. Plus, we don't know who your ex-partner or that guy Trapani talked to."

He looked over and met Mary Kay's gaze. "Besides, the cops start sniffing around this whole thing and they're going turn up other shit I don't want them to." He checked his watch. "Howie, let's go get some food and a couple of beers. We need to talk." He looked over at Mary Kay. "You okay here for a while?"

"Sure, go ahead," she said. "I'm not hungry anyway."

Howie looked up at the clock. "It's nine o'clock."

David nodded. "I like beer in the morning. Get dressed. You've got fifteen minutes. I know a bar that makes a great breakfast."

Howie and David had been sipping their beers in silence for a couple of minutes. Finally Howie said, "You're right, beer before breakfast is just fine. Was she really going to gun down Saladino?"

"Without a doubt, she would have blown a hole in him right there," David said. "And maybe you for a bonus."

"That was crazy," Howie said. "She had already told him to shove the table up his dick, then she ran off and got the shotgun and shot the ceiling for Christ's sake! Then she looked all calm again and two minutes later she fires that goddamn glass fish at him."

David was nodding with just a trace of a smile. "She's an interesting woman. Sometimes you can see it coming, mostly it just appears. She will go from zero to a hundred with no warning, especially if it involves Tommy. Anybody who she sees as a danger to him is in serious shit."

After a few more moments of silence, Howie said, "So, what's really the deal with you and Mary Kay? You two a couple?"

David pondered how to answer and said nothing for an uncomfortably long time. "It's complicated, or maybe it's really simple. That going steady thing is just some shit she likes to throw out there sometimes. She thinks it's funny 'cause people don't know what the hell to say."

"Yeah, I could tell she has no problem saying shit to get a reaction," Howie said.

"We're not a couple like most people would think," David continued. "I guess we're some kind of couple. We are best friends, partners, lovers, we protect each other, sometimes we're going our own ways for a while. I know it sounds weird but it kind of works for us. Hell, maybe we are going steady."

Howie slowly nodded. "That is complicated. Look, man, I know we went through this last night, but I can't get over it. You kept this a secret all these years. It's fucking incredible!"

David just stared back at him for a bit. "I haven't thought about it like that for a long time." He sighed and leaned forward, resting his elbows on the table. "It was all on me to make this whole thing work. I worked hard at becoming as much of a financial genius as I could and learning every trick I could about staying out of everybody's awareness. Tommy and Mary Kay basically went along with everything. The hardest part was keeping Mary Kay and Tommy quiet, especially Tommy, but her too later. Tommy was scared and it's been complicated for him too. He's pickled himself to cope, I guess. Mary Kay is, well, she's Mary Kay. Sometimes she just does whatever the hell she wants. She gets scared too about anyone finding out about our secret but in her it comes out as having one hell of an attitude when she decides to have one. God, it was work! It was easy for a few days or a few months, but now it's years, decades. Don't get me wrong, I was excited about it too but I was always so damn worried that somehow somebody would find out. It was hard, man, and I was a kid too. You know what the weirdest part of the whole thing is?"

Howie smiled and shook his head. "It's all weird, but tell me."

"The strangest thing is that it never was fun like it should've been. Plenty of great outcomes, but it was just never that fun after that first few weeks. And as the years went by it just..." His voice trailed off and he seemed to be staring at nothing and thinking back. He returned his gaze to the present and let a small grin come to his face. "It was pretty fucking incredible, wasn't it?"

"Bet you never guessed finding three million bucks would somehow not be fun."

David downed a long swallow of beer. "All in all, I suppose being rich is better than being poor, even if it's not like you imagined."

"Care to elaborate any on just what you did with the dough after high school?" Howie asked.

David gave him a squinting long look as he rubbed the stubble on his chin. "I could go on for a long time, but since you already know too damn much, here's the basic short version. I opened a few accounts here and in Europe along with a couple of so-called secret Swiss accounts."

"Wait," Howie interrupted. "You just walked into these places with all that cash? You flew to Europe with it?"

"Lot easier then," David said. "That bank secrecy act made it a little harder over here, but not much at first. I would just ask to meet privately with the manager, tell him I was some international investor who wanted things kept private. I ran into a couple of guys who were more than happy to keep it private for a few thousand bucks. Europe was no problem at all."

Howie was shaking his head and smiling.

"So then I did a lot of depositing and transferring back and forth. I set up a phony consulting business and wrote myself paychecks. I bought and sold real estate all over the world. At first I was just trying to hide the origin of the money, but after a while I started making real money with the property transactions, and I mean real money. You know how people flip houses, right?"

"Yeah," Howie said. "Buy a cheap house, do a little work, sell it for a profit. Like that?"

"Exactly," David continued. "Well, I was property-flipping on a grand scale. Starting about the mid 70's inflation was driving up prices everywhere and especially housing prices. I was buying multi-million dollar land tracts and all kinds of huge commercial developments, doing nothing and turning around and selling them and making millions. I did a lot of that over and over and made a goddamn accidental fortune. One time I bought this huge condominium development in Germany. It was something like four hundred units spread out between twenty-five buildings and it was still under construction. I signed papers, the money was transferred and ten days later I turned around and sold it and made twelve million dollars profit. Shit like that."

Howie just smiled admiringly and sipped his beer while the server set down their breakfast orders.

"Wait until you taste that omelet," David said. "They're the best. Anyway, it made it easy to muddle up all the profits with the extra money I was still funneling in. In a few years I was building up legit money and doing more buying and transferring. Early 80s I sold off some Alaskan and Canadian land holdings that had gone up ridiculously and some private offshore oil rights in Mexico that netted about two-hundred million. I took that money, consolidated a couple of consulting and real estate businesses, and DMT International was born."

"Wasn't that kind of fun?" Howie asked.

"I guess it was in a way," David said, shrugging, "but there was always the other side of it. Keeping us all out of the media and everyone's loop and I always had to be as prepared as I could in case someone found out. Part of that was making it increasingly difficult to trace the three of us very far back. I was always working, always planning, always listening. As time went along there was more and more that I needed to keep secret. As much as possible I had to stay aware of everything and try to control everything. I still am."

He leaned in closer. "Everything, Howie. Everything. I know shit that I don't even need to know because someday I might need it. I keep track of people who just might have a connection, but probably don't. I continually check on everything and everyone. Over the years I've even checked in on you every now and then."

"Me?" Howie said. "Did you know I was coming to see you?"

"No, that was a surprise," David said. "But I know you've done pretty damn well as a cop. I've followed your career from time to time. You've done well."

Howie smiled a little and nodded. "Yeah, I did okay. Better than anybody thought I'd do."

David leaned back and folded his arms. "So, I still don't know what to think. You working for Johnny Saladino?"

Howie made a pained face. "No, I told you last night that I'm not, and that's the truth, but I guess he kind of thinks I am. I told you I had a meeting with Heinz, my ex-partner and that guy Trapani. I only talked with those two, but it confirmed some things for me. I already knew about the yacht, but when Heinz told me about the Mary Poppins shit in the note you left, I knew for sure. I needed Trapani because he knew Nicolas Saladino back in the day and he's one of those guys who's always hearing stuff. He didn't know anything about you but I guess he learned about you from me. Now I think pulling him into the conversation was a mistake. A few days later Johnny Saladino calls me and says he wants to meet with me. He's been around, you know, and I knew who he was but I'd never actually met the guy before. I was pretty curious so I agreed to meet him at a restaurant."

"Just the two of you?" David asked.

"At the table at least," Howie said. "I didn't have anybody there but who knows if he did. So he starts in with all that same phony politeness you saw. Tells me who his Uncle Nic is and how Vincent was a cousin he never knew. He says how interesting it is that I grew up in that neighborhood and that I was friends with you three. Chatting me up about the old days. He's an annoying punk. Then he says he found out that I'm going to go visit you guys and how interested he would be in finding out if you actually did steal that money. He says that when I come back he'd like to meet with me and find out what I learned. I hardly even did any talking. I definitely got the idea that he knew exactly as much as I did. That fat ass Trapani tipped him or talked to somebody who went to him or his uncle."

"So, did you agree to meet with him when you returned?"

Howie shrugged. "Not really, but I guess it might've been implied in the conversation. I wanted that meeting to end and I felt like I was just putting him off. So, listen, I didn't come here for him. I was going to tell you about him and that I thought he was a dangerous guy and try to help you out with that. I had no idea he was going to come to town. When he did, it just threw me off. I didn't think you'd even believe for a second that I didn't know about him coming here."

"So for all you know," David said, "he was wired when you met with him or he's talked to his cronies all about it."

"Anything's possible," Howie said, "but I would say probably not. He thinks he's on the trail to some money so I'm pretty sure he wants to keep it to himself and Uncle Nic. I don't like the guy. Thinks he's hot shit. Like I said, he's a punk and I get the impression that he's not terribly bright. And if I was Uncle Nic I wouldn't be trusting him too much either. So what made you tell him that Tommy is probably in Vegas?"

David took a swallow of beer. "Well, like I said, I obsessively stay in touch with everything I can think of that might be related to us. Johnny Saladino is somebody I like to keep up on a little. I know what he's up to in his businesses. He lives in L.A. but he travels to Vegas all the time and a lot of his contacts seems to be there. It was just a guess, but when I said that, just for a second there was a look on his face that told me I was probably right."

David reached into his inside jacket pocket and pulled out two folded sheets of paper. "Two small articles from the LA times this morning." He unfolded the papers and laid them flat in front of Howie. "I have somebody there who texts or emails me stuff. Trapani and your partner Gary Heinz are both dead. Both killed yesterday."

Howie skimmed through the short articles. He looked up with glistening eyes. "So I brought this mess to you and I got Gary and that shithead Trapani killed." He leaned back in his seat and seemed visibly deflated. "Johnny?"

"That would make sense," David said. "Didn't want them hanging around knowing what he knew or talking to anybody."

Howie nodded. "I think that would make sense too, but is that what happened? Was it Johnny?"

"Are you thinking it was somebody else?" David asked.

"Tell me something first," Howie said. "Ever hear of a guy named Janelli, goes by Moley? Another guy named Zuber?"

David stared at him for a long time. "What if I have heard of them?"

"Tell me about them,' Howie said.

"You just stepped into the picture," David said. "I've been dealing with this for a fucking long time. It's some more shit that's complicated." He pointed at the news articles. "Besides stirring up this mess it looks like you dragged yourself right into the middle of it too. So, I'm asking again, can I trust you?"

Howie leaned back and looked hard at David. "I'm telling you, I am absolutely not after you and I'm not up to anything with Saladino. I do want in on helping you in this. So, you going to fill me in on this whole deal?"

David shook his head. "Can't yet. What I have planned is going to get a little hairy. There's a good chance you're going to have to kill somebody and if things don't go just right you might get killed yourself. You sure you want in?"

Howie said, "Did you have Heinz and Trapani killed?"

"I've never had anybody killed," David said, "but that's probably going to change in the next few days."

"What about Zuber and Moley? Do you know who killed them or ordered them killed or what happened when they disappeared?"

David leaned back and after a bit said, "I can't talk about that."

Howie sighed impatiently. "Maybe I'm not asking the question exactly right, but how about you just tell me what I want to know?"

"It's not that simple," David said. "I told you I didn't have them killed."

Howie nodded slowly, glancing down at the table and back

up to David. "I've been getting increasingly concerned about my well-being since I started digging into this whole thing. Oh, and I know about Tommy's shrink disappearing, Dr. Lindsey Robbins. And somehow, Bakersfield keeps popping up in all these cases. So, am I going to disappear too? Am I going to join Moley and Zuber and dear old Dr. Robbins? Or maybe instead of vanishing I'll just turn up murdered like Trapani and Heinz?"

David gave him a long look. "No, and it's complicated."

Howie stared at him hard and sighed. "Okay, I'm in."

David glanced at his watch, checking the date. "Saladino and I are talking later tonight. I've got a message being delivered to him later today demanding some conditions. I'm going to stall so I can make it all come down on Saturday."

Howie nodded slowly, thinking over the timeline. "You're not going to pay him, are you? Besides the fact that you don't trust them to keep the deal I think the whole thing just plain pisses you off."

David nodded. "I could afford to pay them any damn amount they dreamed up. I've worked pretty hard all these years to make this thing work and to protect all of us. I'm not letting them undo it all." He leaned forward and lowered is voice. "I was right about Vegas. I got a call early this morning a little before we all got up. I know where Tommy is. They're guarding him in a house in Vegas. I'm going to suck Johnny into thinking he's double-crossing Uncle Nic and, you're right, Johnny's getting fucked. Somebody's getting paid, but not him. He's just getting what's coming to him."

Howie watched Las Vegas, now just two thousand feet below, as the pilot guided the Hawker 800 over part of the city and began a steep dropping turn to line up the approach for their landing at McCarren Airport. They had boarded the private charter jet at noon, just about two hours before in Seattle.

Before the flight and for most of the flight David had been on cell phones and satellite phones finalizing arrangements for Tommy's rescue and a few related items. After getting practically no information sent his way over the last twenty-four hours, Howie knew better than to ask for details. He knew that details would be coming soon enough.

The private jet rolled to a stop near a couple of other charters and a low building away from the main terminals. David got up, tossed his phones and a folder of papers into a thin briefcase and motioned for Howie to follow.

They approached the cockpit door just as it opened and the pilot stepped out smiling. "Hey, you said two hours max. I did it in a few minutes less. This plane really moves when you want it too."

David handed the man an envelope. "Thanks for doing this with no notice, Dale. Great flight. We're still a go for tomorrow, so I'll see you then."

The pilot took the envelope, smiled even bigger and saluted. "Anytime, Mr. Steiner. See you tomorrow."

They took the few steps to the tarmac just as a grey Escalade pulled up just fifty feet away. "That's ours," David said. "They'll put our bags in." He checked his watch. "I need to take a short chopper ride to check out some arrangements I've made for good old Johnny. You don't need to come. You can head to the hotel if you want and we can meet up there in a little while. But if you're good with helicopters then come along. I'll show you what's up out there and when we come back I'll fill you in on what's happening tomorrow."

Howie said, "I'm good with choppers, especially short rides. I just don't fully trust their gliding ability in case of engine failure."

David smiled and checked his watch again. "No kidding. My guy should be here any minute."

A few minutes later they were lifting off in an A-Star 6 passenger helicopter from Nevada Desert Helo Charter. Normally it would be taking tourists on flights over the Strip, Hoover Dam or to the Grand Canyon. Today, a pilot that David knew well, was taking David and Howie for a little flyover of where a certain mobster would be meeting his demise the following day.

Mandalay Bay Hotel Casino was just off to the right, reflecting shimmering gold in the afternoon brightness as they turned heading southwest across I-15 past the southwest edge of the city, or at least where the spreading edge was today, out over empty desert.

The pilot, David and Howie were all wearing headsets with microphones to be able to communicate. "Charlie, you know where we were talking about, where Silver State is working the ground?"

Charlie laughed. "Hey, I'm way ahead of you, David. We went out early this morning and put down the marker and helped those guys place the nets. You're not going to believe how it all just disappears into the desert. That guy Mr. Ed knows what he's doing. We're almost there."

A minute later, Charlie guided the chopper down to about six hundred feet and did a tight banked right circle so they could see down out that side of the aircraft. "There's the red X where your bad guys will arrive tomorrow."

He broke off the turn and flew straight south for a few seconds then pulled up into a hover, still at about six hundred feet altitude. "Okay, look off to the left here. Believe it or not, that little storage shack has two trucks with trailers and equipment parked behind it. They're covered with netting and a little bit of desert brush. Down on the ground you have to practically walk right up and bump your head on them before you even notice. From up here it looks just like all the rest of the terrain. Incredible job."

"You're right, Charlie. It's beautiful." David nudged Howie's arm. "I'll tell you later what's going to happen here. Right now just believe me when I say that Johnny will barely have time to enjoy it all."

Howie nodded and gave a thumbs up.

"That it?" Charlie asked.

"We're done," David said. "You can take us back. Thanks for

the look."

The two of them stepped off the chopper and waved to Charlie as he went back to his usual business. Seeing their Escalade missing, David called on his cell.

"Okay, thanks." He turned to Howie. "They took our stuff to the hotel and our bags are already in the room. I told them to just put the Escalade in valet parking and we would get it later. Let's call a cab, go get a drink or two and some dinner in a while."

"Sounds good," Howie said. "We can finally talk, I assume?"

David said, "Absolutely. The time has come."

A while later the cab pulled up to a restaurant called Del Fresco's a few blocks east of the strip on Paradise. On the way in the door, David said, "Look, we're getting older but we're not old enough to have dinner this damn early. So, let's just hang out, have a couple drinks, talk things over and work our way into dinner."

There were only a handful of customers in the restaurant, a couple at the bar and a few people at three dining tables. David handed the host a hundred dollar bill. "I'd like that booth right there. We're not going to eat for a while but we're going to sit and talk and drink and take too long to give you the booth back."

"Be my guest," the smiling host said.

Their drinks came along with some complimentary appetizers. After a couple of minutes David said, "Okay, I had to look at that place from a chopper because that's what I think Johnny or one of his guys is going to do in the morning. I'm calling him in a little while to let him know exactly where to make the exchange. Right now he just knows it's somewhere around Vegas. I wanted to make sure they would see what we thought we were seeing which is mostly desert."

Howie was a little confused. "There's going to be an exchange?"

David shook his head. "No, but he thinks that I think there is going to be one. I'm telling him that you and Mary Kay are meeting him at that spot tomorrow to exchange money and he will have Tommy there. I know Tommy won't be there and all he is planning to do is take the money and kill you both."

"So, I'm not going there?"

"Nobody's going there except Johnny and his guys," David said. "This is going to get a little hairy tomorrow. I'm going to Bakersfield to meet with Nicholas Saladino and make a deal. If you want to, you are going to help Mr. Ed rescue Tommy from the house in Summerlin. But listen, you can stay nice and safe at the hotel. He has people if you aren't there."

"No," Howie said. "I'm all in. I helped cause this clusterfuck of a situation. I want to help pull Tommy out of there."

"I already told Mr. Ed that you'd want in on it," David said. "He's planning on working with you. I told him your history and he thinks you'll fit his plan fine. I know he wants to keep it a small operation so besides his backup guys who'll be close by it might just be the two of you and Mary Kay."

"What else do I need to know?" Howie said.

"Not a lot," David said. "I'm taking that same jet out of here in the morning to Bakersfield. It's not even an hour flight. Uncle Nic and I are going to come to a mutually beneficial understanding that's going to keep all of us safe from now on. You are going to pick up Mr. Ed tomorrow at the hotel and follow his directions."

"So, where is Mary Kay in all this?" Howie asked.

David swirled the ice around in his glass and took another swallow. "I told her to let us do this and we would keep her posted, but I knew that wouldn't go. She's going to do whatever the hell she wants. Mr. Ed is expecting her to show up and I told him he might as well just plan on using her because that's what she wants to do. She's definitely got some skills that could be used in this rescue. She might be the most ruthless person he could get to help in this situation."

"So, this Mr. Ed guy knows what he's doing?" Howie asked.

David smiled. "About the only thing we don't have to worry about tomorrow is him. Knows what he's doing is an understatement. You'll see. And listen, man, even the most successful missions have casualties, so you watch your ass tomorrow and don't be one. Assaulting a house to rescue a person is a dangerous deal. I don't really even want Mary Kay in on this, so if at all possible look out for her too."

"Hey, I've made it this long and I've been in my share of hairy situations."

David checked his watch. "Okay, old man, it's past 4:30. You want to order dinner? At least it will be after 5:00 by the time we eat."

Howie smiled. "Sure." He held up his glass. "To Tommy."

They clinked glasses and drank down their first drinks.

Howie was driving the grey Escalade out of Mandalay Bay and heading north up the Strip to Tropicana Avenue as his passenger had instructed. In the passenger seat was a man who had shown up at the same time as the vehicle had been brought up by the valet parking attendant. Howie thought he looked well built, around forty and at least six foot two. As David had told him, he had introduced himself to Howie as Mr. Ed.

"Like the horse?" Howie said, smiling.

"Exactly," the man said. After a few seconds he gave a quick smile. "Okay, here's what I know. We're rescuing a guy named Tommy. He's being held by two mob guys, and a third guy that comes and goes, in a neighborhood house out by Red Rock in Summerlin. David had somebody call from Nevada Power and asked about some billing just to verify the address, cell phone, landline and all that. I cruised by there yesterday, so I know the layout and exactly where we're heading. The priority is getting Tommy out alive. There may be orders for them to kill Tommy. David said you could fill me in on anything else I needed to know."

"That's the basics," Howie said. "I assume David sent you because you know what you're doing?"

Mr. Ed pointed. "Turn right on Tropicana. It's just a few blocks down. I know some shit and I've done this kind of thing before. I know you're an ex-military cop, retired L.A. cop and a current PI. David says you're good so I assume you know some shit too, but I'm going to give you some quick lessons between here and our destination. He pointed to a storage facility ahead. "Second driveway."

Howie pulled in and followed his companion's directions to a doorway. Mr. Ed disappeared through the doorway. A minute later he emerged carrying a sports bag and a large, thin suitcase.

As Howie drove, Mr. Ed unzipped the bag. "There's probably more in here than we need, but it sure beats not having enough."

He held up items as he explained. "Two concussion grenades. Don't do much damage but they scare the shit out of the bad guys and they think they're dead for just a second. Two 40 caliber semi-autos with regular ten round mags and a couple of extras. Two converted full auto MAC 11's with thirty-two round mags and extras. David said you knew how to handle any of these."

"Yeah, I'm good," Howie said. "I like these for what we're doing."

"Like I said, a little more here than you and I can use all at once," Mr. Ed said, "but the more the merrier I say."

As they took the onramp onto I-15, Mr. Ed noticed Howie checking the side view and rear view mirrors several times in just a few seconds. "Mary Kay back there?"

Howie glanced in the mirror again as they merged over to the far left lane. "Yeah, I spotted her as we came out of the storage place. She texted this morning that she wants to meet in front of a store on Flamingo. Friend of hers will watch her car there."

"Did you text her about wearing something that showed a little cleavage?" Mr. Ed asked.

Howie smiled. "Yeah, I did. She sent back something about being the star of the show."

"She might be right," Mr. Ed said. "David told me she was going to do whatever the hell she wanted no matter what we said so to try to keep her safe."

Howie gave him a look and let out a quick laugh. "You ever meet her? We're the ones who need to be kept safe."

"He said she's one hell of a shot and has handled a lot of

different guns. He also told me she wouldn't want to be kept safe and it would just piss her off. So I've got a couple of ideas for how we can use her."

Howie flipped on his signal and went over three lanes and watched her steer her black Corvette with him. He took the exit onto Flamingo. Howie sped to the light, took a left back over the freeway and over to the curb in front of a supermarket parking lot. Both men got out of the SUV and walked to the back of it as Mary Kay steered the black Corvette to a stop just a couple of feet from them.

She stepped out of the car and smiled as she approached. "Hi guys!" She looked Howie's companion up and down. "You're a big boy, Mr. Ed. Okay, listen you two. Clue me in so I don't fuck up. What's the plan?"

"You bring any fire power?" Mr. Ed asked.

She nodded. "I know you have some extra handguns so I'd like one of whatever you're not using. I've got a little pistol grip short barrel 12 gauge with some hot pink accents. Holds five shells. It's a girlie gun. I think you remember that baby, don't you Howie?"

"I remember perfectly," Howie said. "Mr. Ed, whatever you do, don't piss her off."

"David says you're one hell of a shot with anything and you're especially good with shotguns," Mr. Ed said.

"I know what I'm doing," she answered.

"The plan is simple," said Mr. Ed, "and should catch them completely off guard. You're gonna walk right up to the front door carrying a clipboard and a little cardboard box I have in the back here." He reached out and pulled the zipper of her top down a few inches. "There, just push them up a little and the bad guys will be looking in all the wrong places. Thing is, you're going to have to take out whoever's at the door, no questions asked, just boom, done. You okay with that?"

She glanced back and forth at the two men. "If that's what I need to do to get my brother out of there, yeah, I can handle it just fine."

Howie checked his wristwatch. "Traffic isn't too bad so we

should be there just about on time. We have about a half hour. We're heading out toward Summerlin."

"Howie said you're leaving your car here. So grab your shotgun and I'll fill you both in on the way there."

"One more thing," Mary Kay said. She looked up at Mr. Ed. "I know you're the one running this show and David says you know your shit and completely trusts you, but I am dead serious here. We're all expendable. The only person not expendable is my brother. No matter what happens, if he ends up safe it's a successful mission."

She retrieved her weapon from the trunk and brought it back to Howie. "Here you go. I'm putting my car in the parking lot up by the entrance. Meet me up there."

She hopped back in the Vette, fired it up and launched it into a 270 degree smoking left turn burnout the wrong way out across three westbound lanes of Flamingo and back into the parking lot entrance.

Howie and Mr. Ed looked at each other smiling as Howie backed up about eighty feet then made a civilized right turn into the same driveway.

TWELVE

Johnny Saladino was living his life in the blissful ignorance of just how far in over his head he was in his doomed kidnapping scheme. He was accustomed to people being intimidated and following his dictates. In this case he had foolishly and completely underestimated his opponent. At the moment he was just southwest of the latest, and always moving, edge of Las Vegas. He was a mile west of I-15 on a small paved road that ended here, out in the desert, much nearer to the foot of the mountain range than any roads used to run just a few years before. He was driving a beautiful new Mercedes S550 loaned to him by a local dealer on the orders of Uncle Nic.

In the clear desert air the mountains to the south and west seemed close enough to reach out and touch. The edge of almost-new neighborhoods could be seen just three miles to the north. The color spectrum of the houses ranged from light tan to medium tan to a couple shades of darker tan to the darkest, which was given various names by various home builders, like Sienna Dune and Iced Coffee Dusk, but looked just like regular brown.

Close by was rolling desert emptiness surrounded by bare hills. A dirt road led to a small storage shed, a couple of storage containers a half mile away and a two-high stack of concrete pipes a little closer that marked the beginnings of another stab at the city's expansion into the desert.

As David had anticipated, Johnny had instructed his people to make two quick passes over the area by helicopter a few hours earlier. They had reported nothing amiss and judged the construction storage area to be far enough away to not be an issue.

The October late morning desert was a pleasant seventy degrees and Johnny and his two companions got out of the car to await the arrival of the other vehicle. According to the elaborate arrangements made by David and agreed to by Johnny, in that vehicle would be Howie and Mary Kay to make a money delivery. Tommy was to be in the Mercedes and be released to Mary Kay and Howie. None of those three were going to be making an appearance here today.

"Okay, I wanna go over this one more time," Johnny said. "This is gonna go quick and no fuck ups. As soon as those two get out of their car, you take them out. There's not supposed to be anyone else with them, but we have to be ready for that so watch it."

Both men nodded and patted their waistbands where thin windbreakers covered their .45 caliber revolvers. In the back seat were two AR-15s in case things got out of hand and they ended up in some kind of shoot-out.

Johnny checked his watch. "We got here a little early, that's good. It's a nice sunny autumn day in the desert. Not too hot. This should all be over in twenty minutes or so."

He adjusted his sunglasses, leaned against the car, lit a cigarette and blew out the smoke contentedly, confident that all was under control. He was right about the time frame. It would indeed all be over in twenty minutes or so.

David Steiner stepped out of the passenger side of the black BMW SUV as he saw Saladino's car turn into the alley from the south end of the block. As agreed upon, David's vehicle had approached from the north end of the block and they were to meet where David now stood in the alley directly behind Vincent Saladino's former apartment complex. As the car neared, David reflected upon how much his life had changed from being in this alley and how much it was about to change once again.

Saladino's Mercedes stopped just a few feet away and the old man got out of the back seat and stood. "Hello, Mr. Steiner." He took a step as David did the same and the two men briefly shook hands and sized each other up.

"Mr. Saladino," David said, noting the other's still firm grip.

"So, you're the young man who stole my money."

"We were both young," David said. "I was a kid and you were in your thirties. Now look at us."

Saladino gave a quick chuckle and nodded. "This the house where the safe was?" He pointed over the fence to the former Boyd house.

"It's still there. Follow me and I'll show you the chimney." Before opening the gate he stopped and pointed to each end of the alley. "My people have closed both ends of the alley and set up some phony utility workers so nobody surprises us. Can we have our associates stay here so it's just the two of us?"

Saladino motioned to his four men as David opened the gate and directed him to the chimney.

David reached down and opened the ash cleanout. "When you're a kid you just lay down on your belly and do this part. I'll spare us both the grunting and groaning of that. There are two levers in here that unlatch the top part."

He showed him how it worked and opened it for him to inspect.

"Pretty goddamn clever," Saladino said, looking it over and feeling the doors and the empty shelves inside. "I still don't get how a bunch of snot-nosed kids got away with this."

"We were smart and lucky," David said.

Saladino backed away and looked over the patio and the back of the house. "Anyone living here now?"

"I know the people who live here," he said. "I told them we were going to be nosing around today."

They closed up the chimney and the two of them marveled at how the seams were still amazingly hidden.

David motioned to the gate. "I want to take you over to the apartment and show you some things there."

"So where the hell is everybody?" Saladino asked.

David glanced at his watch. "I wanted us to have some time. Don't worry, things will go fine."

Saladino gave him a look and knew he was being lied to.

They instructed their bodyguards to stay with the vehicles and walked across the opposite side of the alley and into the courtyard of the four-plexes.

"It's the last door down here," David explained and gestured for Saladino to go ahead. "We don't have to worry about anybody bothering us." He pointed along the walkway and across the lawn to the other four doors. "I own them, all eight of them. Nobody lives here."

Saladino looked him over. "No shit? They're just sitting here empty? A shrine?"

"Yeah, something like that." David opened the door and stepped in.

Saladino hesitated and glance back toward the alley where his men were waiting.

"I'll explain everything," David said. "Come on in." He reached and flipped the light switch. "You ever been here?"

The elder Saladino shook his head, stepped inside and David closed the door.

David walked the few steps to the kitchen and turned on the ceiling light. "Except for a few minor items the police removed for evidence, a new mattress and some pillows it's just like it was thirty-five years ago when Vincent was killed."

Saladino looked around at the walls crowded with paintings and the table tops strewn with assorted Vegas casino souvenirs. He reached down and picked up a black plastic ashtray with "The Dunes" printed in gold around the outside. "God, he sure cluttered up the place with a lot of shit." He looked around again. "He stole all that dough and he lived in this little dump?"

David nodded. "I guess he was saving it up for a big move that he never got to make. Come on down here." He walked down the short dimly lit hallway and turned left into the bedroom and turned on the ceiling light.

David seated himself in a small upholstered chair near the

head of the bed and motioned to a matching one near the foot for Saladino as he entered.

Saladino seated himself with a grunt and a sigh. "Okay, let's get the ball rolling. What the hell are we really doing here?"

David sat silently for a few seconds. "This is where it happened." He gestured to the bed. "Back on that day in 1968, this is where I found Vincent shot dead. He was sitting up in bed right here, bullet hole right here." He pointed to his own head just above his left eye.

Saladino nodded slowly as he looked over the now clean white sheets and blue comforter. "You didn't kill him?"

"I was twelve years old, what do you think?"

"What do I think?" Saladino said, tensing and showing a menacing smile. "I think you three little bastards were old enough to steal all that money, so who knows?"

"One of the reasons I brought you here was to tell you about that." David said. "Mary Kay killed Vincent."

"No, kidding?" Saladino said. "She was twelve."

"Tommy, the guy you have in custody, is her twin brother," David explained. "I want you to understand why that happened and I want you to keep in mind we were all kids. We were all twelve years old. You may already know that Vincent apparently liked girls and boys."

"I actually figured he was all queer," Saladino said.

David continued. "This room is just like it was then except there was just one of these chairs back then. On top of that safe was a .38 revolver that Saladino kept there when he was home. He had brought Mary Kay into his apartment a couple of times and touched her, and had her touch him. He told her if she told anyone he would hurt her brother. She was confused and scared, probably because her uncle had been molesting her occasionally for a couple of years. When she was talking about it later she said it didn't make sense to her why she went along with what Vincent wanted, but at the time she felt like she should. The day he was killed things went a little further. They were in here. He had all his clothes off and she had just her panties on. He was holding her hand and rubbing it all over him. In a suddenly brave moment she told him she didn't want to do this anymore and she was going to tell her mother. He said that was okay and he liked little boys better. He told her she didn't have to do this anymore if she would bring Tommy over so he could have some fun with him."

Saladino nodded. "So that's probably what he really wanted all along, the bastard."

"The way she describes it," David continued, "what happened next seemed to be a blur. She stepped over to the safe, picked up the gun and pointed it at Vincent. She had been shooting a few times with her father and an uncle so she knew a little about how to handle a gun, but she was no expert. She says it was heavy and she was pointing it at his balls. I guess he told her to put the gun down or he'd kill Tommy. The next thing she knew she pulled the trigger. She was surprised that it hit him in the head."

"What happened after she shot him?" Saladino asked.

"Tommy and I came over a minute later," David said. "We were going to help him paint over at the house. When he didn't answer I walked in. I found Mary Kay sitting by the safe sobbing. I calmed her down, put the gun in my pants, and told her everything would be okay and I would take care of us. She got dressed and I told her to go out the back, go home and just act like nothing happened and we would see her in a few minutes. A minute later Tommy came in. He never knew Mary Kay was the shooter. We took Vincent's keys and left."

"Well, I'm not sorry she killed him," Saladino said. "My two guys would've done the same later that night or the next morning. But not knowing who did it caused me a fucking shitload of problems. I even had this other guy killed 'because I was sure he did it, but, hey, he needed to be killed anyway." Nicolas Saladino shrugged, then pounded the arm of his chair. "But why the hell did you little fuckers take that money? That almost got me killed!"

"Listen," David said, "if your two guys had killed Vincent,

they wouldn't have found the money. Nobody knew about the chimney safe but us. The cops would have found him and then found out he owned that house and they would've discovered the safe just like they did, but with the money still in it, and you still would not have had the money."

Saladino was silent for a long time as he thought all that over. Finally he sighed and said, "I hate to say this but you're right. I'm sorry my pervert nephew put that little girl through all that."

"I'm not done," David said. "I have a couple more things that I know you will be very interested in."

The old man looked him over. "It's kind of creepy in here, don't you think? Can we move to the living room or something?"

Atop one of the storage containers, lying down behind some boxes, was a man with powerful binoculars watching Johnny Saladino. Next to him was a small radio transmitter. A hundred yards closer to Johnny and his companions, three other men were each lying comfortably on foam pads in the deep shadow inside the concrete pipes. Each man was watching Johnny Saladino or one of his companions through the scope attached to his SR 25, one of the world's best sniper rifles. Stationed at strategic positions, well hidden in the surrounding hills, were another four spotters just to make sure that no curious bystanders, day hikers or men sent by Saladino were witnessing the activities below.

Silver State Ground Prep Company had filed a permit with Clark County to do some blasting in the area during several days in October in preparation for underground utilities construction. The cracks of the three quick rifle shots were not noticed by anyone in the neighborhoods three miles away or anyone else in the surrounding emptiness. A few seconds later the first of three larger blasts were heard and felt by quite a number of people, but caused no alarm. There had been a few of them a day for the past several days and they were due to continue for a few more days as more of the desert came under attack by the encroaching tentacles of expanding Las Vegas.

Two minutes later, after the camouflage netting was removed, two heavy duty trucks each carrying six men and towing a flatbed trailer, one with a bulldozer and one with a power shovel, emerged from behind the storage containers stirring up a swirl of dust as they sped toward the Mercedes. Next to the car were Johnny Saladino and his two body guards, lying dead on the ground, dutifully awaiting their next move?

David knew it was a risk to have this many people involved in an operation that needed to stay secret, but he felt very confident about the security of these men for two reasons. First of all, they were all vouched for by Mr. Ed and that by itself was worth a lot. Secondly, they had all been paid a large amount of cash to do a professional job and then to forget about it.

Thirty yards on the other side of the car was the edge of the newly formed crater. Before sunset the crew and their machines would enlarge, shape and reshape the blasted, fractured desert. Monday the asphalt and concrete trucks and the laborers would arrive at their expertly smoothed and prepped area ready to extend civilization a little bit farther into the desert.

At the end of that day, eighteen feet beneath a pristine new residential intersection, Johnny Saladino, his bodyguards and a ninety-thousand dollar luxury automobile would all begin their first full day of never being seen again.

It would've been cheaper and easier, too easy David thought, to just pick up the bodies and take them somewhere else to disappear. This way was more challenging, more entertaining, and had way more style, even if he would never get to enjoy anyone's appreciation of the scheme.

David and Saladino moved to the living room and seated themselves in two stuffed chairs facing each other overlooking a cluttered coffee table.

"Like I said, there are several things you should know," David said. "First of all, my men have secured the alley. Your guys have been disarmed and are being guarded."

Saladino stiffened, "What the fuck's going on?" he snarled.

"Just sit tight and take it easy," David said. "Nobody's been hurt and if everything goes right we're all going to drive away from here in a little while and go back to our lives. Johnny told you that he was showing up here with Tommy, right?"

Saladino shook his head. "No, I was just supposed to meet and wait to hear from Johnny about what we were going to do with you. I'm just stalling you."

David nodded. "He thinks he sent you on a wild goose chase here while he is going to make a phony exchange for Tommy at a meeting place in the middle of nowhere just south of Vegas. He plans to take out a couple of my people at that meeting, but that won't be happening. You should know that Johnny thinks I'm going to kill you here today. He's okay with that and he thinks he's getting an extra ten million for his trouble."

Saladino seemed calm and unsurprised. "You gonna kill me?"

"Depends on how this conversation goes," David said, "and if I think I can trust you."

Saladino chuckled softly. "Shit, can I trust you?"

"We'll see," David said. "Here's what I want. I want Tommy to be released. I want you to take the twenty million and leave us alone forever. Johnny's a dead man because I do not trust him to keep his word to let Tommy go or to not come after us."

Saladino took a deep breath and sighed. He looked around the small room. "Why have I been cursed with such shitty nephews? So, you don't need my permission to take out Johnny, do you?"

"True," David said. He glanced at his watch. "In fact if everything is running on schedule I should be getting a call soon confirming he is dead. But I wanted you to know why and that he was giving you up. By the way, he and his two bodyguards will be disappearing. Nobody will be seeing any of the three again."

"Wouldn't it be easier to just kill me than to trust me?" Saladino said.

"I considered it," David said, "but I need you. I want you to call off everyone else. I want your word that we're declared off limits. Nobody comes after me, Mary Kay, Tommy or any of our families or anyone connected to us. In return, like I said, you walk out of here with twenty million and you and I become silent partners. You can call on me if you ever need anything."

Saladino raised his eyebrows. "Like what?"

David shrugged. "I know a lot of the right people and I have a ton of money. In this world, a ton of money can accomplish a lot of shit, for both of us. A stack of money can open mouths, close mouths, change people's minds, convince people to do things or not do things. It can do a lot. But I want this deal to work both ways. I can call on you too. There might be things I need done that would take something other than money. You might have access to just the right people with just the right skills and the abilities to accomplish things in ways that I just can't, or won't. You know I'm opening a hotel casino in Vegas soon and that could come in handy."

Saladino nodded slowly to himself. "So, you're buying your way into working with me?"

"That's one way to put it," David said.

"Okay, let's say I agree to all that," Saladino said. "What happens next?"

David's cell phone buzzed. He picked it up from the table and listened, glanced at his watch then hung up. "That was about Johnny. It's done. There are several people guarding the house where Tommy is being kept in Las Vegas. I'm pretty sure Johnny has left instructions for Tommy not to make it out of there alive. Can you call them off?"

Saladino shook his head. "Don't even know who's there. In fact I don't know where it is except he mentioned it's out by Red Rock. But, you're right about Johnny not releasing your guy. He figured all three of you were going down today, and I know something else that I think you don't know."

"Okay, maybe we can start building some trust right now," David said. "I know where the house is, but what do I not know?"

Saladino studied his wristwatch, "Their orders are to kill your boy and torch the house in exactly an hour and fifteen minutes."

David sighed. "In a half hour or so, a few people I know are going to storm that house. My people are good, real good, and I think they can get Tommy out of there alive. If they can't and Tommy is killed then we need to do some more talking and maybe you do die here today." David stood and walked to the refrigerator, took out two bottles of beer, twisted off the caps and set one bottle in front of Saladino.

Saladino took a long swallow and set the bottle down. "Let's hope your people are as good as you say."

Inside the house on a quiet street in the southern end of Summerlin, a community running along the northwestern edge of Las Vegas near Red Rock, Tommy was sitting in a recliner in the bedroom that had been his prison for several days, sipping straight vodka from a plastic glass and thumbing through that day's USA Today. He had finally convinced his captors to supply him with something other than a couple of cans of beer, but he was anything but relaxed. They figured he deserved it since it was to be his last day. Tommy figured he deserved it because he was goddamn sick and tired of being held prisoner in this house and it was beginning to piss him off.

It was three days ago when he had plugged in the desk phone from the closet and called David. As soon as he got him on the line he quickly explained the situation then followed David's instructions to keep the line open for a few minutes. He shoved the phone under the bed in case one of his guards came in while David had people trace the number and the address. After a few minutes he picked up the phone and David told him to be ready on Saturday. Then he quickly unhooked the old phone, wound up the cord and placed it back on the closet shelf.

If he got out of this mess he had decided he was going to ask David how in the hell he would have found him if he hadn't made that call.

In the living room, two of his guards, Arty and John, were looking at the television while Arty endlessly flipped through channels to find something they both could agree to watch.

"Yeah, ESPN, that's good," John said. "Wait and see what's coming after the commercial."

Arty set the remote down on the table in front of him. He checked his watch for the fifth time in the last five minutes. "We've only got forty-five minutes."

John waved a dismissive hand. "Don't worry. All our stuff is in the car. I'll take care of Tommy boy."

Arty eyed the gas can sitting by the closet door across the room.

The third man, Gabe, was in the hall bathroom, on the toilet, thumbing through the latest issue of Maxim magazine.

It was a mild October morning and the front door was open with just a screen door to let in the cool air. Arty got up, as he had also done five times in the last few minutes, paced to the kitchen and back to the living room. He heard a noise from outside and walked to the screen door. "Hey, there's some good-looking chick across the street. Looks like she's selling something."

Mary Kay was just walking away from the front door of the house across the street. She had a clipboard in one hand and a briefcase in the other with a long rectangular cardboard box squeezed under her arm against her side. She stopped on the sidewalk and pretended to study something on her clipboard, hoping the men in the house across the street would see her, become less suspicious rather than having her surprise them when she came to the door.

David had called Howie on the way here and told him they were now on a time limit and what Nicolas Saladino had told him about the plan to kill Tommy at a specified time. That call had taken away any apprehension Mary Kay may have had about gunning down whoever was at the door. She had already made up her mind that there was no way around it, but after the call she had taken on an even stronger resolve. Initially they were rescuing him from his captors. Now they were saving him from his would-be killers.

She unzipped her tank top a little more and fanned herself unnecessarily with the clipboard as she looked up and down the street, knowing that it moved her shoulder length hair a bit and hoping it made her even more interesting and non-threatening.

She knew she looked good enough to pull this off.

In the driveway next door, just out of sight from the front of the target house, Howie and Mr. Ed were sitting in the Escalade behind dark tinted windows, waiting and watching. After dropping off Mary Kay down the street they had quickly added U.S. Marshals Service markings on the side and back of the vehicle. Mr. Ed knew from past experience this would cause most nosy neighbors to hesitate to interfere when the commotion started. At both ends of the block was a parked car with three of Mr. Ed's crew in each one just in case they were needed.

"Hey, she's walking over here," Arty reported.

"Good," John said. "I haven't even seen her, but I know she's better-looking than you."

Arty laughed. "I think you're right." He checked his watch again and chuckled, happy for the distraction from thinking about what he did not want to do soon.

Mary Kay walked to the small front porch, set her briefcase down, moved the clipboard to her left hand and set the tall cardboard box standing up in front of her. She rang the doorbell and reached into the top of the box and wrapped her right hand around the shotgun's pistol grip, her index finger just to the side of the trigger.

Arty opened the screen door hoping to get a closer look at her, a goofy smile on his face. Standing in the middle of the room several feet behind him was John, holding his 9mm Glock behind his back, a little wary but mostly just checking her out.

Mary Kay moved the clipboard behind her back and waved it back and forth several times to let Howie and Mr. Ed know that the door was open.

"Hello, gentlemen. My name is Magdalena and I have two reasons for coming to your door today. The first is a very short survey. Seriously it will only take about two minutes. Then, depending on your answers, I have a few product samples to show you and really that will also only take a minute or two."

She could see Arty's gaze shifting from her eyes to her

cleavage and back several times. In the next few seconds several things happened in quick succession.

As Arty was asking, "What kind of products?" Howie went over the side fence to the back of the house, Mary Kay dropped the clipboard and threw the box off the shotgun. Mr. Ed sprinted to the living room window, a concussion grenade and a Mac 11 in one hand, a large landscaping rock from the flower bed in the other. In the bathroom, Gabe had just flushed the toilet and was zipping his pants. As Mr. Ed reached the window, Mary Kay fired twice at Arty standing right in front of her and twice more at John behind him. She caught both men in the upper abdomen and chest, spewing blood and tissue throughout the living room. They both received the walloping devastation of 54 pellets of #4 buckshot from a 12 gauge shotgun at close range and were now quite dead. As planned, she saved one shell for whatever popped up next and threw herself down flat in the doorway.

At the same time, Mr. Ed smashed a hole in the front window with the cantaloupe sized rock and tossed in the concussion grenade as he continued to the front door. The grenade went off, breaking several more windows in the house and knocking items off shelves and tables. He then stepped over Mary Kay into the living room, dropped a .40 caliber semi-automatic in front of her, and shouted "Tommy, stay down!"

Howie kicked in the French doors from the back patio and stepped into the dining area, quickly checking the kitchen and signaling all clear to Mr. Ed.

Mr. Ed pointed and hurried to the hallway that led to the bedrooms and bathrooms in the back of the house followed closely by Howie.

Gabe had already switched off the bathroom light, picked up his .45 caliber revolver, opened the bathroom door halfway and stepped behind it waiting for whatever was to come next as the two men rushed right by the bathroom.

Mr. Ed slapped on the hall light and sprinted to the end of the hallway to the open master bedroom. Finding nothing, he turned and hurried to the next door, also open, showing another small bedroom.

Howie was standing at the door to Tommy's room, pointing at the padlock securing the door. Together they waited for just a second then Mr. Ed threw his weight against the door, breaking the door frame and flinging the door open.

Both men crashed into the room, Howie crouched low, Mr. Ed standing tall, Mac 11's at the ready. Neither of them had yet to fire a shot.

Tommy rose slowly from behind the recliner, hands in the air. Both men relaxed and looked relieved. "Tommy," Howie greeted.

"Anyone in there?" Mr. Ed asked, pointing to the adjoining bathroom.

Tommy shook his head.

"Let's get out of here," Howie said, as he grabbed Tommy by the arm hurrying him to the living room.

Mary Kay was standing just inside the front door, shotgun at the ready, pistol tucked into her waistband. "Tommy!" she took two steps toward him and hugged him.

"Hey, M.K." he greeted.

"Gotta go!" Mr. Ed prompted. "He grabbed Tommy and pushed him toward Howie at the front door. "Let's go," he said to Mary Kay as he walked by her.

She was turning to follow them when Tommy, just stepping out onto the porch, having seen the two dead men on the floor, said, "Hey, where's Gabe?"

"Another guy, shit!" Howie pushed Tommy toward Mr. Ed, then stepped back into the living room to hurry Mary Kay. As he did so, Gabe stepped out of the darkened bathroom, emerged from the hall, leveled his gun in the direction of Mary Kay and Howie and opened fire.

Mary Kay was facing Howie, just as he leaned to his right and fired a quick burst from his fully automatic weapon, hitting Gabe seven times in a line from his left knee up to his jaw, but it was too late. Gabe had fired three shots. One of them missed wide, the second one caught Mary Kay in the outside left shoulder and the third hit Howie square in the chest.

Howie watched Gabe fall and looked down at his own chest. It had felt like someone punched him. A blood spot showed but he wasn't feeling much pain. Mary Kay looked at him, he grabbed her good arm and ran with her out the door toward the Escalade along with Tommy and Mr. Ed.

As he ran, the nick in his aorta separated further and by the time he reached the Escalade, it had torn wide open and was gushing blood into his chest cavity. They jumped in, Mr. Ed took the wheel and they sped away down the street. It had only been seventy-five seconds since Mary Kay had fired the first shot.

"Mary Kay!" Tommy shouted, looking down at her blood-soaked shoulder.

"I think I'm okay," she said. "Howie's bad."

Howie was sprawled awkwardly next to her, knees on the floor and torso on the seat face down. The exit wound in the center of his back had blood-soaked his entire shirt and more was still bubbling up but slowing. He had stopped breathing and his blood pressure was near zero. His heart was slowly going through the motions of its last couple of contractions.

Mr. Ed turned the corner and slammed on the brakes. He jumped out the driver's door and jerked open the door on Howie's side. After lifting him up, checking his wounds and looking for a pulse he gently put him back in his face down position. Quickly checking Mary Kay's wound, he reached in the back, grabbed a towel and pushed it against her shoulder. "Keep pressure on it. Nothing too serious. We'll get you fixed up and you'll be fine."

He got back behind the wheel and sighed. "Howie's dead."

He waited several seconds then put the shifter back into drive and continued down the street. A few blocks away they pulled over and moved Howie's body into the car that had followed with Mr. Ed's men. Tommy, Mary Kay and Mr. Ed hurried into a white SUV and continued on their way.

Two days later, David, Mary Kay and Tommy gathered for another "annual meeting" aboard the Chimney Sweep, moored at Bell Harbor in Puget Sound. Following some minor surgery on her shoulder at a very private clinic, Mary Kay and Tommy had spent some time together flying in from Las Vegas and then waiting half a day for David to arrive onboard.

After some quick hugs, kisses and greetings, David showered, changed clothes and joined them in the salon of the yacht. They were spaced around the leather sectional in the sunken seating area of the space, all of them feeling a combination of exhausted and adrenalin-pumped after their ordeal of the last two days.

"Did you take care of Howie?" Mary Kay asked.

David nodded. "All taken care of. His sister still lives in Bakersfield and she said he wanted to be cremated and didn't want any kind of service. I referred her to one of our funeral homes there and let her know there would be no charge."

Mary Kay nodded slowly and gave David a questioning look.

"So how are you doing Tommy?" David asked.

Tommy took a swallow from his drink and let out a long sigh. "Great now. That was a pretty hairy deal. Those guys treated me okay but they wouldn't give me enough booze."

David and Mary Kay shared a look and a smile.

Mary Kay leaned over and put her hand on her brother's knee. "I didn't want to bring it up there or on the plane but we got there maybe a half hour before they were going to kill you and set the house on fire. That's why it didn't really bother me taking out those two who answered the door."

Tommy glanced at David and got a nod of confirmation. "I thought they were being extra nice that morning. That's pretty scary. We might not be sitting here, huh?"

Their eyes darted around as the three exchanged quick looks.

"So who was that guy Mr. Ed?" Tommy asked. "Where did he come from?"

Bringing back his impression of Detective Lassiter from the summer of 1968, David answered, "Can't tell you, can't tell anybody."

Tommy took just a second to remember the comment and turned expectantly to his sister.

Mary Kay was staring hard at David as the barest hint of a smile came to her eyes. "I've only got one good arm at the moment, but I'll put you on your ass again!"

Tommy slapped his seat cushion and laughed out loud while David and Mary Kay pointed at each other smiling widely.

"Seriously I can't tell you and you really don't want to know," David said. "He's a one of a kind. It's kind of complicated but I met him accidentally through a business acquaintance eight or ten years ago. He's definitely not the kind of guy I would think I would ever get to know at all but we hit it off. It was a damn good thing I had him to call on. He's ex-military, ex-mercenary, and ex-a lot of other stuff. Never know who you might need. He's returning a large chunk of the money I paid him to take out Johnny and his crew and to plan your rescue. He feels really bad about Howie and says it's his fault. That guy came from the bathroom that he should've cleared but he and Howie ran right by it to Tommy's room. Anyway, we should all be safe from now on. I had a long talk and came to an agreement with Nicolas Saladino. It's over and our safety is guaranteed now by him personally. Cost twenty million and he's happy."

Mary Kay looked hopefully at David. "Are you sure we can trust him?"

"No," David said. "but I've made a good deal here. He and the people around him would be fools not to abide by the agreement. But there's no guarantee that another lone wolf like Howie won't pop up."

They were all silent for a bit as they thought over the implications of finally not having to worry about the mob anymore. David was doing his best to make them feel good. Their situation was much better but it still wasn't perfect. He knew he still needed to keep control as much as possible and he knew that no matter what happened, he would never be relieved from his job of protecting them and their secret.

"And Johnny is really gone?" Mary Kay asked.

"Johnny Saladino is as gone as gone can get," David said. "And Uncle Nic is just fine with it."

With no emotion Mary Kay said, "David stopped me from killing him when he told us they were holding you prisoner."

Tommy shook his head and let out a quick laugh. "I would've liked to see that whole scene. I bet you scared the shit out of him."

"She did," David said, "and me too. Listen, I have a question for both of you. I've been putting some thought into this. They're still just doing the foundation and underground infrastructure stuff. We can call it off at this point or find a buyer who wants to finish it out their way. We still want to go forward with Chill?"

"Absolutely," Mary Kay said. "We thought it would be our coming-out party and it sure as hell was a coming out. I think we're in even better shape to enjoy it now. You say we are protected from the mob and I still think it will be fun to create it and watch people enjoy it. What about you Tommy?"

"I agree. Let's do it."

"Great," David said. He stood and walked to a small closet in the corner. "I was thinking this over a lot on the flight back here." He pulled out a tube of papers and returned to the seating area, unrolling them out onto the table in the center.

"Oh good," Mary Kay said clapping. "The design ideas."

All three of them sat up and leaned forward to get a good look.

"So you remember this restaurant area where we penciled in some ideas? I still like calling this café Mary Kay's or maybe just MK. We've got plenty of time to finalize that. But the steak place in the corner here, what do you think of calling it Howie's?"

"Great idea," Tommy said. "I like that."

Mary Kay was nodding agreement. "I wish he was here instead of us just talking about him." She sighed. "It's not fair that he had to pay the price. I was starting to like him and, Tommy, I don't know if rescuing you would have worked without him."

David grabbed a pencil and wrote in the name for the future steak restaurant.

"Okay, I've got another idea," David said. "I'm not sure if it's dopey or cool. Won't mean anything except to us, but that's okay." He rolled out another design sheet showing the floor plan for the western half of the casino. "Okay on this side we've got two wide walkways and a long two-sided bar in between. I was thinking…"

"I already know what you're going to say," Tommy said. He stood to reach the table better and put his finger down onto the paper. "The two walking areas, street signs naming them First Street and Second Street. The bar in between can be The Alley Bar."

David had a growing grin. "Exactly."

"It's cool," Tommy said. "Way cool. I don't care if anyone else gets it, we do."

"Sure," said Mary Kay. "I like it. It's kind of dopey and cool."

Tommy sat and drained the last of his drink. "So the sports store with that great golf pro department is still going to be Tommy's, right?"

"Still sounds good to me," David said.

"So what about you?" Mary Kay asked. "Something going to be called David's?"

Tommy stood and walked to the galley counter to make himself another screwdriver. "Maybe the casino cage, huh? Or maybe the whole damn place."

"Tommy may have an idea there," Mary Kay said. "I know you don't care if anything gets your name on it. The world is going to know it as Chill, but to me, to us, it's going to be David's Place."

David smiled a small smile. "Thanks. By the way, it's right next door to The Rio which is pretty big and been sitting there by itself across the freeway from the Strip. Opening Chill will be good for both of us. We can feed off each other and bring people across from the strip to visit both places. Also, we still need to keep in mind that even though we don't need to worry about the mob so much anymore wanting their long-lost money, we still need to keep it a secret. The less information we put out there the better. We still don't want to attract any extra attention from the IRS, the cops, somebody from the old days thinking they can shake us down, or another fucking kidnapping. I'm sure people would be interested but we don't want our real story out there.

People might start asking too many questions and finding out more than we want them to."

David looked back and forth between the twins, wanting what he just said to really sink in. Tommy nodded and leaned over to examine the casino design plans.

Mary Kay nodded as well, and continued locking eyes with David. "Absolutely," she said.

THIRTEEN

September, 2005

David and Mary Kay were standing behind darkened glass in a second-level VIP room overlooking Chill's casino floor. Below them was the central rectangular area of the sprawling 160,000 square foot casino. From their vantage point they could see the central main casino area, the mezzanine level that ran around the perimeter of the main casino floor, the entrances to several of the restaurants, the top of the wide staircase leading down to a lower lever with shops and more restaurants, and three wide openings leading from the casino floor to the hotel lobby and more shops and restaurants. In the center of the casino floor was the very long Alley Bar with First Street and Second Street running along each side of it, paved in black with a street sign at each end.

In keeping with the visual theme of Chill, various sizes of "icicles" hung down from the high ceiling, some of them dripping into pools and fountains below.

Mary Kay pointed to a wide section of the mezzanine level about halfway across the casino. "He is loving this." She was smiling widely and genuinely enjoying watching her brother.

"And it fits right in with his concept of giving away all our money," David said.

Tommy was holding court. With a putter in his right hand he was addressing the crowd of about a hundred who had gathered to see just what the man was up to. Standing on a platform that put him just a couple of feet above the growing crowd, every thirty seconds or so as he spoke, he was tossing a crumpled up bill into the crowd. Some were just ones, but several had been fives, a few had been twenties and, so far, two of them had been hundreds.

"If any of you are interested in golf, you are in the right place," Tommy shouted. "We have a beautiful driving range just behind the property and adjacent to that, and just about to open in the next week or so, is the most amazing miniature golf course you've ever seen. We don't have our own regular course but there are several close by and we have all kinds of specials for play there and free transportation to and from."

He tossed another crumpled bill into the crowd. The woman who caught it opened it and began squealing and hopping up and down. "It's a hundred dollar bill!" she shrieked, and returned to her squealing.

"Our miniature course is called Double Trouble," Tommy continued. "It's the damndest thing you've ever seen. It's a spectacle that you'll want to see even if you don't play on it. It's huge and I guarantee it will make you think of the Caddy Shack movies, but no gophers! At least I hope not. Every hole has an adult starting tee and a kid's tee. That way the kiddies can play along with the parents and the parents can actually be challenged along the way. Or, if you're just feeling lazy, or maybe you've had too much to drink, go the kiddie route! Or switch back and forth as you go through the course. Some of the holes are shorter, some longer. And of course at the end is the Nineteenth Hole. Just a small bar with a few tables and some very attractive cocktail servers." He tossed another bill to a woman right in front. It turned out to be a twenty, which produced just as much squealing and commotion as the hundred had.

With 2800 rooms, seven restaurants, and a variety of shops big and small, Chill, Las Vegas' newest mega hotel casino, was still in the midst of their "grand opening" celebration activities even though they had officially been open for six weeks. Construction had taken just over a year and a half and the cost came in at just under 1.5 billion dollars. Reflecting the same theme and design elements as the inside, all around the exterior of the huge building "icicles" of various sizes hung from the roof's edge and from other levels around the building. Some were several stories in length and what appeared to be melt water fell from them into pools and fountains below. David, Mary Kay and Tommy had gone to great expense to get the design right and the result was spectacular. The illusion of giant melting icicles had been a popular topic on local news channels and had even made several appearances in the national news and celebrity gossip shows.

Up behind the darkened glass, David was watching Mary Kay's genuine smile as she watched her brother. He had to admit he was enjoying all the hoopla surrounding the opening of Chill more than he thought he would.

Over the nearly two years of meetings with architects, designers and construction bosses, it had all gone smoothly and the process had been both interesting and energizing, but as with everything in his life he could only enjoy it to a certain extent. He knew he should feel relieved compared to what their situation had been for most of the past thirty-seven years, and in many ways he did. But with the attention a new mega resort hotel and casino brought he was constantly working to keep their personalities mostly behind the scenes and out of the the public awareness beyond brief mentions.

But one of his main concerns was still dealing with the mob. He had been in regular contact with Saladino's representatives and they had repeatedly assured him that the three of them and everyone they knew were indeed protected. He no longer had to worry about keeping the secret from them about what had happened but it was still a secret to the world at large. The real problem now was that he didn't trust them. David was certain the fact that they had gotten away with taking such a huge amount of mob money, kept it a secret for so long and now turned it into such an obvious display of wealth and success rubbed some of the organized crime figures the wrong way. He felt that if some "young gun" came along and wanted to make a name for himself, they could still be in some danger.

So he had decided to keep doing all he could to make sure their stock in the organization was so well thought of that maybe nobody would consider going against the status quo. Which was exactly the reason for the meeting he was about to attend.

He tapped Mary Kay on the arm. "My meeting with Ape Face is in a few minutes. Have fun watching Tommy."

Mary Kay slowly shook her head and gave him a grin. "You're going to mess up and call him that to his face someday. Hey, you haven't mentioned your headaches lately. What did the doctor say?"

"He said they could be stress related," David said. "They've been a little better, maybe."

She reached and caressed his arm. "You had the dream again last night. That's several times in just the last couple of weeks."

"I'm fine," he said, "Go on down and walk the property if you get bored. Give away some more money. It's fun."

She watched him as he walked away and wondered again, as she had several times lately, what was going on with him. There was something different about him over the last few months that she couldn't quite figure out and it wasn't just the headaches or the dream. Stressed? Nervous? Tired? She wasn't sure. But she didn't feel good about whatever it was and it was always on her mind lately.

Like all casinos in Las Vegas, Chill was under the constant scrutiny of the Nevada Gaming Commission. Compared to the free-wheeling days of the 50s and 60s, the business was now tightly controlled by the state. Any hint of cheating or money diversions to avoid taxes came with the very real threat of losing your gaming license. The state now prided itself for having brought the gambling industry to modern respectability and long ago broken the hold that organized crime once had on it, although it had never been cleaned of mob influence to the extent they liked to advertise or believe. Operating in that climate made certain things more challenging for David Steiner, but he knew plenty about how to make supposedly impossible financial situations work.

David walked into the private office where he knew the man was waiting for him. "Mr. Opificio, good to see you. Something to drink?" He walked to the bar in the corner and poured himself a Wild Turkey on ice.

"Whatever you're having is fine," Opificio said.

Anton Opificio was the man who lately was most often in contact from the Saladino organization. He was in his early forties and no real boss of any kind as far as David could tell, but he seemed to be one of their more important errand runners with some kind of limited authority and a direct line to Nicholas Saladino.

David handed him his drink. "So, you mentioned yesterday that you might need some help with a gaming agent. If it involves infusing some money into the situation, I'm pretty sure I can help."

"I appreciate that," he said. "This is a little more delicate than money. I have a member of the gaming commission in my pocket, as the old-timers used to call it. It's not an easy thing these days. They are well paid with good retirement systems and health benefits. But I have someone who likes the idea of an extra $5,000 a month coming in. As you are well aware, it's always good to have a little influence to call on if you need it. I've had him on my payroll for a couple of years but now he may have become a problem for both of us."

"Really?" David said. "Let's hear about it."

Fifteen minutes later, David walked up beside Mary Kay as she strolled slowly through the main casino space.

She smiled and patted his butt. "So how'd your meeting go with you-know-who?"

"Went fine," he said. "He brought up a concern though. It's about Tommy, but don't worry. He thinks it's handled."

Mary Kay said nothing but turned her head toward him and put on an expectant look as they continued walking.

"According to him," David continued, "there is a local gaming commission agent who they are having a little trouble with. The guy has been on the take to them for a number of years and for some reason he has let them know lately that he has recorded some conversations and created some written accounts of just what has transpired between him and the organization. Says he has copies of these somewhere and if anything happens to him they will be made public."

"Does he think it's going to keep him safe?" Mary Kay asked.

"Ape Face thinks it may actually work for a while," David said. "They are going to work on who knows where the information is."

"So how is this connected to Tommy?"

"It isn't really," David said, "According to Ape Face this guy brought up Tommy out of nowhere and said something like he's going to bring down that asshole golfer one way or the other."

"What the hell?" Mary Kay said, her anger rising. "Why?"

"I guess they asked him about it but he wouldn't say anything. So he had a couple guys look into it and it looks like it has to do with back when Tommy was trying to break into the PGA. You remember there were qualifying tournaments and it seems that Tommy and this guy kept coming up in the same qualifying rounds and Tommy kept beating him. There were some words exchanged along the way and I guess this guy has been blaming Tommy for years for him never making it in pro golf."

"Oscar Ramone," she said.

David looked surprised. "So you know about this guy?"

"I remember the name from hearing Tommy complain about him. So what do they think he meant by bringing him down? How?"

David sighed, regretting he had even brought it up to her. "Some confusing stuff about finances and taxes and theft. They're not sure where to go from here since they don't know exactly what he's got on them and if he really has plans to release damaging information. This guy worries me." He stopped walking, turned toward her and lowered his voice to a hoarse whisper. "And don't go getting any ideas that you should try to fix this problem! We don't want to mess up anything the organization has planned for him. I didn't get the impression Ramone was planning anything right away. I'll keep you informed."

They resumed walking. "Okay," she said. But she had no intention of following what he had just said and he knew it.

Jerry was already seated at a booth in a small, worn out Mexican restaurant called El Matador waiting for Mary Kay. She walked in and he waved her over to the table, thinking as he often had that she was still one of the best-looking women he had ever known. But he knew better than to think that was her strongest asset.

As requested, the owner had kept the booth on each side of theirs and a small table close by empty. She slid into the booth across the table from him and set a file folder between them. "So how you like my favorite dive restaurant?"

"So far so good," he said and washed down a mouthful of chips. "Sounds simple but not everybody has great chips. These are great." He pointed to the folder. "So what have you got for me? I remember the last time we met in a restaurant you had a laughter orgasm."

Mary Kay smiled and softly chuckled under her breath. "Yeah, I did. This one isn't funny and it gets complicated. Names and key points are in the folder. Here's the rundown. Some guy named Oscar Ramone is a gaming board agent on the take to the mob. He has come up with some scheme that he thinks is going to keep him safe. I think it's going to get him killed. He's got some information that he says he will release if anything happens to him. I don't really care so much about that, but I am curious about just what he's got on them. Here's the part I really care about. He mentioned to someone, who then let David know, that he's holding a grudge against Tommy and wants to bring him down too."

"A grudge?" Jerry asked.

"Back when they were both trying to break into the PGA. He thinks Tommy kept him from succeeding and at the time there were some hard feelings between them. It's stupid crap, but I need you to find out what he's got on Tommy. It could be something that would affect all three of us. Also, on the mob info, who he has holding the information or how it is stored to be released if anything happens to him. It must be something big or really sensitive for them to not just kill him outright."

Jerry nodded and chewed for a bit. "So you're more interested in what he's got on Tommy but you'd like me to find out the other if I can."

"Exactly," she said, "but we have to make sure the information about Tommy won't be released if something happens to Ramone."

Jerry opened the folder and scanned the names and facts on the first page. "Well, damn Mary Kay, this is a bit of a hairy one, organized crime and all. Is this going to be worth all the trouble and risk I'm taking on?"

She shook her head slowly and smiled. "Have I ever let you down? I'm giving you ten thousand today just to get you started. Depending on how successful you are, you think twenty grand will get you by?"

"I think that will do just fine," he said. He glanced at his watch and stood. "You said you're sticking around and eating with Tommy when he gets here, so I'm going to take off and get to work on this."

"Okay, Jerry. Nice seeing you again and good luck with this."

As she waited for her brother, Mary Kay mulled over again, as she had done increasingly often lately, what was going on with David. She was so engrossed in her thoughts that she didn't notice Tommy walking in and was startled by his sudden appearance.

"Hey M.K," he said as he plopped into the booth across from her that Jerry had vacated. A second later the server set a drink in front of him.

"Hey yourself," she answered. "You know I'm very proud of

you for cutting back so much on your drinking the last few months, but I knew you couldn't be in this place without at least one margarita."

He took a long sip. "You're just an enabler. Seriously, the whole designing and opening of Chill and the golf thing has just occupied my mind, in a good way. But don't worry, I won't be attending any AA meetings or anything."

"I didn't think so. Okay, we almost started a conversation the other day that I wanted to continue in a little more depth."

"David?" he said. "You know what's up with him these days?"

"No," she said, "but I'm concerned. He keeps bringing up the old neighborhood and the four-plexes. I guess maybe we all do once in a while, but he just starts talking about it right in the middle of other stuff."

Tommy nodded. "Like the other day, I was having breakfast with him over at the Rio."

Mary Kay raised her eyebrows and patted his hand to stop him. "You were having breakfast?"

"Well, yeah, but it was around noon," he explained, smiling. "Anyway, we were talking about how good the reaction has been on the minigolf and he says, 'Did you ever think it was weird that we hardly ever saw the other people who were living right around Vincent in the four-plex or the other four across the grass? I remember a couple of them but mostly nobody was ever out and about, watering their plants, getting their mail or whatever. So I think I kind of stared for a second before I answered and told him that yeah, we never saw anybody much and maybe they were afraid of Vincent."

Mary Kay was nodding. "When we're together lately, he does bring up things out of nowhere from back in the day. He never used to do that very much and, thinking back over this the last few months, I think it's a lot more often than I even realized. And the other thing is, he has randomly brought up the name Max a few times. I asked him and he says he is some computer geek that used to work for our company and he sometimes has him do errands and computer searches." She stopped and sighed.

"And he just seems, I don't know, different lately."

"Yeah," Tommy said, "but I don't know exactly what I mean either. He's been really busy with the opening of Chill. Maybe he just has brain overload."

"Maybe," she said, but she didn't really think that was it. "He's been complaining about headaches and have you heard him do that little nervous giggle? That's new. And he sometimes just laughs at loud at odd times."

Tommy nodded. "I have noticed that a few times, and it's kind of random where it doesn't really seem to fit the conversation. So, what do we think?"

Mary Kay shrugged. "He's been having his disturbing dream more often and not sleeping well. I don't know but let's keep sharing whatever we see, okay?"

Tommy nodded. "Yeah. In the meantime, I'm hungry and I'm ordering another drink."

It was just a few days later when Jerry called Mary Kay for a meeting, so she had them meet in El Matador again. They had just settled in at the same table and spent a couple of minutes on idle small talk.

Jerry tapped the folder that he had set on the table. "I think I have found out some interesting stuff for you. It was a bit confusing at first but I had a couple of lucky sources that got to the bottom of this deal pretty fast. What I've turned up changes what you thought was going on."

"Really?" Mary Kay said. "Again, this is why I keep you on the payroll. Sounds interesting. So what've you got for me?"

"Details are in the folder, but here's the main stuff. The mob, or more accurately I think, a couple of mob guys, don't seem to be having any contact at all with Oscar Ramone. They have been watching him and we caught a few snippets of conversation where they are talking about him." He opened the folder and glanced at the first page. "Anton Opificio and Denny White have met several times and they are the ones passing along that he has some information that would hurt the mob. But, they are just using his name. They have some financial shenanigans information that's designed to expose some things about your brother Tommy. We're pretty damn sure these two jokers, Opificio and White, are working on their own and trying to pull some kind of scam on their bosses. It looks like they're going to make it look like they saved their bosses from some kind of trouble from this guy Ramone."

"I know that one name," Mary Kay said. "So Ramone is not pressuring them that he has information they don't want exposed?"

Jerry nodded. "They are creating the whole thing themselves and Ramone doesn't know what's up at all. These two are just trying to use this whole charade of a feud between your brother and Ramone to take out your brother and blame it on Ramone. They're probably going to end up taking out both of them to play up their phony story. I did find out the keeper of their phony information is some computer geek named Max Nguyen. I don't have any current employment info but at one time he worked for your DMT Company. He's kind of dropped off the grid since then, but I did manage to find a current address. He lives in Bakersfield."

Mary Kay stared at Jerry for a few moments then reached and opened the folder and saw the address on Second Street. "I'll be damned," she said softly. "The Boyd's house."

FOURTEEN

David hung up the phone, leaned back in his desk chair and tried to figure out what he thought about Mary Kay having disappeared for four days now. It wasn't out of the ordinary for her to just do whatever the hell she wanted for a day or two, but she would always answer his calls or messages after a day or so. He didn't know if he should be worried or just pissed. He was mostly worried because something had been different about her since he had let her know about Oscar Ramone holding some kind of information about Tommy.

He decided to text her again and to his surprise she replied right away with "I'm fine, I'll explain later. Might do some shopping in L.A. I'll stay in touch."

He took a couple of deep breaths and sighed. "What the hell is she up to?" he said aloud. He picked up his phone and punched in Tommy's number.

"What's up?" Tommy answered.

"How'd you like to fly to Bakersfield with me tomorrow?"

That caught Tommy off guard. "Why you going there?"

"I go there every now and then," David said. "I've decided it's time I clued you in on something I've been keeping secret from you and Mary Kay. I think you'll find it pretty amazing. You need to know, and besides that, we can do a little sightseeing around the old neighborhood. It'll be interesting for you. I can come by around noon. We can just hang out, do dinner somewhere and hit the old neighborhood the next day."

Tommy thought David sounded a little too enthusiastic but nervous at the same time. It sounded fishy. After he hung up he called Mary Kay to tell her where he was traveling to with David the next day.

"I can't say anything right now," she said, "but I know what he's taking you there to show you. Don't tell David we talked, but I've been avoiding him for a few days and he's probably wondering about that. I think you'll see me when you visit the four-plexes day after tomorrow. I'm more worried than ever about his mental state. Stay safe."

Tommy stood and announced he was getting a shower. In the bedroom doorway he stopped and turned back to David. He still couldn't quite put his finger on it, but as he had discussed with his sister just days before, something had been different about David lately and it worried him. It mostly worried him because nothing was ever different about David. He was always the same, but not the past couple months. "You sure you want to go to the old neighborhood tomorrow?"

"Hell yeah," David said. "That's why we're here. I've been there a few times in the last few years or so. There are some things I want you to see and we need to talk about the past and the future. When's the last time you were there?"

"Long time ago," Tommy said. "I think I had just turned twenty-one so, going on thirty years."

David shook his head. "Where'd the time go, huh? Remember that day we first met Vincent?"

"You know, I've thought about that day so many times," Tommy said. "Sometimes it seems like a million years ago, but every once in a while I remember back to then and it seems like it just happened yesterday, man."

"I know," David said. "It'll be fun for you to check it out. A lot has changed but some of it is just the same. It'll take you back. And I've got some surprises for you."

Tommy nodded, still wondering about David and the way he was staring at him right now and thinking he sounded just a bit too enthusiastic about tomorrow. "You okay?"

David stared at him a little longer. "Why?"

Tommy shrugged. "I don't know."

"Hell, just go get your shower," he said. "I'm fine."

The next day after a late breakfast at the hotel by the airport they headed out with David driving the rental Camry sedan. "I know the owner. He offered us a nice Jag but this will blend in better. We don't want people wondering too much who we are."

David drove toward the older part of town. It was just a few miles from the airport to the old neighborhood. He turned onto First Street and slowed.

"Hey, there's the liquor store where your old man worked," Tommy said. "I don't remember it being that small."

"I guess we were small, so it seemed bigger," David said.

They neared the block of four-plexes that ran along First between Princeton and Simpson streets and David slowed to a crawl as they passed in front of them. "Check these out. Lot different."

"No kidding," said Tommy. "Geez, look how some of them have a fence right down the middle of the courtyard where the lawn was. That looks like shit."

David pulled over, stopped the car and pointed.

"This one looks just like they all did back then," Tommy said. "Same open lawn in between and the brick wall along the sidewalk. This Saladino's?"

David nodded as he pulled back onto First and continued slowly, nearing the north end of the block.

"This one still looks pretty good too," David said. "They put in a swimming pool where the lawn used to be. Decent-looking place."

Tommy nodded. "Good idea. Maybe they should all have pools."

David turned right at the corner onto Simpson.

Tommy pointed. "You should head down the alley."

"I want to cruise our old block first," David said. "We can go into the alley from the other side."

"There's where Mary Kay knocked you on your ass after those detectives stopped and talked to us," Tommy said.

David smiled and turned onto Second Street and drove slowly.

"There's the Boyd's old place and Mrs. Palmer's," Tommy said. "Some of these places look kind of crappy now, but a lot of them still look pretty good." He turned one way then the other checking out both sides of the street. "A couple places actually look better, but mostly not, huh?"

David nodded, slowing to a near stop in front of Tommy's old house.

Tommy was smiling and taking it all in. "Looks about the same. Still has the bricks where that lamp post was. Man, how many times did we run into that damn thing with bikes or our bare feet?"

David stopped in the middle of the street when they pulled even with his old house. "Look at that," he said, pointing to the narrow strip along the north side of the house which was full of weeds. "Somebody's not doing enough digging and playing along there."

Tommy nodded. "Look at the rest of the yard. Hardly any shrubs or anything. Looks kind of bare. And the house was green before, wasn't it? Everything looks smaller, like the liquor store. We used to play football on your grass and look how dinky it is. Does it look smaller to you?"

"A lot smaller," David agreed.

He drove forward again and turned the corner at Princeton. He pulled to the curb just short of the alley entrance, shut off the key and opened his door to get out of the car. "Let's do some walking," he said as he grabbed his windbreaker from the back seat. Tommy stepped out and zipped his sweatshirt. The two of them stood together and looked around at how much everything had changed and also stayed the same.

"The clouds look painted on," Tommy said, turning his face to the grey sky. "Not too cold but it feels like it could rain. Feels ominous." He was also feeling something like danger and he didn't know why. Something about seeing the old neighborhood combined with the weather and David's strangely upbeat mood was unsettling.

"Yeah, it's not bad," David said. "But you can feel that impending chill in the background. The season is changing. Might rain a little, but that's okay. Let's head down the alley."

The two friends, now forty-nine years old, turned and walked into the great divide.

"Man, this sure looks shittier than when we were kids," Tommy said.

"Yeah, it looks kind of run-down," David said. "This was all pretty new when we were kids. The houses are almost as old as we are now and the apartments are older than that. I've seen it since you have, though. I just like to come by once in a while and see how things are doing."

"Why?" Tommy asked.

"You'll see," David said. "I've got something really special to show you."

Their route was still cheap pavement half covered by sandy dirt. The fencing that once stretched for a long block of uniform five and a half foot high cedar pickets along the back of the houses on Second Street had transformed into a display of assorted styles at various heights. Some of it was sagging outward, some was sagging in, some had broken fence boards or posts and some looked like it had been recently built.

They continued in silence for a bit and the only sound was the crunching of their shoes on the sandy pavement.

"This is my best pair of doorbell shoes," David said.

They both laughed softly.

"You ever wonder how different things would be if we had never found that money?" Tommy asked.

"We'd be poorer," David said.

"Probably," Tommy said. "But Howie might still be alive. We would've never met any other Saladinos. We'd all be living different lives. Maybe husbands, wives, kids, grandkids."

David shrugged. "Yeah, maybe. Might've been boring. Think we would've been any happier?"

Tommy didn't answer for a few steps. "You know, if we were unhappy it would've been for a lot different reason than having to spend our lives keeping a secret from the whole damn world."

"Rich is better than poor," David said. "Listen, I brought you here today because it's time I filled you in on some things. First of all, your sister never wanted you to know that she killed Vincent Saladino. But I think it's time you knew."

"I know," Tommy said.

David stopped and faced him. "She told you?"

Tommy motioned and they resumed walking. "Long time ago. It was a short conversation right around high school graduation. She said she wanted me to know but she never wanted to talk about it again. The strange thing was while she was telling me I somehow kind of already knew. I think it's a twin thing. We never did talk about it again and even after I knew different I always just pretended that he was killed by the unknown bad guys. I don't know why, but it just seemed easier that way."

They walked some more in crunching silence.

"Killing Cadillac Vinnie did something to her," Tommy said. "I think she figured out that she had some power she could use. That whole thing when she hit our dad with the book really stuck. It changed him for real. It wasn't just getting hit, it was something different about her."

David nodded. "It turned that protective streak of hers into something really powerful and complicated, something even she didn't completely understand."

They took more steps in silence. "So, back in the day, Saladino was the only one with a garage door," Tommy said. "Now it looks like they separated all of the common parking spaces into separate garages. All these different styles and colors of doors looks kind of crappy too."

David just nodded, then stopped and pointed. "This was Saladino's." He stepped toward the other side of the alley. "I want to show you something."

"Then this is where the Boyds lived," Tommy said. "Man, this block wall looks pretty good. The whole alley should be this way."

David stepped to an arch-top redwood gate in the wall, lifted the hasp and pushed open the gate and stepped into the yard. "This is usually locked but I had them leave it unlocked today."

Tommy followed him into the yard. "Man, this yard looks just like it did back in the day. Who the hell lives here?"

David turned, pushed the gate closed and slid the hasp to hold it shut. "A guy named Max. I hired him a long time ago to live here, keep an eye on some things, do a little cleanup here and there. I bought the house even before that."

Tommy remembered Mary Kay talking about Max. "You bought this house? Why?"

"I like owning a piece of our history." He smiled at the look on Tommy's face. "Here, I want to show you something."

He walked to the chimney, pulled a key ring from his pocket, squatted down and opened the small lock on the ash cleanout door. He opened it, reached inside, moved the levers and stood back up with a groan. "Man, this was easier when we were twelve."

"Jesus, the thing still works," Tommy said with a laugh.

David opened the brick fronted doors, opened the lock on the inside and opened the steel door wide.

Tommy stared for several seconds. "What the fuck are you up to? Is that real?" He reached in and pulled out a bundle of hundreds. "Son of a bitch," he whispered.

"Want to guess how much is in here?" David asked.

Tommy put the bills back and stared some more. "Oh, I suppose it's about three million two hundred twenty-five thousand."

"Almost, but you'll see! Pretty cool, huh?" David said, sounding cheerful. Then he giggled in a way that made Tommy stare at him and wonder again just what was going on with him. "I just like having a little stash in case we need it. I have some plans for it."

"So, who knows about this?" Tommy asked.

"Just me and Max and now you," David said. "I pay him a stupid amount of money to just keep an eye on the house and some other things and to not wonder too much about anything."

"Mary Kay know about this?"

"No, just me. I just loaded the money in a little while after I made the deal with Saladino. I showed him the empty safe that day we rescued you."

They closed it up and locked both locks. They both stood there for a bit feeling the bricks and mortar lines.

"It's still amazing," Tommy said. "You think Vincent made it himself?"

"Don't know," David said. "Whoever it was knew their stuff. I'm guessing Vincent made sure that the guy wouldn't be around to get curious about what it was being used for."

"I'm sure," Tommy said. "Aren't you afraid somebody's going to break into your chimney?"

David gave a dismissive wave of his hand. "Not likely. People move, time goes by, everyone forgets. There's not one person living on this block of Second Street or in any of the four-plexes that was living here back in '68. Last person moved about ten years ago. I don't think most people had the story straight anyway back then. There was never a real explanation about the safe in the news. It was mentioned in a couple of articles but not in any detail about it opening up and how it worked. Everybody just knew Vincent was killed, he owned a house where he hid stolen mob money. It was a big deal thing to have happened in Bakersfield, but after a while it's blah, blah, on to the next big thing. The Vietnam War, Woodstock, Charles Manson, all the rest of the shit from the late 60s into the 70s and everything since."

Tommy was scowling and nodding. "Yeah I guess, but I still don't get why."

"Because I can," David said, adding a small chuckle again. "It's a little bit of private fun and now I can share the secret with you. But like I said, I've got plans for it."

"So this is what's so special that you wanted me to see?" Tommy asked, still trying to figure out what was going on with David.

"Oh, this is just part of it," he said. "The really special thing is across the alley. I have a lot to show you and we have a lot to talk about."

Tommy followed him to the gate, feeling more apprehension with every passing minute. He glanced up at the darkening sky and he couldn't shake the feeling it was lowering and closing in around him. They walked across the alley and into the former Cadillac Vinnie complex. David led Tommy out onto the lawn. In the middle of the grass area was a three foot tall marble fountain shaped like a sphere. Water softly burbled out of the top of it and cascaded down the sides onto beach pebbles. On each side was a curved concrete bench.

Tommy stood next to him watching the fountain. "You going to tell me you own the apartments too?"

"All eight of them," David said. "Old man Saladino knows it. This is where we met that day we rescued you." He pointed to the corner apartment. "I took him in there and told him about Mary Kay killing Vincent. Showed him where it happened. That's when we came to our understanding."

"So, these people don't care that we're nosing around in their courtyard?" Tommy asked.

"There isn't anybody to bother," David said. "I don't rent them out. You want to see inside Vincent's old place? Looks exactly the way it did back then."

"Wait." Tommy grabbed David's arm as he started to walk away. "You're telling me nobody lives in these apartments? All eight of them?"

"Right," David said. "There's nobody living here. Max across the alley keeps an eye on the place."

"Max." Tommy was staring at him with a look of concern. "This sounds crazy, man. Is this some kind of shrine or something?"

"I guess it's something like that," David said. "That's exactly what Nicolas Saladino asked me."

"No, I don't want to see inside Vincent's place." Tommy gazed around, feeling the memory closing in around him of the last and only time he had been in that apartment. "It looks good out here, kept up nicely. Let's go."

"Listen, there are some things you need to know," David said. They were strolling slowly toward the low brick wall and Vincent's apartment, "I have kept as many layers as possible between anything Mary Kay or I have done and you."

"Okay," Tommy said slowly. "And by the way, how come she's not here too?"

"Good question," David said. "She's been staying out of touch for a few days now. Who knows what she's up to."

"So why are we needing to talk about this?" Tommy said.

"Because I want you to know that you're the innocent one," David began. "Mary Kay and I have done a lot of things over the years to keep the secret. In the process we created more secrets. You know nothing about any of that or about the inner workings of the business. In case anybody ever asks, you can say you don't know and really be telling the truth."

Tommy was smiling. "Me the innocent one. Pretty funny."

"Yeah, I thought you'd like that. Everything Mary Kay has done was out of loyalty to the secret we shared, loyalty to me and especially loyalty and love for you. When we got you rescued the deal I made with old man Saladino was to keep the three of us protected."

"Saladino is getting up there," Tommy said. "What happens to you when he kicks it?"

"Yeah, he's in his eighties," David said. "His close associates know me. I'm sure they want the relationship continued so they still have my money as a resource. As long as they still guarantee our safety it'll all work out. What I'm trying to tell you is that everything we did was to keep us safe."

Tommy pointed to a rusted, dented metal drum standing near Vincent's former front door. "What's that for?"

David laughed out loud. "You are going to flip when I tell you. You're gonna love it. Here's a hint—seventy-one pounds."

Tommy tilted his head and looked at David through squinted eyes. "What's seventy-one pounds?"

"Mary Kay ever tell you about my recurring dream?" David

asked.

Tommy sighed. "Not really. Just that you've had one that's been disturbing you for years." He glanced at the drum again and thought he recognized some familiar marks in the rusted and charred steel. "Is that the barrel that used to be in my backyard, the one my dad would burn stuff in sometimes?"

David pointed at him. "Very good Tommy boy! It is that very barrel. I took it out of the yard from whoever lives there years ago and moved it here and stored it in Saladino's garage. You, me and Mary Kay are going to make good use of it. Seventy-one pounds is how much three million, two hundred twenty five thousand dollars weighs in hundred dollar bills." He leaned toward Tommy and in an exaggerated whisper explained, "Not exactly, of course, but pretty damn close, I rounded just to keep it simple." He returned to a normal voice. "In my dream it's always nighttime and flaming bills, hundreds mainly, are falling from the sky in the rain. Never could figure out that part but I finally did! We need to have a little bonfire, a tribute fire, a cleansing fire. Three million will fit nicely into the drum. We're going to ceremoniously burn every damn dollar that's sitting in that chimney."

Tommy saw there was a can of lighter fluid and a box of matches sitting by the drum. He studied David's face for a few moments. It wasn't just what he was saying, it was how he was saying it. He was excited, enthusiastic and talking fast. "Why?"

"I figured it out!" David said. "It's Cadillac Vinnie's money. That's the money in my dream. Why is it burning in my dream? It's a sign. It means we need to burn it. I think when I do then my dream will vanish. We need to do it at night because it's nighttime in my dream and, hey, it'll be more fun to watch at night anyway."

"When are we doing this?"

"Tonight if I can track down Mary Kay," David said. "Maybe tomorrow if she can't make it until then. The three of us can move the money with no problem. Seventy-one pounds! We did it before. Just to get things started I already moved a few bundles into the drum. Seed money!" He laughed out loud again.

"But we don't have Vincent's money anymore," Tommy said. "This is our money."

David was vigorously shaking his head. "I thought of that! It's symbolic, plus it's been in his chimney so it qualifies." He laughed out loud. "It's my dream! I get to make the rules."

"So this is the special thing we came here for today?" Tommy asked.

"It's part of it, but there's more." He patted Tommy on the top his shoulder. "Come on, man, don't look so serious. This is pretty great stuff! Wait here."

He walked to Vincent's old apartment, pulled a set of keys from his pocket and opened the door. A few seconds later he came out, locked the door and walked back to Tommy carrying a large manila envelope.

"There have been a few times Mary Kay found out about some people she thought were getting too close to the secret about Vincent's money. For her, protecting the secret was protecting you. She felt bad that you were haunted by the whole thing. She still trusted me to protect us, but she felt like she needed to do her part to make doubly sure nobody stumbled onto us. She knew I would still protect her and I did, but to do that I had to make sure nobody ever found out about how Vincent was killed. Later she got a bit, uh, shall we say, too enthusiastic about making sure nobody ever discovered what she had done and especially about protecting you. He handed him the envelope. "It's all in there. I have to step across the alley and talk to Max about some things."

David took a few steps then stopped and turned back around. "I'll be back in a couple minutes. Check out those articles and take a good look around, especially apartment two. Take a look at the mailboxes over there."

Tommy walked slowly back to the fountain and set the items on the bench. He opened the envelope, peeked in and pulled out two key rings with several keys on each. One looked like it was all door keys. The other had some that looked like door keys and several smaller keys.

He pulled out the papers and began leafing through them. They were all photocopies of newspaper articles. He quickly skimmed the headlines and the first few sentences of each one and saw that the ones about the same people were clipped together. There was an ex-cop named Zuber who disappeared in Bakersfield in 1992, another one about some mob-connected guy named Janelli who disappeared in 1997.

"Janelli," Tommy said to himself. "I remember that guy from school."

The next one made his heart start beating faster. He read the entire article about his former therapist, Dr. Lindsey Robbins, who disappeared in 2002 after attending her high school reunion in Tulare.

"Tulare," he said. "Hell that's just an hour up the freeway. I didn't know she was from around here."

He stopped and stared around at the empty apartments that surrounded him. He grabbed the key rings again and looked them over and counted that there were eight keys on the one that looked like front door keys.

His gaze fell on a group mailbox David had pointed out by the low brick wall and he walked over to it. There were eight small doors in the box with an apartment number on the front of each one and a key lock.

Tommy looked closer at the key ring with the smaller keys on it and saw they were labeled with apartment numbers. He put key number one in and opened the small door. Just inside on the bottom ledge was written the name Saladino. He closed it and opened the next door. His hands began to shake as he saw the name Robbins. He opened the next door and, as he feared, he saw the name Zuber. He knew before he opened it what he would see inside the next door. It read Janelli. He opened the next one and was surprised to see the name Williams.

"Howie?" he said to himself.

He turned and looked at each of the apartment doors, recalling David saying nobody was living in any of them. He stood motionless and stared as his chest started pounding. "No," he whispered. It was a completely insane thought, but he already knew it was true.

David returned from across the alley and walked into the courtyard.

"What have you done?" Tommy said, mainly to himself. He looked around quickly at the apartment doors then back to David. Yelling this time he repeated, "What have you done!"

He ran to apartment number two and fumbled through the keys with shaking hands. Finally he got the right key, inserted it into the lock and turned it. He pushed the door open but instead of the living room he found himself facing another door a few feet in front of him. This one was metal with a deadbolt lock. He used the same key on this door as well and pushed it open as the front door closed behind him.

It was completely dark inside. He brushed his hand against the wall until it hit a switch. A dim light appeared from a lamp sitting on a table by the window. He turned and looked at the living room and kitchen and saw that it was furnished just about like he remembered Vincent's apartment looking. Walking the few steps to the edge of the kitchen he found the wall switch and realized he'd been holding his breath. The bright light from the kitchen ceiling did little to push back his rising panic.

He peered down the short hall leading to the bedroom and bathroom. It was only dimly lit from the reflected light and too dark to see the back door at the end of the hall. As soon as his foot took a stride toward the hall his heart began pounding harder again. It was only a few steps to the end of the hall but as he took each one he felt like he was twelve years old again and the only thing he could think of was that there would be a dead Vincent Saladino sitting up in his bed, with a hole over his eye and his brains splattered on the wall behind him.

He reached the shadowy, nearly dark end of the hall. His heart was hammering and his breathing was beginning to transform to ragged shallow panting. Resisting his sudden craving for light and open space and the nearly overwhelming urge to turn and break into a screaming run out of the apartment, he turned his body to the left and took the two steps that put him in the open bedroom doorway. He could feel Vincent Saladino's lifeless eyes staring back through the darkness. He was working hard to convince himself that the dead mobster would vanish when the light came on. He took another step, reached for the light switch and flipped it on.

Tommy let out a quick involuntary shout then stood staring, trying to really believe what he was seeing. The light did help his claustrophobia a bit but it surely did not take away any of the dread that had brought him into the apartment in the first place. His hands began to tremble uncontrollably. Where the bed should be was a dark wood grain coffin sitting on a platform. Next to it was a display stand with a blue placard. On it was an 8 by 10 color photograph and in large black letters the name Dr. Lindsey Robbins – Born March 20, 1964—Died September 28, 2002.

Tommy found himself standing outside, hands on his knees taking deep breaths under an increasingly cloudy sky, not remembering for sure how he had gotten there. Tears were running down his cheeks. He stood up straight and used both hands to wipe his face and clear his eyes. He walked shakily out to the center of the courtyard lawn near the fountain, looked down at the keys in his hand and slowly turned in a circle as he looked at each of the eight apartment doors. David stood some distance away by the short brick wall near Vincent's front door.

Tommy turned and stomped toward David.

"Now you know what this place is all about," David said with a smug smile.

When Tommy was closer he looked down at the cluster of keys on the rings in his hand and hurled them, hitting David in the chest. "You had Dr. Robbins killed because I told her about us!" he yelled.

David looked annoyed. "That was Mary Kay."

"Well, I don't think you tried very damn hard to stop her,"

Tommy said. "I liked her and she was helping me! She was a nice person! You two killed her?" He was rubbing his head with both hands and his breathing was puffing out his cheeks. "But why do this? What the hell is wrong with you?"

"Secrets needed to be kept," David said calmly. "I had to control everything. Do you understand? Everything! Nobody would ever find out about this. This way I could keep total control and know exactly where everybody was."

He stopped and looked at Tommy who was staring back in shocked silence. David returned an arrogant smirk and continued his explanation. He pointed at each door as he loudly recited the names. "Robbins, Janelli, Zuber. On this side, a couple guys you didn't see articles about, we have Franks, Carpenter, Hatfield and Wu. All of them, all in their proper places. The most recent one is Wu over in number eight. He's the guy from the funeral home that helped me make this happen, but he was a loose end that I couldn't just leave hanging. Most people can't be trusted to keep secrets you know. That one was a little tricky because, well, it had to be DIY on my part, but I learned a lot from Wu over the years so it all worked out. So I thought doing this had a certain style to it, don't you? A definite bit of in-your-face, unexpected panache, as my Uncle Harry would say. I like to think of it as paying a fitting homage to where this all started, plus it was a kind of hobby for me to see how well I could pull it off. I really like how I brought it full circle to where it all started for the three of us."

Tommy's eyes widened and he yelled. "In whose face?" He stepped up to David and grabbed the front of his windbreaker with both hands. "Style? Homage? A goddamn hobby! What the fuck! I thought you were guarding the secret, not creating a freak show. You always thought you were so goddamn smart about all of this and so did we, but look what you've done!" He let go of his jacket with a hard push and pointed at apartment number two and lowered his voice. "There are three urns in there along with Dr. Robbins. How many people's remains do you have sitting in these apartments?"

"There are eleven," David said. "There's a few coffins, but most of them are urns. Easier to move and store, you know?"

"Mary Kay killed eleven people?" Tommy asked.

David shook his head. "She only killed five, and all of those were a few years ago. Since your rescue and my working relationship with Saladino I've provided them with some storage space as well. And Lee was my own project. But with him gone I think I'm calling it. No vacancies."

Tommy slowly shook his head and stared hard, trying to wrap his mind around all of this. "Why did you suddenly want to tell me about this today?"

"I thought it was time to finally let you and Mary Kay in on my brilliant secret instead of keeping it to myself," he announced, spreading his arms wide. "I made the luck of being a chimney sweep work for real! I protected us all. Nobody knew until Howie and that goddam Johnny Saladino. It was the whole world against me and I won! Nobody would've ever suspected such a brilliant idea. I thought the money burning ceremony could be part of the celebration. It's in my will and other confidential legal papers I have filed. When the last of us three dies, it triggers an opening of documents that will direct the authorities to this property. It will be a sensation and we'll be famous!"

"I hate to interrupt this lovely conversation," Mary Kay announced loudly as she walked toward them, carrying her favorite shotgun pointing down at the ground by her right leg.

Tommy looked back and forth, wondering if this was some further insanity.

"What's with the gun?" David asked, immediately suspicious and a bit scared of what she might be up to.

She held the shotgun down at her side in her right hand and continued strolling toward them. "You just never know when it might come in handy." She stopped ten feet from them.

"You haven't answered any of my calls or texts for several days," David said, trying to size up her emotional state.

Mary Kay made a grim smile. "I've been very busy meeting with Max and taking care of some things."

"Max?" David said, raising his voice again, his eyes popping open wide. "Taking care of what things? Is this why I couldn't get into his house just now? No answer and my key didn't work. What the hell are you up to? Max works for me and I take care of things! What did you do with Max?"

"Don't worry." Mary Kay said. "He's fine and he and I have developed a whole new working relationship. Did you know that Max had been forced into doing some computer work for that guy you like to call Ape Face?"

David looked incredulous and slowly shook his head.

"There never was any information being held over the head of the mob by Oscar Ramone," Mary Kay said.

"Oscar Ramone?" Tommy said, looking utterly confused "The golfer? What the hell is going on?"

Mary Kay held up her hand to hush Tommy. "It's crazy and I'll get you caught up later. Anyway, there never was anything threatened by Ramone. It's all made up by Opificio, who was going to kill him for no reason at all just as a decoy. They had some information about Tommy that was going to be released and that would be blamed on Ramone. Somehow Opificio found out that Max was working for you, but he had no idea what was going on here. He had Max keeping information in a computer and he was probably trying to recruit Max to make bigger moves down the road. Max was trying to manage the situation himself because Opificio convinced him if he didn't play along he would do something that would hurt us, all three of us."

"Why was Ape Face stirring all this up?" David asked. "What was he trying to accomplish?"

"Never did get an answer from him that completely made sense," Mary Kay said. "He was going to kill Tommy and make it look like Ramone did it to lend some credence to their bogus story. That is the reason he is now at rest in apartment six. It seems he was trying to make a reputation for himself with his associates. Apparently the three of us are so legendary that some in the organization, in spite of our guaranteed safety, still consider us to be some kind of intruders who should not be protected. I guess he figured he would get some respect coming his way when he let it get out that he had engineered something that hurt us."

David glanced over at Tommy and they both slowly shook their heads in confused disbelief.

"Max filled me in on just what you have going on here," she said, taking another step toward them. "I've taken the grand tour through every apartment. This is beyond crazy. Keeping us all safe all these years was hard on you, David. I feel very sad for you and very sorry that I had a part in driving you to this utter madness. I know about your idea to burn the money to stop your dream. I don't think that will help anything."

Two rather large men wearing suits and ties who David did not recognize walked in from the alley behind Mary Kay and walked forward until they were flanking her. David figured them to be bouncers or some kind of cops. He could see a holster under one of their unbuttoned jackets and he guessed the other one was armed as well.

Mary Kay's tone softened. "David, I'm so sorry but we are getting you some help and we're going to help you get better. Come here, Tommy."

Tommy walked to her as the two men walked past him. Just as they were about to put hands on him, David lunged forward, intentionally tripping one of the men and grabbing his gun out from under his jacket. Mary Kay took several steps back, pulling Tommy back with one arm and raising her shotgun with the other. David raised the pistol, pointing it at her chest just inches away, and gripped the barrel of her shotgun with his left hand.

With pleading fear she screamed, "David no, no, no!" and pushed Tommy aside as she took more steps back with David stumbling forward still clenching the barrel of her gun and aiming the pistol at her. He was pulling the trigger over and over but the safety was on and the gun wouldn't fire. One of the men finally tackled him from behind and Mary Kay wrenched the shotgun from his grip and managed to keep her fingers away from the trigger.

The two men took hold of him by each arm, twisted the pistol out of his hand, lifted him to his feet and dragged him back away from Mary Kay. "This was my masterpiece!" he shrieked, flecks of saliva flying. "This was for both of you, but especially for you, Mary Kay! I thought you'd be impressed with the genius of it all. And burning the money was going to stop my dream and we could all celebrate. You ruined everything! Do you hear me? Everything!"

Mary Kay laid the shotgun at her feet and sobbed. The two men struggled to put handcuffs on David as Tommy held his sister in his arms and tried to console her.

After a bit she quieted, sniffed and wiped her tears away. David was no longer fighting his guards and he stood calmly, panting, his hands cuffed behind him, gazing at Mary Kay as they flanked him, still gripping his arms. Watching her crying, which he had seen just a handful of times, had softened his reaction and the expression on his face.

The two men both tightened their grip as she walked closer to David. "Don't worry," she said just above a whisper. "These guys are going to take good care of you. It's a great place in Vegas and the staff there will treat you right. Tommy and I will see you in the next day or two. When you're better, the three of us will get back to making Chill better than ever. Right now you don't have to protect us. You don't have to protect the secrets. You're off duty. You can relax."

"What about all this here?" he asked, sounding exhausted and defeated.

"I'll catch you up when we visit," she said. "It's going to be fine. Don't worry."

"Car keys," Tommy said, holding out his hand. One of his guards reached into David's pocket and tossed the rental car key ring to Tommy.

Mary Kay leaned forward and kissed David on the lips. Hoping he was hearing it just as he had back in 1968, she said in a shaky whisper, "I love you David Steiner. I always have and I always will."

The two of them exchanged a quick look, then he turned and allowed himself to be escorted to the waiting SUV.

She hugged Tommy, "Let's sit."

They walked to the bench by the fountain and sat next to each other.

"I didn't know about this place until a few days ago," she said. "It never remotely occurred to me that such a thing would be going on."

"I don't know why he brought me here today to tell me all about it."

"I think it was just building up inside him," she said. "Maybe he thought sharing this with you would share the burden. Maybe it was the stress of opening Chill and worrying about still keeping our past hidden from the rest of the world. I don't know. Maybe it was the stress of keeping the secrets and all of it since 1968." She looked up at the gray sky. "Feels like it's going to rain."

Tommy thought that over. "So what happens now? We think David has been driven over the edge. What about you?"

She reached and held his hand in both of hers. "I did what I thought I needed to do to keep us safe, especially you. So did David. It wasn't just me imagining threats, they were real. They were people who were on the trail of what happened and if they found out just the right things it would lead them to us. I was always so scared of someone finding out I killed Vincent and about us taking the money. I was afraid of going to prison and of us losing everything. You were so tortured by it all and you seemed so, I don't know, fragile? I was afraid for you and what it would do to you if we were found out. I knew he was taking care of my victims, but I never thought he would…" She gestured at the apartments and said nothing for a bit. "Listen, I don't know exactly how things are going to go but we're going to go back to Vegas and keep making Chill the best ever."

"What about this?" He gestured at the apartments.

"I started a discussion with Max about that," she said. "I'm going back across the alley to finish up the details with him. We're going to have Mr. Ed bring a team in here, take care of the remains, fix up the place and sell it. Once that happens we're moving Max to Vegas to work for us. He's a computer genius and he knows a lot of money stuff too. I think David can make good use of him."

"Don't forget to clean out the chimney," Tommy said.

Mary Kay chuckled softly and stood. "I won't."

"I'm going to sit here for a bit then head back to the hotel and fly back to Vegas in the morning," he said.

"I think I might be back tomorrow too." She reached down and poked his shoulder. "And you know I've been over the edge all along. I needed to be."

He looked up at her and nodded. "Yeah, M.K. you did."

Tommy watched her walk to the alley. She turned and waved as she crossed and walked through the gate she had left unlocked into the Boyd's yard, as they still referred to it.

Large raindrops began to fall as he sat and contemplated things, watching the softly burbling water at the top of the sphere in the fountain. Glancing around at the apartment doors, the low brick wall along the street, the neatly manicured landscaping, he thought it was a peaceful scene for anyone who didn't know what it really was.

It was difficult to comprehend just how their lives had led to this. After what he had learned today and seeing David like this, an awareness that he had not fully grasped before came to him. The stolen money had stolen from them. All three of them had become something they would never have been. It didn't just change their lives and their fortunes. It changed their true selves and their destiny.

Tommy stood and walked across the grass to the metal drum. He looked down into it and saw that David had dropped three bundles of hundreds into it. "One for each of us I guess," he said to himself. He reached down, grabbed the lighter fluid and matches, soaked the bills and tossed in a lighted match.

As the flames from the burning money rose as high as the top of the drum he walked along the brick wall for several steps and glanced over it remembering how, in that exact spot, he and David had laughed themselves silly before Vincent Saladino interrupted them. A colder breeze kicked up, swirling a few leaves across the courtyard lawn along with some smoke as the rain began to fall a bit harder. The season was deepening.

He pulled the hood of his sweatshirt up onto his head and thought back to how their youthful ingenuity allowed them to make an amazing find. They had been so uniquely clever and bold and so proud of themselves. As he reminisced over all of that, he wondered again how it would have been if they had never known about Cadillac Vinnie and not taken his secret fortune. He turned, leaned against the wall, put his hands in his pockets as the rain continued from the darkening sky, and gazed around at the place where early one summer evening in 1968, without any of them knowing it, their lives veered off course and never came back. They were ingenious finders, lucky takers and achieved incredible success beyond their wildest dreams, but would never know what their lives would have been, or just who they might have been, on the path not traveled.

THE END

ACKNOWLEDGEMENT

Thanks and appreciation for their skills and talents in proofreading, editing and advising to

Francesca Fairbrother

and

Dava Parks

BOOKS BY THIS AUTHOR

War Paint

www.ingramcontent.com/pod-product-compliance
Lightning Source LLC
Chambersburg PA
CBHW030251200626
46816CB00002BA/594